Also by Otto Penzler

The Private Lives of Private Eyes, Spies, Crime Fighters
  and Other Good Guys
Whodunit? Houdini? (editor)
Encyclopedia of Mystery and Detection (with Chris Stein-
  brunner)
Attacks of Taste (with Evelyn B. Byrne)
Detectionary (co-editor)

The
Great
Detectives

The Great Detectives

edited by

Otto Penzler

Little, Brown and Company

Boston   Toronto

Second Printing

Library of Congress Cataloging in Publication Data
Main entry under title:
The great detectives.
  Bibliography: p.
  1. Detective and mystery stories, American —
History and criticism. 2. Detective and mystery
stories, English — History and criticism. 3. Detective
in literature. I. Penzler, Otto.
PS374.D4G7   813'.0872   77-25487
ISBN 0-316-69883-0

The author is grateful to the following publishers and individuals for
permission to publish copyrighted materials:
Ngaio Marsh, for her piece "Roderick Alleyn." Copyright © 1977 by
Ngaio Marsh Ltd.
Kenneth Millar for his piece "Lew Archer." Copyright © 1977 by
Kenneth Millar.
Richard Lockridge for his piece "Mr. and Mrs. North." Copyright ©
1977 by Richard Lockridge.

Designed by Christine Benders

*Published simultaneously in Canada
by Little, Brown & Company (Canada) Limited*

PRINTED IN THE UNITED STATES OF AMERICA

To my mother and my brother —
With thanks for caring so much

Contents

Foreword

THE SEASON OF THE HERO appears to be ended. While that may be cause for mourning, it should be no cause for surprise. Whether art imitates life, or whether the influence is the other way around, literature, inarguably, is the mirror of its time.

It is a commonplace of literary history that the rise of naturalism in the late nineteenth century is primarily responsible for the interment of the romantic hero. Knights in shining armor, performing selfless, fearless deeds, galloped down the road to oblivion. Readers of contemporary literature will find few protagonists in "serious fiction" who appear to be stronger and wiser, more courageous, more compassionate, than themselves. The glorious hero of the kind of story that held listeners and readers spellbound for a thousand years or more — that lifted up their hearts, gave them models to emulate — is almost no more. The *Übermensch*, the superman, has almost vanished with the culture that extolled singular men performing singular deeds. Almost — but not quite. The detective story still flourishes.

With the creation of C. Auguste Dupin in "The Murders in the Rue Morgue" in 1841, Edgar Allan Poe fascinated an international body of readers with the astonishing feats of deduction of the first great literary detective. When Arthur Conan Doyle introduced Sherlock Holmes in *A Study in Scarlet* in 1887, the ultimate literary detective — dedicated to the pursuit of excellence, justice, and truth — was born. (Holmes bears not a little resemblance to the concept of that ultimate human being, the *Übermensch*, as developed by Friedrich Nietzsche in the series of narratives published as *Thus Spake Zarathustra* between 1883 and 1892.)

Holmes, of course, was not *entirely* unflawed. We know that he was, for a time, if not an addict, then an irregular user of cocaine. And, in several instances, Holmes was defeated in his quest to bring a case to a successful conclusion.

Yet the great detective in fiction today still carries the aura of invincibility, the power of omniscient ratiocination, the unwavering determination to see the game through, the infallible knowledge of truth and justice, that characterized Holmes.

Naturalism, to be sure, has had its impact on this species of hero. Although some English detectives (Dorothy L. Sayers's Lord Peter Wimsey, Margery Allingham's Albert Campion, Ngaio Marsh's Roderick Alleyn) have been actual (or at least nature's) aristocrats, the type of American detective who came to flower with Dashiell Hammett's Sam Spade and Raymond Chandler's Philip Marlowe has been a more dubious sort of hero — troubled by many of the failings to which the flesh is heir, from being occasionally lustful to being frequently broke.

Today's literary detectives are hardly perfect heroes. Consider the weary cynicism of Ross Macdonald's Lew Archer, the alcoholism of George Harmon Coxe's Flash Casey, the self-effacement of H. R. F. Keating's Inspector Ghote, and the collective roughnecked opportunism of Ed McBain's 87th Precinct squad.

Yet the idea of the Great Detective still grips us. Flawed though they may be, as a class great detectives are a testimony to the concept of the superhero. Where else can we read of a protagonist who risks life, limb, and often reputation for little recompense? Who persists doggedly to the grim end of the trail, unraveling the case? Who ultimately apprehends the villain? And who upholds the law and — more important — glorifies the concept of justice?

We know that, in life, detectives do not always triumph. The odds, in fact, favor the felon. And if captured, the criminal often goes free because of overloaded, ineffectual, bureaucratic systems more concerned with law than justice.

So the mystery story, the saga of a detective at work, is characterized, not unfairly, as escape fiction. It not only permits the reader to share vicariously the experience of the detective hero, but to escape from an imperfect society. In detective literature, the detective is invariably victorious. And such victors must endure.

What makes a great detective in fiction? Is it his winning personality? Who would be enchanted by Quiller, Van der Valk, or Pibble? Is it his commanding presence? If so, how can one account for Ghote, or Cockrill? Is it the style, the subtlety, the magisterial prose of the detective writer? Rarely. Pulp magazine writers drew their characters with only the broadest strokes, in hundreds of thousands of words a year. Yet The Shadow is not forgotten.

The characters, the heroes, immortalized in the literature of detection do tend to be more memorable than the corner greengrocer or the mousey blonde down your apartment hallway, or the bored cop who interrogates you about the theft of your TV set.

The genre of the detective story has produced more recognizable and unique (and, yes, desirable, in the sense of craving their company) characters than all other forms of fiction combined. This phenomenon has never been more evident than in the fiction of the last three decades.

How many readers can recall the appearance, habits, or even the names of the protagonists in novels by, say, Norman Mailer, Saul Bellow, John Fowles, John Updike, William Styron, or Thomas Pynchon? Can you name six of them? But millions will not forget the introspective Lew Archer;

two-fisted Mike Shayne; ruthless Quiller; aristocratic Roderick Alleyn; tough, raunchy Matt Helm; phlegmatic, schnapps-loving Van der Valk; or even the charming Nancy Drew.

The enduring detectives of fiction have recognizable traits that remain consistent throughout their adventures. Their points of prowess and their frailties draw us to them. And we welcome their return, in case after case.

The accomplishments of some are known to us through the scantest literary legacy. Mark McPherson, the sleuth of Vera Caspary's *Laura*, has had only that one recorded case. On the other hand, Maxwell Grant's narratives about The Shadow exceed three hundred. Some of these detectives conduct investigations that are meticulously planned and that have, to an extent, a predictable end. Others habitually become embroiled in cases that seem bizarre beyond the wildest roll of fortune's dice.

This book, then, is a mixed collection of diverse personalities and varied styles, reflecting a slightly idiosyncratic (and certainly personal) taste.

A lifetime of savoring the rich flavors and abundant textures of detective fiction had proved inadequate. I wanted to know more about some favorite characters — more than was contained in the books and stories, more than could be inferred from the texts, more than had been written. Convinced that others shared a curiosity about the origins of the great literary heroes of our time, I decided to ask the creators of those detectives for additional information. On what real-life people might their heroes be based? How did the adventures come to be written? Did they *like* their creations? What is the secret of inventing a character who will outlive its author?

Doubtless another addict of detection would put such

questions to a somewhat different group of authors. These detectives were chosen after considerable deliberation. There were some limiting criteria. Only authors who write in English were invited to contribute to the book (because of my inability to read anything else). Only authors still alive were asked (as the others could hardly testify). And, regrettably, a very few authors had to decline the invitation because they found writing directly about their heroes impossible, either physically or psychologically.

It is my hope that the gracious and highly individual contributions which follow will provide useful clues for a fuller understanding of these great detectives. An even greater hope is that they will recruit new readers to share the pleasures of one of literature's most entertaining and enduring forms.

— Otto Penzler
September 1977

Roderick
Alleyn

Ngaio Marsh

*Handsome socialite detectives are a mainstay of "Golden Age"
British mystery novels of the 1920s and 1930s, and are not unknown to the American writers who affected Britishisms for
their prose style and the language mannerisms of their detectives. Lord Peter Wimsey is a notable example of the former,
and Philo Vance and the early Ellery Queen are examples of the
latter.*

*Dame Ngaio Marsh's Roderick Alleyn is one of the few
aristocrats officially connected with Scotland Yard, rising
quickly from inspector to superintendent, and he has found his
familial connections of invaluable assistance on cases that might
have proved a trifle sensitive to police officers of a different
social stratum. He is also one of the few who have survived into
the 1970s.*

*The supporting cast in Alleyn's exploits includes Inspector
Fox, whom he persists in calling "Br'er Fox" or "Foxkin," and
Nigel Bathgate, a reporter for the* London Clarion, *who sometimes chronicles the cases of Scotland Yard's most attractive
detective.*

*Dame Ngaio Marsh (she was made a Dame Commander of
the British Empire in 1966) was born in New Zealand in 1899
and has divided most of her adult life between that country and
England. Her unusual first name (it is, actually, her middle
name, since she was born Edith Ngaio Marsh) is the Maori
word for a regional flower; it is pronounced NY-o. Much of
her time has been devoted to the theater: first writing plays,
then acting in them, and finally directing and producing them.*

Roderick Alleyn

by Ngaio Marsh

HE WAS BORN with the rank of Detective-Inspector, C.I.D., on a very wet Saturday afternoon in a basement flat off Sloane Square, in London. The year was 1931.

All day, rain splashed up from the feet of passersby going to and fro, at eye-level, outside my water-streaked windows. It fanned out from under the tires of cars, cascaded down the steps to my door and flooded the area: "remorseless" was the word for it and its sound was, beyond all expression, dreary. In view of what was about to take place, the setting was, in fact, almost too good to be true.

I read a detective story borrowed from a dim little lending library in a stationer's shop across the way. Either a Christie or a Sayers, I think it was. By four o'clock, when the afternoon was already darkening, I had finished it and still the rain came down. I remember that I made up the London coal-fire of those days and looked down at it, idly wondering if I had it in me to write something in the genre. That was the season, in England, when the Murder Game was popular at weekend parties. Someone was slipped a card saying he or she was the "murderer." He or she then chose a moment to select a "victim" and there was a subsequent "trial." I thought it might be an idea for a whodunit — they were already called that — if a real corpse was found instead of a phony one. Luckily for me, as it turned out, I wasn't aware until much later that a French practitioner had been struck with the same notion.

I played about with this idea. I tinkered with the fire and with an emergent character who might have been engendered in its sulky entrails: a solver of crimes.

The room had grown quite dark when I pulled on a mackintosh, took an umbrella, plunged up the basement steps, and beat my way through rain-fractured lamplight to the stationer's shop. It smelled of damp newsprint, cheap magazines, and wet people. I bought six twopenny exercise books, a pencil and pencil-sharpener and splashed back to the flat.

Then with an odd sensation of giving myself some sort of treat, I thought more specifically about the character who already had begun to take shape.

In the crime fiction of that time the solver was often a person of more-or-less eccentric habit with a collection of easily identifiable mannerisms. This, of course, was in the tradition of Sherlock Holmes. The splendid M. Poirot had his mustaches, his passion for orderly arrangements, his frequent references to "grey matter." Lord Peter Wimsey could be, as one now inclines to think, excruciatingly facetious. Nice Reggie Fortune said — and he said it very often — "My dear chap! Oh, my dear chap!" and across the Atlantic there was Philo Vance, who spoke a strange language that his author, I think I remember, had the nerve to attribute, in part, to Balliol College, Oxford.

Faced with this assembly of celebrated eccentrics, it seemed to me, on that long-distant wet afternoon, that my best chance lay in comparative normality — in the invention of a man with a background resembling that of the friends I had made in England — and that I had better not tie mannerisms, like labels, round his neck. (I can see now that with my earlier books I did not altogether succeed in this respect.)

I thought that my detective would be a professional policeman but, in some ways, atypical: an attractive, civilized man with whom it would be pleasant to talk but much less pleasant to fall out.

He began to solidify.

From the beginning I discovered that I knew quite a lot about him. Indeed I rather think that, even if I had not fallen so casually into the practice of crime-writing and had taken to a more serious form, he would still have arrived and found himself in an altogether different setting.

He was tall and thin, with an accidental elegance about him, and fastidious enough to make one wonder at his choice of profession. He was a compassionate man. He had a cock-eyed sense of humor, dependent largely upon understatement, but for all his unemphatic, rather apologetic ways, he could be a formidable person of considerable authority. As for his background, that settled itself there and then: he was a younger son of a Buckinghamshire family and had his schooling at Eton. His elder brother, whom he regarded as a bit of an ass, was a diplomatist and his mother, whom he liked, a lady of character.

I remember how pleased I was, early in his career, when one of the reviews called him "that nice chap, Alleyn," because that was how I liked to think of him: a nice chap with more edge to him than met the eye — a good deal more, as I hope it has turned out. The popular press of his early days would refer to him as "The Handsome Inspector," a practice that caused him acute embarrassment.

On this day of his inception I fiddled about with the idea

of writing a tale that would explain why he left the diplomatic service for the police force but somehow the idea has never jelled.

His age? Here I must digress. His age would defy the investigation of an Einstein, and he is not alone in this respect. Hercule Poirot, I have been told, was, by ordinary reckoning, going on 122 when he died. Truth to tell, fictional investigations move in an exclusive space-time continuum where Mr. Bucket ("of The Detective") may be seen to go about his lawful occasions, cheek-by-jowl with the most recent of fledglings. It is enough to say that on the afternoon of my man's arrival I did not concern myself with his age and am still of the same mind in this respect.

His arrival had been unexpected and occurred, you might say, out of nothing. One of the questions writers are most often asked about characters in their books is whether they are based upon people in the workaday world — "real people." Some of mine certainly are but they have gone through various mutations and in doing so have moved away from their original begetters. But not this one. He, as far as I can tell, had no begetter apart from his author. He came in without introduction and if, for this reason, there is an element of unreality about him, I can only say that for me, at least, he was and is very real indeed.

Dorothy Sayers has been castigated, with some justification perhaps, for falling in love with her Wimsey. To have done so may have been an error in taste and of judgment, though her ardent fans would never have admitted as much. I can't say I have ever succumbed in this way to my own investigator, but I have grown to like him as an old friend. I even dare to think he has developed third-dimensionally in my company. We have traveled widely: in a night express through the North Island of New Zealand, and among the geysers, boiling mud, and snow-clad mountains of that country. We have cruised along English canals and walked through the streets and monuments of Rome. His duties have taken us to an island off the coast of Normandy and the backstage regions of several theaters. He has sailed with a psychopathic homicide from Tilbury to Cape Town and has made arrests in at least three country houses, one hospital, a church, a canal boat, and a pub. Small wonder, perhaps, that we have both broadened our outlook under the pressure of these undertakings, none of which was anticipated on that wet afternoon in London.

At his first appearance he was a bachelor and, although responsive to the opposite sex, did not bounce in and out of irresponsible beds when going about his job. Or, if he did, I knew nothing about it. He was, to all intents and purposes, fancy-free and would remain so until, sailing out of Suva in Fiji, he came across Agatha Troy, painting in oils, on the deck of a liner. And that was still some half-dozen books in the future.

There would be consternation shown by agents and publishers when, after another couple of jobs, the lady accepted him, but the acceptance would be a *fait accompli* and from then on I would be dealing with a married investigator, his celebrated wife, and later on, their son.

By a series of coincidences and much against his inclination, it would come about that these two would occasionally get themselves embroiled in his professional duties, but generally speaking he would keep his job out of his family life and set about his cases with his regular associate who is one of his closest friends. Inspector Fox, massive, calm, and plain-thinking, would tramp sedately in. They have been working together for a considerable time and still allow me to accompany them.

But "on the afternoon in question" all this, as lady crime-novelists used to say, "lay in the future." The fire had burned clear and sent leaping patterns up the walls of my London flat when I turned on the light, opened a twopenny exercise book, sharpened my pencil, and began to write. There he was, waiting quietly in the background ready to make his entrance at Chapter IV, page 58 in the first edition.

I had company. It became necessary to give my visitor a name.

Earlier in that week I had visited Dulwich College. This is an English public school, which in any other country would mean a private school. It was founded and very richly endowed by a famous actor in the days of the first Elizabeth. It possesses a splendid picture gallery and a fabulous collection of relics from the Shakespearean-Marlovian theater: enthralling to me who have a passion for that scene.

My father was an old boy of Dulwich College — an "old Alleynian" as it is called, the name of the Elizabethan actor being Alleyn.

Detective-Inspector Alleyn, C.I.D.? Yes.

His first name was in doubt for some time but another visit, this time to friends in the Highlands of Scotland, had familiarized me with some resoundingly christened characters, among them one Roderick (or Rory) MacDonald.

Roderick Alleyn, Detective-Inspector, C.I.D.?

Yes.

The name, by the way, is pronounced "Allen."

John
Appleby

Michael Innes

As one of the most erudite of all detectives, particularly of those officially connected with a police department, John Appleby of Scotland Yard was uniquely suited to handle his first recorded case, a murder at Oxford University. And, although many of his subsequent cases have also involved academic settings — with their inevitable academicians — he is never intimidated. To the contrary. Appleby's education has apparently been so extensive (if less formal than that of the professors with whom he deals so competently) that he amuses himself by quoting appropriate lines from the classics at opportune moments.

Appleby is not an effete amateur, dabbling in detective work because he thinks it good sport. He began his police career as a uniformed bobby and rapidly progressed through the ranks of inspector, assistant commissioner of Scotland Yard and ultimately, commissioner of London's Metropolitan Police. He was knighted just before retiring to a not very serene life punctuated with frequent criminal encounters.

Michael Innes began writing detective fiction as an escape from a more sober professorial life. Recently retired, he was known to students of literature at Christ Church College of Oxford University as Professor J. I. M. Stewart, Reader in English Literature, under which name he has produced numerous scholarly studies and biographies. Curiously, the 71-year-old creator of one of mystery fiction's most memorable detectives believes that in-depth characterization is inimical to crime fiction. Professor Stewart also considers the reading of detective novels addictive and decided to fight the disease by writing his own.

John Appleby

by Michael Innes

JOHN APPLEBY CAME INTO BEING during a sea voyage from
Liverpool to Adelaide. Ocean travel was a leisured affair in
those days, and the route by the Cape of Good Hope took
six weeks to cover. By that time I had completed a novel
called *Death at the President's Lodging* (*Seven Suspects* in
the U.S.A.) in which a youngish inspector from Scotland
Yard solves the mystery of the murder of Dr. Umpleby, the
president of one of the constituent colleges of Oxford
University. It is an immensely complicated murder, and
Appleby is kept so busy getting it straight that he has very
little leisure to exhibit himself to us in any point of character
or origins. But these, in so far as they are apparent, derive,
I am sure, from other people's detective stories. I was simply
writing a yarn to beguile a somewhat tedious experience —
and in a popular literary kind at that time allowable as an
occasional diversion even to quite serious and even learned
persons, including university professors. (It was to become
a rather juvenile university professor that I was making this
trek to the Antipodes.)

Appleby arrives in Oxford in a "great yellow Bentley"
— which suggests one sort of thriller writing, not of the most
sophisticated sort. But "Appleby's personality seemed at
first thin, part effaced by some long discipline of study, like
a surgeon whose individuality has concentrated itself within
the channels of a unique operative technique." This is alto-

gether more highbrow, although again not exactly original. And Appleby goes on to show himself quite formidably educated, particularly in the way of classical literature. "The fourteen bulky volumes of the Argentorati Athenaeus" (and for that matter Schweighaüser's edition of the *Deipnoso-phists*) he takes quite in his stride when he encounters them in Dr. Umpleby's study. This must be regarded as a little out of the way in a London bobby lately off the beat. And there is no sign that Appleby is other than this; he is not the newfangled sort of policeman (if indeed such then existed) recruited from a university. Research in this volume will show that he is definitely not himself an Oxford man. This has frequently been a contentious issue, and I fear that the evidence becomes a shade confused in some later chronicles.

What Appleby does possess in this early phase of his career is (I am inclined to think) a fairly notable power of orderly analysis. Had he been a professor himself, he would have made a capital expository lecturer. But I am far from claiming that he long retains this power; later on he is hazardously given to flashes of intuition, and to picking up clues on the strength of his mysteriously acquired familiarity with recondite artistic and literary matters. He also becomes rather fond of talking, or at least of frequenting the society of persons who prefer amusing conversation to going through the motions of being highly suspicious characters, much involved with low life and criminal practice.

What I am claiming here (the reader will readily perceive) is that Appleby is as much concerned to provide miscellaneous and unassuming "civilized" entertainment as he is to hunt down baddies wherever they may lurk. And I think this must be why he has proved fairly long-lived: and by this I mean primarily long-lived in his creator's imagina-

tion. In forty years I have never quite got tired of John
Appleby as a pivot round which farce and mild comedy and
parody and freakish fantasy revolve.

If I finished the first of these stories before reaching
Australia, I think I am right in my reckoning when I say that
I had written a dozen of them before coming away again
ten years later. This suggests more application than, I fear,
actually went into the activity; one is rather freely inven-
tive when one is young, and the stories seemed to get themselves on the page out of odd corners of my mind at odd
times and seasons. I never brooded over them as I was to
brood over ordinary "straight" novels later; and here I was
only being faithful to that first *ethos* of the "classical" English detective story as a diversion to be lightly offered and
lightly received. Yet the circumstances of my diurnal life
and my immediate physical and social surroundings during
those years must have had some impact upon them. Where
did this lie?

I think a species of naive nostalgia was at work. English
life and manners had a compelling fascination for me — and
the more so because, as a Scot who had scarcely crossed the
border as a boy, my experience of them had been comparatively brief. And at once keen but impressionistic! So as
Appleby moves through his early adventures he reflects
something of this situation. He is within a society remembered rather than observed — and remembered in terms of
literary conventions which are themselves distancing themselves as his creator works. His is an expatriate's world. It is
not a real world, controlled by actual and contemporary
social pressures, any more than is, say, the world of P. G.
Wodehouse.

But the sphere of Appleby's operations is conditioned by
other and, as it were, more simply technical factors. Why

does he move, in the main, through great houses and amid
top people: what an Englishman might call the territory of
Who's Who? It might be maintained that it is just because
he likes it that way. We never learn quite where he comes
from. He has a sister who has been an undergraduate at
Oxford, and an aunt of somewhat imperious aristocratic
manners who lives in Harrogate; he has married into an
eccentric family, the Ravens, who are country gentry. But
wherever he comes from (and it appears to me to be some
quite simple station of life), he is a highly assimilative person, who moves, or has learned to move, with complete
assurance in any society. Eventually he makes a very convincing commissioner of Metropolitan Police, which is
Britain's highest job in a police service. I'm not sure that
he isn't more verisimilar in this role than he is as a keen
young detective crawling about the floor looking for things.
So one might aver that he finds his way into all those august
dwellings because he fancies life that way.

But this isn't quite the fact of the matter. In serious English fiction, as distinct from a fiction of entertainment, the
great house has long been a symbol — or rather a microcosm
— of ordered society; of a complex, but on the whole har-
monious, community. And indeed French, Russian, and
American novelists have tended to see life that way; in the
"English" novel the grandest houses of all have been invented by Henry James.

Something of this has rubbed off on the novel's poor
relation, the detective story — the more readily, perhaps, because in England itself that sort of story was in its heyday
rather an upper-class addiction.

But Appleby, like many of his fellow-sleuths in the genre,
roams those great houses for a different and, as I have said,
technical reason. The mansion, the country seat, the ducal

palace, is really an extension of the sealed room, defining the spatial, the territorial boundaries of a problem. One can, of course, extract a similar effect out of a compact apartment or a semidetached villa. But these are rather cramping places to prowl in. And in detective stories detectives and their quarry alike must prowl. At the same time, they mustn't get lost. And this fairly spacious unity, the Unity of Place in Aristotle's grand recipe for fiction, conduces to an observance of those other unities of time and action which hold a fast-moving story together. And just because Appleby is leisured and talkative, urbane and allusive; just because he moves among all those people with plenty to say themselves; just because of this he wisely seeks out that rather tight *ambiance*.

There is one other point that strikes me about him as I leaf through his chronicles. They *are* chronicles in the sense that time is flowing past in them at least in one regard. The social scene may be embalmed in that baronets abound in their libraries and butlers peer out of every pantry. But Appleby himself ages, and in some respects perhaps even matures. He ages along with his creator, and like his creator ends up as a retired man who still a little meddles with the concerns of his green unknowing youth.

Michael Innes

Lew
Archer

Ross Macdonald

Ross Macdonald's private-eye stories reflect our time. It is difficult to know precisely what drives Lew Archer. A sense of chivalry and honor, surely, yet he strays easily and frequently. Justice, yes, but his own definition of it. Paradox and mystery obscure the outlines of his personality. What does Archer look like? Macdonald says he doesn't know; he's never thought about it. Is he based on a real-life character? Yes, he admits, himself, but not completely. Is Paul Newman's portrayal accurate? Well, says Macdonald, he is a wonderful Harper but Harper is not Archer.

Read the short stories and novels, and you will find a few clues to the real Lew Archer: what he thinks, how he acts, what his intentions are, what his destiny is. But Macdonald writes about him indirectly, always, as if triple-thick gauze had been placed over the camera lens. A little more about this lonely "underground man" emerges in Ross Macdonald's essay. Like the author's Lew Archer stories, the image of the Los Angeles private detective is a glimpse through a fog, rather than a studio portrait.

Ross Macdonald is the most honored active American writer of detective fiction. Writing in the New York Times, *William Goldman described the Lew Archer series as "the best detective novels ever written by an American"; he has been the subject of a* Newsweek *cover story; he has received a coveted Grand Master Award from the Mystery Writers of America; and his is that rare detective writing reviewed and treated as "serious" fiction by critics. Born Kenneth Millar, the 62-year-old author adopted his famous pseudonym in 1949 to avoid confusion with his wife, mystery writer Margaret Millar. They live in Santa Barbara, California.*

Lew Archer

by Ross Macdonald

IN THE EARLY MONTHS of 1929, when I was thirteen, the
most important figure in my imaginative life was Falcon
Swift the Monocled Manhunter. Swift was a fictional detective who was regularly featured in the *Boys' Magazine*, a
thin pulp magazine with a pink cover which was imported
from England and sold for five cents a copy. I bought it
every Saturday at a little store on North Main Street in
Winnipeg, across the street from the semi-military school
where I passed the long Manitoba winter.

The school library was open only on Sunday afternoons.
But my nights were enlivened by Falcon Swift's war on evil,
his hundred-mile-an-hour journeys by high-powered car
across the green face of England, the harsh justice which he
meted out to criminals. Reluctant to leave Falcon Swift at
Lights Out, I rigged up a mirror which reflected the light
from the hallway onto my pillow and enabled me to read,
with some difficulty, far into the night.

The stock market crash which took me out of the school
in Winnipeg may have saved my eyesight. I never saw another *Boys' Magazine* or heard of Falcon Swift again. But
for good or ill he had left his mark on me. Fantastic as his
adventures undoubtedly were, they prepared me for (as
they derived from) Sherlock Holmes's more cerebral war
on evil, Lord Peter Wimsey's towering egotism, and Sap-
per's low blows. Even when James Bond rose like a Sputnik

on the horizon, he seemed not wholly unfamiliar. The Monocled Manhunter was riding again, armed like a battle cruiser, rescuing England from evil, domestic and foreign.

A deeper sense of evil (which I associate with Dickens and Wilkie Collins) has come back into the detective form in more recent decades. It reminds us that we live on the slopes of a volcanic history which may erupt again at any time. The evil we are aware of is both public and terribly personal, like an unruly child or an insane relative who has taken up permanent residence in the basement of our lives. At its very best, where it grazes tragedy and transcends its own conventions, detective fiction can remind us that we are all underground men making a brief transit from darkness to darkness.

The typical detective hero in contemporary American fiction speaks for our common humanity. He has an impatience with special privilege, a sense of interdependence among men, and a certain modesty. The central vice of the old-fashioned hero like Holmes or Wimsey, who easily accepted their own superiority, is hubris, an overweening pride and expectation. The central vice of the underground man is moral and social sloth, a willingness to live with whatever is, a molelike inclination to accept the darkness. Perhaps these are the respective vices of aristocracy and democracy.

The private detective is one of the central figures of fiction in which the shift from aristocracy to democracy has visibly occurred, decade by decade. This is true of the real-life detective as well as the fictional, for each imitates the other. The relationship of the imaginary and the actual is further complicated by the fact that fictional detectives tend to be idealized versions of their authors, the kind of men we would choose to be if we were men of action instead of the solitary fantasists we are. Everyone knows this, including the present writer. ("I'm not Archer, exactly, but Archer is me.") What everyone may not know is the extent to which actual detectives, both privately and publicly employed, read detective stories and watch crime movies for clues as to how to conduct themselves. One reason why detective fiction is important is that it serves as a model for life and action.

Detectives are human like other men, and the perfect detective will never exist in the flesh. But the several good detectives I have known have certain qualities in common. One is a rather selfless chameleon aspect which allows them to move on various levels of society, ranging from the campus to the slums, and fade in and out of the woodwork on demand. They are able to submerge themselves in the immediate milieu and behave according to its customs and talk the language: a little Spanish in East Los Angeles, a little jive in Watts, a little Lévi-Strauss in Westwood. This is something different from the miming of the actor because it is played out in the actual world and is subject to its pressures and uncertainties. The stakes are real.

One night a few years ago I had a phone call from a man who wanted to come out to my house and talk. I remembered his name. A few years before, as a local university student, he had joined the campus branch of the John Birch Society in order to expose its purposes. Since then, he told me in my study, he had carved out a career as a private detective.

Perhaps carved is the wrong word. My visitor was gentle in manner, though he told me he knew karate. Over a period of a year or so, in the Bay Area, he had apprehended some fifty criminals. I was surprised by his reason for coming to me. He wanted to establish a code of ethics for private detectives, and thought my Archer stories might serve as a starting point.

Nothing came of that. Events carried him away, as they tend to do with young men of action. I saw him once more, in Superior Court, when he was gathering evidence for the defendants in the Isla Vista trial. Then he went underground on another case, and I haven't seen him since. But let me describe him. He is built like a middleweight, dark and slightly exotic in physical appearance, his dress faintly mod, his hair neither long nor short. His style could be that of a graduate student or an artist, or possibly a young lawyer for the defense. But he is more diffident than self-assertive. He watches and listens, and talks just enough to hold up his end of the conversation. For all his goodwill and energy, there is a touch of sadness in his expression, as if there had been some trouble in his life, a fracture in his world which all his investigative efforts had failed to mend.

I think self-knowledge, and a matching knowledge of the world, are what the serious private detective may be after. I've known a couple of older detectives who had found these things. One of them, an experienced operative from Los Angeles, went into a minority neighborhood where a crime had been committed. Within twenty-four hours, with his white hair and his outgoing democratic manners, he was the friend and virtual confidant of half the families on the block. I know a Nevada detective who works six days a week running down the losers who flock to the gaming tables. On the seventh day he acts as the ombudsman and unofficial justice of the peace for his working-class neighborhood in Reno. He is a good and gentle man, nondescript in appearance, short in height, casual in speech and dress, profoundly offended by violence.

I don't wish to imply that all private detectives scatter kindness. But the ones I've known tend to be reasonable men. If there are sadists and psychopaths among them, they don't last very long in this rather exacting work. The fictional detectives who revel in killing don't belong to the real world. They inhabit a sado-masochistic dream world where no license is required, either for the detective or for the wild dreamer at the typewriter.

What makes a private detective, then? Why does he choose the shadow instead of the sunlight? Why does his interest in other men's lives often seem to transcend his interest in his own?

A good private detective has an appetite for life which isn't satisfied by a single role or place. He likes to move through society both horizontally and vertically, studying people like an anthropologist. And like an anthropologist he tends to fall a little in love with his subjects, even if they happen to be the most primitive savages of the urban jungle.

Possibly he became a detective originally in order to make his concern for and knowledge of people possible and then useful. He felt a certain incompleteness in himself which needed to be fulfilled by wide and extraordinary experience. He discovered a certain darkness in himself which could only be explored in terms of badly lighted streets and unknown buildings, alien rooms and the strangers who live in them.

If my detective sounds just a little like a potential criminal or a possible writer, he is meant to. But the criminal seeks out people in order to steal their money or their secrets, or to project himself against them in a rage for power. The detective is tempted by power and knows its uses, but he subordinates a hunger for inordinate power to the requirements of the law and his own desire for understanding and knowledge. The knowledge he seeks is ultimately self-knowledge, and like his sedentary brother the writer he finds himself in the course of his life if he's lucky.

Ross Macdonald

Father
Bredder

Leonard Holton

The normal function of detectives is to apprehend criminals and to see that they are brought to justice, usually in a court-room. A case generally is considered successful if the felon is caught and punished. It is altogether different when the detective is a clergyman. He is concerned with the laws of God, not Man, and is successful only when a soul is rescued from damnation. For him, success is far more difficult to achieve — and it is more difficult to verify.

Father Joseph Bredder is a priest at the Franciscan Convent of the Holy Innocents in Los Angeles, but it is difficult to imagine a man who looks less like a clergyman. No doubt his years as an expert amateur boxer and as a marine sergeant contributed to the tough appearance of this gentle man. His adventures are recounted in eleven novels and he has served as the inspiration for the television series Sarge, *which ran for thirteen one-hour episodes during the 1971 season, following a highly rated two-hour pilot film starring George Kennedy.*

Leonard Holton is one pseudonym of Leonard Wibberley (also known as Christopher Webb, Patrick O'Connor), the prolific author of some one hundred juveniles and novels. Wibberley's most popular novel is The Mouse That Roared, *the hilarious story of Grand Fenwick, a tiny European country that launches an attack on the United States with an invasion force of twenty longbowmen. It was made into a successful motion picture starring Peter Sellers. A native of Ireland, the 62-year-old Wibberley now lives in Hermosa Beach, California.*

Father Bredder

by Leonard Holton

ABOUT TWENTY YEARS AGO, having at the time written some forty books of various kinds, I decided for my amusement to try my hand at a detective story. The field was not entirely new to me, for at the time I had written two detective stories for juveniles: *The Watermelon Mystery* and *The Five Dollar Watch Mystery* under the pen name Patrick O'Connor, which are actually my middle names.

The detective stories written by men these days are usually full of tough talk and tense action and casual sex. Women on the other hand tend to deal with minutiae of appearance, of habit, of thought, or dress, weather and surroundings; of remarks or absence of remarks. These form a truer but quieter picture of life as life is. As a result women in my view are far superior to men in writing detective fiction. Indeed, when I think of the great detective story writers of the twentieth century, I don't think of Edgar Wallace (remember him?), Dashiell Hammett, or Ian Fleming, or the magnificent Ross Macdonald. I think of Dorothy Sayers, Josephine Tey, Agatha Christie, and (a recent find for me, but certainly a writer of the first water) Emma Lathen.

Now I'm not fond of bashing people around or shooting them, and casual sex I disagree with. On the other hand I have no great talent for the threads of detail which form the smooth and satisfactory web of the detective story as written by women writers. It occurred to me then that I had to devise a nonfussy and nonviolent sort of detective — a detective with an entirely different personality and motivation from the usual private eye; although on reflection few of them are usual. This decided me that if I made my detective a priest I could give my stories a background and quality others lacked — a spiritual quality. I reasoned that from the point of view of a priest, a crime is not merely an offense against the laws of Man. It is (infinitely more important) an offense against the laws of God. "Thou shalt not Kill," "Thou shalt not Steal" are not, after all, reckoned man-made laws in their origin. When a criminal is caught and brought to justice, nothing at all has been achieved from the priestly point of view unless the offender acknowledges his offense against his Creator and repents it. Indeed, if the crime is murder and the culprit is executed unrepentant, he faces a sentence of eternal damnation.

My detective, then, I made a priest whom I called Father Joseph Bredder. He would, I decided, be a priest first and a detective much later and he would always have as an urgent motivation in solving any crime the need to bring the criminal to repentance while there was still time.

The first book I wrote in this vein was called *The Saint Maker*. It involved a nice old lady who killed people when they were in what is called a State of Grace — right after being absolved from their sins in confession for instance — so that, dying, they would go immediately to Heaven. She thought such killing an act of perfect Christian charity and was so sure of the rightness of what she was doing that, leaving the head of one of her victims in Father Bredder's church, she lit a candle before the statue of Saint John the Baptist (who was, of course, beheaded).

The lighting of the candle before the statue is what Father Bredder, my detective, called a "spiritual fingerprint." It is with the aid of such "spiritual fingerprints" that he often solves the crime which confronts him. This outrages his friend Lieutenant Luis Minardi, of the Los Angeles Police Department Homicide Division, who likes a more material approach. Minardi, by the way, is a Sicilian by birth and of an upper-class background. Although now an American citizen, the Sicilian remains — the tight cultural code which he feels he should impose on his daughter Barbara, a student in most of these books at the Convent of the Holy Innocents of which Father Bredder is pastor.

Now when an author devises a detective series with a priest as a hero, it is immediately assumed that his inspiration was Chesterton's Father Brown. Although I had certainly read a couple of the Father Brown stories, I wasn't particularly struck by them. Chesterton spent much of his life battling the Dragon Paradox, and Father Brown isn't, in my view, so much of a priest as he is a Paradox tamer. I'm not an expert on him, but I was never particularly struck by his spiritual depth. I don't recall him ever visiting, as a priest, the inmates of seamy flophouse hotels, or trying to explain to children the mystery of the Christian Trinity. Father Bredder does all that appertains to the priesthood while examining bodies and diving on sunken barges for evidence which a "spiritual fingerprint" has suggested should be there. There is not in all this a whit of criticism of the classic Father Brown. I merely hope to point out that Father Bredder isn't in the slightest degree related to Father Brown. I don't suppose I will succeed.

Father Joseph Bredder is a big man, well over six feet, and weighs about 180 pounds. He was born in Twin Oaks,

Ohio, or Red Oak, Ohio (the detail here is confused). His father was a farmer and he was on his way to being a farmer too, when World War II broke out. He joined the Marines, was promoted to the rank of sergeant, and fought in many of the Pacific Island battles; it was this experience that made him a priest.

Since his conversion to the priesthood is important, I'll quote the passage concerned from the first book about him — *The Saint Maker*. The scene is a Pacific Island battle:

The shout had gone back for phosphorous grenades and flame throwers, and two Marines had crawled forward with tanks on their backs. Three grenades were flung into the cave and after what seemed an eternity, half a dozen men came out. Then there was the roar of the flame throwers and the men struggled in the flames, clawing with burning hands at burning clothing, and collapsed on the ground, still burning and writhing. Suddenly he [Sergeant Bredder] had been very sick and wondered whether that was why he had been raised in a good country, with a bounteous earth and gone to church and said his prayers as hard as he could say them every night — to kill terrified men who had been brought up pagans and did not know what they were doing. That was why and when and how he had decided to become a priest.

I had a model for this conversion. At Cardinal Vaughan's School in London in my day, the sportsmaster and the man in charge of punishment was a priest. I still recall the deep regret I used to feel when I had to disturb him in his cozy study and say I had "come for punishment." He was often settled before a fire with a book and a pipe and it seemed to me the height of bad manners to intrude.

On the wall of the study was his "kit bag" (*knapsack* is the modern word), a sword-bayonet in its scabbard and his "tin hat," or combat helmet as they call it these days. They were all souvenirs of World War I — The Great War — in which he had been an infantryman. His years in the Flanders trenches, among the mud, the rats, and the moldering dead, with the ever-present chatter and mutter of the guns, had made him a priest. He was a very decent man, for when he had administered punishment (which was done with a wooden stick with a broad tongue of leather on the end) he let the victim remain in his study until he had got hold of himself, lest he be seen sobbing by some boy in the hall outside. We were all grateful to him for that, and sometimes after punishment he would give us a hint about handling a cricket bat or trapping a football which helped to take our mind off the pain and indicated that the whole matter was over, and without enmity, which would have been unbecoming among gentlemen.

In Father McClimant then (for that was his name though I am dubious of the spelling) was one source for Father Bredder. Another source was Father Joseph Brusher, S.J., now deceased, who used to teach history at Loyola University near Los Angeles. I mention him only because I stole his first name, Joseph, and intended to model Father Bredder on him. But the two are entirely different. What struck me about Father Brusher was that although he had cancer and some degenerating condition of the cells, and was supposed to age two years for every year of living, he had a huge zest for life. There was a lot of boy in him — right up to his last breath. There is a lot of boy in Father Bredder too.

To backtrack a little: the first book was of course rejected by several publishers. Nobody understood it. It wasn't a simple murder story. It wasn't a beat-'em-up-and-love-'em story. The motive for the murder was queer, to say the least. And of course the rules of detective-story writing properly outlawed any trace of insanity on the part of the criminal.

I happened to be in New York when the last rejection came in and my agent (who didn't understand the book either) suggested I might have a chat with Ed Bond who was then in charge of detective fiction at Dodd, Mead. I had at this point rewritten the manuscript to play down the spiritual content of the book, following the well-known motto, so different from that of M-G-M, *Pecunia Gratia Artis.* I explained to Mr. Bond what I had been trying to do — write a book in which the real crime was against God, not Man.

"Put that back into the manuscript," he said, "and I'll buy it." And he did. That was the first of ten Father Bredder stories published by Dodd, Mead.

Right now it would be nice to say that they swept the nation, but the fact is that they didn't even sweep half a block of Madison Avenue. Nobody had any explanation for this, for everybody at Dodd, Mead loved Father Bredder. I think it was based in the religious trauma that had seized the whole of the Western world and centered around the proposition that God may be nothing more than a psychological response to an unfaceable fate — death. Father Bredder is not worried about this trauma. He goes on mediating as best he can between God and Man. He is worried about his own worthiness, about his lack of eloquence and his clumsiness of mind. He continues growing roses, comforting children, down-and-outs, alcoholics, millionaires, and policemen. If you were to tell him that God is merely a psychological response, et cetera, he would say quietly that God had never sworn an oath not to use psychology in His attempt to capture the love of Man.

To complete the portrait of Father Bredder, he has a vast assortment of somewhat seedy friends and acquaintances, many of whom appear in each adventure. There is Soldier Sam who runs a coffee stall in the Main Street area of Los Angeles. He has flat feet, massive varicose veins, and bones enlarged by rickets, and he shouldn't be alive at all except that he has also so valiant a spirit that nothing can defeat it. Hence his name — Soldier Sam.

There is Mrs. Cha, Japanese manageress of a flophouse hotel in Los Angeles. She is a Buddhist who lives among derelicts without losing an iota of her wizened Oriental dignity. There's Cagey Williams, a retired pug who runs a gymnasium in East Los Angeles where he trains hopefuls for any kind of a prizefight he can find anywhere. (Father Bredder was himself a boxer of some standing during and after his Marine Corps service.) And there's the Senator, who is a ward heeler and makes no apologies at all for his outspoken opposition to "Papists."

There is also Reverend Mother Theresa who runs the Convent of the Holy Innocents and is of county English stock. She finds it very difficult to get along with Father Bredder, who lacks "breeding" and keeps involving the convent in the "police columns." And there's Mrs. Winters who keeps house for Father Bredder and wears a straw hat anchored firmly to her head with a hat pin to advertise that that is all she keeps for him.

Father Bredder has the ability to get into a crime in a wide variety of circumstances. He is involved with werewolves in Portugal (*Deliver Us from Wolves*), with the drug scene in California (*The Mirror of Hell*), with the fabulous Golconda Diamond which has an Indian background (*The Secret of the Doubting Saint*), with scuba diving (*Out of the Depths*), with international yacht racing (*A Touch of Jonah*), with an attempt to murder a baseball player coming home from second base (*The Devil to Play*), and with violin making (*A Problem in Angels*). Scuba diving, international yacht racing, ball playing, and violin making are all interests of mine, and since I also believe in immortality and Hell and Heaven, it is plain that Father Bredder and I have much in common.

Most of the books about Father Bredder have sold to book clubs, and some appeared in paperback. There was also a television series, *Sarge,* based on him, or inspired by him. But the scripts departed from the original character and Sarge became (in my view) merely a policeman disguised as a priest. Still, television has paid Father Bredder the compliment of stealing several gimmicks in his plots — as for instance the burial of a body, which could not be found, in the hole dug for one of the supporting pillars of a big building in downtown Los Angeles, and the use of a musical score as a code for secret information (someone pointed out to Father Bredder, who is not musical, that the score made no sense since it changed into unrelated keys without reason).

To complete the picture, Father Bredder sticks very closely to his vow of poverty, to the extent that he cannot bring himself to buy a tobacco pouch but keeps his tobacco in a paper envelope. He smokes a cheap, dark Carolina tobacco. He loves baseball and is an ardent fan of the Dodgers. Other than ball games he watches very little television, has a great fear, in giving advice, of sounding pompous or pious, does not carry a gun, and is opposed to violence though he will defend himself if need be. He is fond of gardening, children, and down-and-outs. He likes reading and buys old novels for a quarter or so when he feels he can afford them.

As far as the final repentance of the criminal is concerned, he sometimes has had to be content with the very slightest of signs. But then, so also does God.

Leonard Holton

Flash
Casey

George Harmon Coxe

Jack "Flashgun" Casey began his career as a crime photographer for the Boston Globe, *but, when he vigorously opposed the newspaper's suppression of one of his pictures, he was fired. Casey thereupon moved over to the rival* Express. *The editors at both papers were less than enthralled by the number of crimes in which Casey became personally involved, but his frequent scoops made his apparent penchant for trouble somewhat more endurable. He had little to fear from criminals. At 6'2" and 215 pounds of solid muscle, he could handle himself — and often had to because of an unpredictable temper and a healthy taste for alcohol.*

Casey is one of the two important journalists in Boston's violent world of murder and mystery. The other is Kent Murdock, also a crime photographer — and also the creation of George Harmon Coxe. While the two characters have many similarities, Murdock is slightly less tough, less disheveled, and less surly. He has appeared in twenty-one books while Casey has enlivened only six. But Casey appeared first and has been the principal of magazine stories and serials, a radio series, two motion pictures, and a television series. Darren McGavin starred in Crime Photographer *on the CBS television network during the 1951–52 season. Casey had also inspired an experimental series in the 1940s, before network television, which never made it to a nationwide audience.*

Born in Olean, New York, Coxe spent several years on newspapers in California, Florida, and New York, then worked for an advertising agency for five years before turning his full attention to writing fiction. The 76-year-old author has spent recent years with his wife in Old Lyme, Connecticut; the Coxes winter on Hilton Head Island, South Carolina.

Flash Casey

by George Harmon Coxe

I THINK Jack (Flashgun) Casey might be surprised to find himself included in a volume listing the names and exploits of well-known, perhaps even famous, fictional detectives. That he often found himself involved in a murder case and just as frequently happened to be around at its conclusion, that he was able to contribute something important to the often violent solution of such cases, needs little explanation since his job as a top press photographer took him where the action was and the camera he carried was in itself an instrument of detection.

Casey's vital statistics and background remain obscure. I'm not sure of his birthplace but I suspect it was not far from Boston; his accent suggests this. There was a high school diploma, possibly a year or two of higher education, although I have no proof of this since he never mentioned it. Physically he stood a straight six two, his weight varying from 210 to 220, a big, rangy-looking man though hardly in a class with the football linemen and basketball players of today. His rugged, not unattractive face became distinctive only when one noticed the dark eyes which were observant, questioning, and occasionally suspicious, but seldom without humorous glints quick to surface. Topping a forehead already beginning to crease was a thick head of dark brown hair which seemed always to be needing a trim.

The reason I can't be more specific about Casey's background is that I first knew him as a full-grown adult, already with a top reputation, even though his character had been rounding out in the back of my mind for some time. I had about five years of newspaper work behind me in California, Florida, and New York (City and Upstate). I had read and enjoyed the fiction exploits of reporters from time to time, but I also knew that it was the photographer accompanying such newsmen who frequently had to stick his neck out to get an acceptable picture.

For this was before the days of the long-range telescopic lens, the electronic flash, the strobe, the rapid-sequence shutter. In the beginning Casey had to use what was called a "spread-light," the flashbulb just coming into use. A "spread-light" was a narrow metal trough into which was tapped a certain amount of magnesium powder, a volatile substance kept in a tightly corked bottle since it was both highly combustible and dangerous when improperly used. Beneath the trough was a handle, a dangling wire trigger for the finger, and a sparking device not unlike that in a cigarette lighter. The resulting brilliant light flash with its puff of white smoke provided the necessary illumination, the effect depending on the amount of powder and the proximity of the photographer to the subject to be recorded. This in turn meant that while the reporter with his pad and pencil could describe a warehouse or dockside fire from a safe distance, the guy with the camera had to edge far closer to get a negative that would merit reproduction.

So why not give the cameraman his due?

If a reporter could be a glamorous figure in fiction, why not the guy up front who took — and still does take (consider the televised war sequences) — the pictures?

At the time I had been selling shorts and novelettes to such magazines as *Argosy*, *Detective Fiction Weekly*, and *Blue Book*. *Black Mask*, by reputation a difficult market to crack, demanded a story of a style quite unlike the others. Under the skillful guidance of its editor, Joe Shaw, it had become a showcase for such writers as Hammett, Gardner, Nebel, and later, Raymond Chandler. I wanted to be published in that market, and against the advice of my agent, in those days a transplanted Britisher and a fine gentleman named Sydney Sanders, who said my writing was too subjective, I went ahead and wrote the first Casey story. I named him Jack — the Flashgun, reduced later to Flash, was the invention of someone on the magazine — and gave him a young assistant named Tom Wade to serve as a foil. Using a style I hoped would fit the market, I banged away.

To my delight, that first story was accepted (as were all those that followed). By the time I had the good news, and now full of enthusiasm, I was well into my second yarn.

I wrote Joe Shaw to say so. His reply, while cordial, stated flatly that he was not looking for another series character. But since the second Casey was by then completed I sent it off anyway, making it longer since pulps paid by the word. Apparently this second effort was sufficiently professional to make Shaw change his mind because his following letter was simple and heartening, saying in effect, "Write another, George."

So Casey, having been launched, never appeared in any other magazine. There followed three or four books, published by Alfred Knopf, the first two of which were serialized in *Black Mask* years later. The editor then was Ken White, who published each in three installments.

As suggested in the opening paragraph, Casey was something of a paradox in that he was not really a detective. What put me straight about this was the sage advice of one of the shrewdest editors I ever met. Along about my third story I had Casey playing the detective's role and the letter of acceptance warned me always to remember that Casey was not a detective and should not compete with others who were — amateur, private, or official — that in addition to the character of the man himself his job provided the plus factor that set him apart from the others. To quote from memory, Shaw wrote, "Look, George. I have a whole bookful of detectives of one kind or another every issue, but only Casey carries a camera."

Casey's involvement in the action and violence necessary for *Black Mask* — see Hammett's *Red Harvest* and *The Dain Curse* — was usually motivated by personal reasons: an attempt by some shady character to steal a negative others wanted; the occasional invasion of the paper's darkroom for a similar purpose, or the abuse of an associate; the interference in any manner by some hired hands, with or without a gun, as well as any attempt to damage his equipment. These were the things that prompted an immediate reaction sometimes more reckless than wise.

It is a well-known fact that without their snitches, the batting average of most city detectives would suffer drastically. Casey also had his sources of information, but with a difference. With the police it is sometimes a few well-spent bucks here and there, but the lever, the weapon they carry, is not the badge or gun but blackmail. Charges of one sort or another on which the officer has evidence to convict are withheld to be traded for information; the threat, always present, of a six-month or two-year stretch becomes surprisingly effective in applying pressure on those who might be reluctant to pass along helpful information.

Casey's tips came from friends and acquaintances. For small favors given and returned. Because he was by nature a friendly and sympathetic man, it was no big deal for him to come up with a pair of hard-to-get tickets to sporting events at the Garden, or choice seats at Fenway Park. Sometimes a photograph could be cropped to avoid embarrassment to someone in the background. Now and then a picture of no great importance never reached the picture editor's desk. Such things together with the fact that he was a soft touch with those down on their luck sometimes paid off handsomely. Those who knew him best knew also that beneath the bluff exterior there was a compassionate heart and a wide streak of sentiment.

This sort of edge often brought him to the scene of a crime well ahead of the competition, the source of the tip perhaps a phone call from a taxi driver, a bartender, a waiter, a small-time crook, a minor politician, even on occasion a city cop who owed him. Yes, and women. Perhaps a friendly waitress, a hatcheck girl, a barmaid. Sometimes a jealous mistress, a street hustler, or even a more expensive call girl he had met in the past. For while Casey had never married — that would be unlikely in a *Black Mask* hero of the day — his sexual appetites were normal and adequately served, not by sweet young things, but by companionable youngish widows and divorcées without ulterior motives, whose needs were compatible with his own.

But like everyone, he had his faults and admitted most of them: a quick impatience, especially with bores and phonies, a touch of irascibility too often quick to surface, a sharp and cutting tongue, frequently regretted, to express displeasure when some wrong, real or fancied, had been done, especially to those who lacked weapons to defend themselves.

On another level, and speaking from experience, Casey

has been very good to his creator. In my first book I made my hero a smoothed-up version named Kent Murdock. For some reason, perhaps from inexperience, I thought such a character, not unlike Casey in many ways as a photographer, but better dressed and better mannered, would be more appropriate for a book. Murdock, too, has been good to me and has appeared in far more books. Complimentary letters and personal comments assure me that women like him. But with men, and they have been the helpful and influential factors in my career, it was always Casey and *Black Mask*, a magazine few women ever heard of.

As an example, my first book, *Murder with Pictures*, had been turned down by Little, Brown and what was then known as Farrar & Rinehart. Alfred Knopf's people accepted it with no rewriting or revision, except for a request for a short introductory chapter to indicate that it was indeed a murder story and not a straight novel. Why then did Knopf, certainly second to none in prestige, take my reject and establish a relationship that has lasted forty years? Quite possibly because Bernard Smith, the editor, and Joe Lesser, Alfred Knopf's right-hand man, were *Black Mask* readers and Casey fans.

Shortly after starting my first stint with M-G-M a well-known director of big pictures and a noted playwright, neither of whom would I have expected to read *Black Mask*, and both unknown to me personally, stopped me on a company street to tell me how much they liked my Casey stories. Years later another fan, a vice-president at CBS — there were two or three VPs then instead of thirty — suggested that I create a radio show around Casey. The result was *Casey, Crime Photographer*, which then gave me six years of welcome royalties for doing little more than writing an audition script and then making suggestions for improvement for the first air shows, written, until he went into the army, by Ashley Buck.

How old is Casey now? Let me illustrate. Some years ago I was a guest at a luncheon given by Alfred and Blanche Knopf for salesmen who had come to town for a week of meetings — this was before Random House entered the picture. A salesman whom I had met before was sipping his preluncheon drink right next to me when he said something like, "How old is Kent Murdock these days?"

I thought a moment, recognizing the humor in the question, before replying. Murdock had made his debut in 1935. In my imagination I pictured him as a young man of, say, 28 to 30. Now, twenty years later and I don't know how many books — this was around 1955 — I grinned back at him and said, "About thirty-eight, give or take a year."

It is the same with Casey. Unlike Nero Wolfe and Archie Goodwin, unlike Ellery Queen, a trio that never seemed to age, Casey got older; his hair showed some gray, the bathroom scales pointing to another ten pounds. I had him in my mind back in 1933 as perhaps 32. In the last book I did about him in 1964, published as always by Knopf, I saw him as a man of 45 or thereabouts. So in a matter of thirty-one years Casey had aged no more than fourteen. Wouldn't it be interesting if we could all age in a proportionate fashion?

I don't know where Casey is now. He always was a lousy correspondent. He quit the *Express* some years back when it merged with another paper. He had some money, and this plus a fat hunk of severance pay should be keeping him well above the ranks of the indigent.

I suspect he is somewhere in the South or Southwest and I have an idea that along with his fishing or golfing or whatever, the local newspaper or the nearest metropolitan one carries a Casey picture credit on an exclusive from time to time, if only to keep his hand in. He may even have found an attractive widow to share bed and breakfast.

George Harmon Coxe

Pierre
Chambrun

Hugh Pentecost

When Pierre Chambrun investigates crimes (which are, too frequently, of a violent nature), he does it for one reason, and one only: he wants nothing to interfere with the smooth operation of his hotel and wants nothing to damage its reputation. As the manager of New York's finest luxury hotel, the Beaumont, he has both the motivation and the resources to guarantee that no untoward events should disturb his guests.

The Beaumont, to Chambrun's mind, is his hotel, and the smallest fuss is regarded as a personal affront. Because of his consuming devotion to the hotel, and the suave efficiency with which he has conducted its management for the past thirty-five years, he has become as much of an institution as the hotel itself. He maintains the highest standards for himself and his staff, and has as his credo: "The Beaumont is not only a hotel, it is a way of life."

Judson Philips took the name of his granduncle, a prominent attorney in the 1890s, for his pseudonym. Chambrun is one of several successful series detectives to appear under the Hugh Pentecost by-line. Others are John Jericho, a huge, red-bearded Greenwich Village artist, Luke Bradley, a soft-spoken New York City Police Department inspector and later lieutenant for Naval Intelligence, and Julian Quist, a public relations man. Under his own name, he recounts the suspenseful adventures of Peter Styles, a one-legged magazine columnist.

Philips, 74, was the third president of the Mystery Writers of America and received the organization's Grand Master award in 1973 for lifetime achievement. He lives with his wife in Canaan, Connecticut.

Pierre Chambrun

by Hugh Pentecost

IN THE 1920s, when I first became a professional writer, which means that I actually paid the rent and fed myself on the product of my typewriter, the pulp magazines flourished. I found myself turning out thousands of words a month for the Munsey magazines and Street & Smith. Almost instantly running characters developed, which meant I wrote over and over again about the same heroes. When the pulps began to fade I made the transition to the "slicks" and found myself writing a running series for *Liberty*. Then came radio, and a running character once more. I felt trapped in backgrounds I had invented and couldn't change.

Somewhere along the way I began doing novelettes for *American* magazine. I persuaded them that working in a new and fresh background each time was an asset. But each time a story went particularly well *American* would suggest that I do another one about the same character. The one place I was free was in books. Each one was separate, individual, and I enjoyed working with new characters and new backgrounds. But there was gentle pressure from Ray Bond, the fabulous mystery editor at Dodd, Mead, to get a running character going. So I would write three books about the same character and then beg off. Then I would write three books about another character and beg off.

Searching for fresh backgrounds I met an attractive lady who was doing public relations for a famous luxury hotel in New York. It was to be the basis for a one-shot, crammed with the details of hotel management, the glamour of the home-away-from-home of the very rich, the facts that demonstrated that a big hotel was like a city in itself with its own government, police force, hospital, restaurants, nightclubs, bars, shops. The manager, with a thousand details at his fingertips, was an obvious central figure. And so I wrote a novel called *The Cannibal Who Overate* and the Hotel Beaumont and its legendary manager, Pierre Chambrun, were born.

Chambrun may have been modeled, physically, after the manager of the hotel on which my background was based, a gentleman of French descent. But his personality, his talents, his special gifts for dealing with crime just happened. I built a story that could only happen in a hotel, and a crime that could only be solved by a man who knew all the details of a hotel's machinery. Where Chambrun came from, what his background was, didn't matter. He was, you might say, the star of a one-night stand. His song-and-dance routines for that one performance didn't involve structuring a past for him.

He was a short, square man with bright black eyes set in deep pouches, eyes that could show compassion or could look as if they belonged to a hanging judge. He had, I said in that first novel, a kind of built-in radar system for sensing the approach of danger, disorder, violence before there had been a sign of them anyone else could see. The hotel was his love, his passion. Anything that disrupted the Swiss-watch efficiency of its operation brought down Chambrun's wrath and even vengeance on the person responsible. In his position he dealt with kings, with presidents, with diplomats, scientists, movie stars, business tycoons. Many of them were friends, grateful for some special service. The blue-period

Picasso on his office wall, a gift from the artist, is one example of an expressed thanks.

In that first Chambrun novel he was seen through the eyes of a young woman who did public relations for the Beaumont. I had learned long ago that when you are dealing with a special background you have to avoid telling it from the point of view of someone who knows everything about it. If you do, you have to know everything yourself, an impossibility with only relatively superficial research. You view your expert from the outside; everything he says about his specialty is true and accurate; but you stay out of his head because you couldn't possibly describe the thinking of that expert and make it sound real.

So Chambrun was seen in that first book by the young woman who worked for him, and by the young man with whom she fell in love in the course of the story. Through them we met Jerry Dodd, the Beaumont's security man, Betsy Ruysdale, Chambrun's fabulous secretary, the various maitre d's, desk clerks, bellhops, doormen, all a part of the Beaumont's handpicked staff. We saw for the first time the Trapeze Bar, hung like a birdcage over the Beaumont's lobby, the Blue Lagoon Nightclub, the Spartan Bar, a remnant of male chauvinism, where old gentlemen play backgammon and chess without the danger of intrusion by females and where they reminisce about the days when their joints didn't creak and when if they whistled at a girl, she might pay attention.

All this was there to surround the cannibal of that first novel and to watch his undoing by Pierre Chambrun, who seemed to know how the dice would come up before they were rolled.

That was to be that. I, figuratively, said goodbye to Pierre Chambrun and set about looking for greener fields. I forgot

about him for some months until the book came out and
the public response came in. Ray Bond was very stern this
time. I must do another Chambrun book.

There were problems. The young girl and her lover who
had been the objective observers of Chambrun in the first
book had, so to speak, ridden off into the sunset. There had
to be a new "viewpoint character," so Mark Haskell was
born. Mark is a brash young man who took over the public
relations job at the Beaumont. He falls in love forever about
once a year, which means that, by and large, he has a new
girl interest in each book. He views with some cynicism the
daily problems at the Beaumont, problems faced by any big
luxury hotel: the drunks, the deadbeats, the call girls, the
endless cantankerous and baseless complaints, the heart attacks suffered by elderly gentlemen in the wrong rooms.
He found out something that might have disturbed Beaumont guests: there is a card on each registered guest indicating his financial and business standing, whether or not he is
an alcoholic, whether he is a husband cheating on his wife
or she is a wife cheating on her husband, his political affili-
ations (particularly if he is one of the many United Nations
people who stay at the Beaumont). Finally Mark found
himself caught up in what he calls "the Chambrun disease,"
a passion for the smooth running of the hotel. Every night
he checks through the bars, the restaurants, the nightclubs,
the ballrooms, "like Marshall Dillon putting Dodge City to
bed for the night."

Pierre Chambrun had to be more than the somewhat one-
dimensional figure he'd been in the first book, the expert on
hotel management who used his knowledge to solve a particular crime. He had to become a fully rounded human
being, but we could only find out about him through what
other people observed. I still had to stay out of Chambrun's

mind because I couldn't begin to know all that he is supposed to know about his special world.

Mark is continually surprised to find that when he takes a piece of information to Chambrun the Great Man already knows about it. "When I don't know what's going on in my hotel it will be time for me to retire," Chambrun says. And he knows because everyone on his staff, from dishwasher to accountant, from floor maid to security personnel, instantly reports anything out of line. People who work for Chambrun have learned long ago that they won't be blamed for mistakes, only for covering up on them. If anyone has any doubts about how to handle a situation, they come to Chambrun. He then shares in the responsibility for any decision made, right or wrong. If you don't know for certain how to handle a situation and you don't go to him and you muff it, you've had it.

But what about the man as a human being? He began to grow, almost without my having thought about him in advance. His habits were easy. He eats only twice a day, a very hearty breakfast and a gourmet dinner at night, prepared by the Beaumont's French chef. He drinks Turkish coffee all day long, prepared by Miss Ruysdale in a coffee maker in his office. He smokes Egyptian cigarettes. He lives in a penthouse which he owns, on the roof of the hotel, but in his whole history we have only been in it once when the owner of the hotel was loaned it for security reasons. If he has a private life there, not even Mark or Jerry Dodd, the shrewd security chief, knows truly what it is. There are rumors about Miss Ruysdale, the cool, chic, and efficient secretary who seems able to anticipate Chambrun's needs in any crisis. Chambrun calls her simply "Ruysdale," as impersonal as you can imagine. And yet Mark thinks that she may supply needs of Chambrun's that have no relationship to the business. "If Ruysdale is ever in any danger we may find out the truth about them," Mark has said. Someday that may happen, and then, perhaps, we will know.

Where did Chambrun come from? What do we know about his past? Well, he is French, English educated, with a later degree in hotel management from Cornell. The presence of foreign diplomats who stay at the Beaumont revealed, early on, a whole segment of Chambrun's past. The outbreak of World War II sent him back to his native country where he fought in the Resistance in Paris. It is hard to associate the dapper little man sitting behind his carved Florentine desk in his office in the Beaumont with the violence of those times. He calls those "the dark days": a time when he was involved in hanging Nazi war criminals from the nearest lamppost. So we know that he was imbued with unusual physical courage, had a gift for secret stratagems and a passion for justice.

So it developed that the Hotel Beaumont, regardless of who owns the real estate and the building, is Chambrun's creation. It is a very complete world in itself with Chambrun the king, or the president, or the mayor, or whatever title you like to use. In the simple yet complex things involving service to the guests, Chambrun can take pride in what he offers. No two suites in the Beaumont are decorated alike, the artwork on the walls is real and not reproduction; the cuisine is unsurpassed anywhere in the world, the wine celler incomparable. The service is elegant, courteous, quiet, and totally efficient. You want privacy, you get privacy; you are a movie star or a politician and you want it known you are in town, it becomes known. If you have a problem and you need help, there is a man sitting in a plush office on the second floor who will provide assistance and compassion if you ask for it. His name is Pierre Chambrun.

But there is one key thing about Chambrun, I think, and he has put it into words. "We live in an unjust world," he has said. "We live in a world corrupted by the super-rich, the super-powerful, who use bribery and terror to satisfy their greed for more wealth and more power." His eyes, buried in their pouches, glitter brightly as he says this. "But they will not play their games here in the Beaumont, *my* hotel! We will cater to their tastes in caviar and champagne, but not to their games of violence and terror. Let them try to use the Beaumont as a stage for their kind of evil and they will find themselves crushed and thrown out on the street. And I am the man who can do it!"

This from the man whose square, stubby-fingered hands can make Chopin's music sing on the grand piano in his apartment. A man of contrasts, Pierre Chambrun: a gentle and compassionate man who can turn into a cold and implacable enemy of evil.

That's how he has developed over the years, and I expect I will learn more about him as time goes on.

Hugh Pentecost

Inspector
Cockrill

Christianna Brand

Shrewd and acerbic, the aging and birdlike inspector of the Kent County Police is one of the kindest and gentlest of detectives. His irascibility tends to conceal a genuine humanitarianism.

Cockrill has not appeared in many books, and in no recent novels, but his cases have been unfailingly memorable. Curiously, the popularity of both the detective and the author have lagged behind critical acclaim. Erik Routley, in The Puritan Pleasures of the Detective Story, *describes* Green for Danger *as "one of the really great detective novels of all time." A motion picture was made from the book a year after its publication, and noted film authority William K. Everson wrote, in* The Detective on Film, *"Despite the admitted entertainment value of literally thousands of movie mysteries, barely a handful have really matched the skill, cunning, and meticulous construction of their source novels. The British* Green for Danger *was one that did." The demanding Everson listed only two others. And the dean of American mystery critics, Anthony Boucher, wrote, "You have to reach for the greatest of the Great Names (Agatha Christie, John Dickson Carr, Ellery Queen) to find Brand's rivals in the subtleties of the trade. . . ."*

Mary Christianna Milne was born in Malaya in 1907 and lived there and in India before attending an English convent school. She worked as a governess, dress packer, receptionist in a nightclub, professional ballroom dancer, model, secretary, salesgirl, interior decorator, demonstrator of gadgets at trade fairs, and ran a club for working girls. Married to a surgeon, she makes her home in London, and has resumed writing mysteries after a twenty-year hiatus.

Inspector Cockrill

by Christianna Brand

TWO THOUSAND WORDS, he says — "or thereabouts." Am I, then, to squeeze this important biography into a mere two thousand words? Is Inspector Cockrill, with all my devotion to him, to be crammed hugger-mugger into so narrow a pint pot?

Well — none better, you may think: for Cockie, it must be admitted, is a little man — unique in being several inches below the minimum height for a British policeman. He came into being in the fine, free, careless days before I became hagridden by the necessity for accuracy in detail. At intervals during his literary career, I have tried to add a bit to his stature, he "looks shorter than he actually is," and so on; but for the most part we find him described as a sparrow, a small, dusty brown sparrow — "soon he was, sparrow-like, hopping and darting this way and that in search of crumbs of information." "What a funny little man!" thinks Louli, in *Tour de Force*, and "A little man, he is," says one of the twins in a short story, "Blood Brothers." He adds, I'm sorry to say: "And near retiring age, he must be. He looks like a grandfather."

For not only is Inspector Cockrill too short to have been in the force; he does also seem to be a bit too old.

True, in *Fog of Doubt* (British title: *London Particular*), his hair is said to be gray, but, were it not so entirely out of character, we might here suspect him of having taken a leaf out of M. Poirot's book. For elsewhere, it is indubitably white: "a little brown man with bright brown, bird-like eyes deep-set beneath a fine broad brow, with an aquiline nose and a mop of fluffy white hair fringing a magnificent head." "Fringing" does even suggest a touch of baldness but this, I swear, is no more than a thinness on top. He is old enough, at any rate, to be wondering rather anxiously whether he may not be in danger of becoming a dirty old man — dearly loving, as he does, a pretty girl. Nothing could be further from the truth — Venetia and Fran, the loving and confiding sisters, sad, gentle Esther Sanson, enchanting Louli, so comic and so vulnerable, even the bouncy little sexpot Rosie — they were all safe enough with him; and when the dreadful Grace Morland sets her cap at him, "though half-heartedly, for he was not to be considered her equal in education or birth," he thinks of her without rancor merely as a sentimental goat. I mention it only to suggest that he *is* old enough to be already a little in dread of the approach of senility. There is even a terrible moment in *Tour de Force* when the local police chief of the island of San Juan el Pirata refuses to believe he can be in the British police. The tourist guide is forced into apprehensive explanation: "Inspector, he says — he says that you are too old."

"*Too old?*" said Cockie in a voice of doom.

If he is elderly, however, the inspector has made up for it by remaining, like the matinee idols of his youth, at the same age for something like thirty years. Any further comparison would hardly stand up; one could by no means describe his attire as the pink of sartorial perfection. He has a habit of picking up the first hat to hand; "Well, never mind — it's quite a good fit," he will say. Any hat that does not deafen and blind him is quite a good fit to Inspector Cockrill. " 'I must have picked up my sergeant's by mistake,' he said, irritably, pushing the enormous hat up from over his eyes for the fifth time. 'I'm always doing it.' He seemed perfectly indifferent to anything but the discomfort involved by this accident." The hat will be crammed sideways on to his head as though he might at any moment break out into an amateur rendering of Napoleon's Farewell to his Troops. True, on his one visit abroad — Cockie simply hates Abroad! — he does acquire a rather splendid straw, but "contrary to custom, he had bought it, not two sizes too large for him, but considerably too small, and it sat on his splendid head like a paper boat, breasting the fine spray of his greying hair." He wears a rather rumpled gray suit and, far ahead of his time, a disreputable old mac trailing over his shoulder. He smokes incessantly, rolling his own shaggy cigarettes, holding them cupped in the palm of his right hand so that the fingers are so stained with nicotine as to appear to be tipped with mahogany.

But by no means suppose my hero to be a figure of fun. "I hadn't counted on its being Inspector Cockrill," says the young villain in "Blood Brothers," "and to be honest it struck a bit of a chill to the heart of me. His eyes are as bright as a bird's and they seem to look right down into you. . . ."

He came into being when, having set my first book in London, I wanted a country background — which necessitated a detective from the local force. He is attached, therefore, to the Kent County Police: a tricky job for his author, getting him to London when a crime must be set there — he is obliged to interfere only in an unofficial character, as personal friend of one or another of the suspects. As he disapproves strongly of the innocently brash young Chief Inspector Charlesworth of New Scotland Yard, it makes for some difficulty all round, not to say an occasional unseemly touch of triumph. "*Et, avec un clin d'oeil satisfait, l'Inspecteur Cockrill s'en alla, clopin-clopant dans la nuit,*" says the French translation, rounding off *Death of Jezebel;* and *clopin-clopant* does seem to just about sum it up.

But at home in Heronsford, matters are very different. "Cockie was sitting with his feet up on the mantelpiece — which fortunately was a low one or his short legs would have been practically vertical and his behind in the fire," musing on the horrors of eventual retirement. He'll have to buy a couple of disguises, that's all, and set up as a private detective, to stave off the boredom. But it had better be elsewhere. "Here in Heronsford, no such attempt would be of the smallest use; no density of beard or whisker could long conceal *him* from the sheep, black and white, among whom he had moved, the Terror of Kent, for so long. . . ."

And indeed he can be pretty fierce. "He was widely advertised as having a heart of gold beneath his irascible exterior but there were those who said bitterly that the heart was so infinitesimal and you had to dig so far down to get at it, that it was hardly worth the effort." Long ago, his wife had died, as had their only child; and with them had died also "all his hope and much of his faith and charity." The heart is there, nevertheless, however deeply buried. He can be very tender and kind, very understanding with all those pretty girls caught up, innocent, in the ugly toils of murder; with the enchanting old grandmother in her room on the top floor of the house in Maida Vale, enlivening her boredom by pretending to be a good deal more dotty than she actually is. And he will have compassion for the guilty, drawn by inner compulsions to the committing of a single crime. On the other hand, he can be forthright and stern. "He thought it unwise and unhealthy that, because she had died for her sins, she should be allowed to grow into a martyr in the family's eyes. He thought they should face the facts. 'She made up her mind to do this thing and she worked it all out thoroughly, and acted quickly and cleverly. . . .' " There is no false sentiment about Chief Inspector Cockrill, none at all.

The secret of his success? — which, strange to say, is unfailing — well, I wonder. He is not a great one for the physical details of an investigation: "meanwhile his henchmen pursued their ceaseless activities" writes his creator, not too sure herself exactly what those would be; and he is content to leave fingerprint powder and magnifying glass to the experts, using their findings in a process of elimination, to get down to the nitty-gritty from there on. He has acute powers of observation, certainly; a considerable understanding of human nature, a total integrity and commitment, much wisdom; and as we know a perhaps overlong experience of the criminal world. ("And buns in the oven is the net result," says naughty little Rosie, confessing, in *Fog of Doubt* [British title: *London Particular*] to conduct unbecoming a young maiden, on a recent visit to the continent. She adds that now she supposes he will be shocked. "My *dear* child," says Cockie, "you should come to the Heronsford police court some time!")

Above all — he has patience.

And spell it another way, and you have his biography, not only in a pint pot, but reduced right down to a nutshell. For Detective Chief Inspector Cockrill is the dead spittin' image of my father-in-law; and my father-in-law was for over fifty years a medical practitioner in a Welsh mining town about the same size as Heronsford.

Above all, therefore — Cockie's progenitor had patients. And what does a doctor bring to the study of his patients, but those very qualities that we claim for the chief inspector? Observation, understanding, the ability to cleave through the irrelevant to the right and only diagnosis; a keen appreciation of cause and effect, an ever-increasing experience; integrity, wisdom . . .

Shrewd and wise he was, my father-in-law, and so is Inspector Cockrill shrewd and wise. Like a good doctor, he inquires into every detail. A young man confesses to the murder of a girl. He has laid upon her breast a brooch in the form of a cross, "to show I was sorry, like."

"You're telling lies," says Cockrill. "The brooch was lying there crooked, with the pin upwards. That doesn't sound much like reverence, does it?" But later, someone discloses that, finding the body, he has picked up the brooch and just dropped it back again. When he had first seen it, it had been the right way up. "I thought it could have been placed there — well, because it was a cross." He added: "Is it important?"

"It depends on what you call important," says Cockie in his acerbic way. "It's going to hang a man."

But in fact he was wrong that time; and often he *is* wrong — till the last hour. He is by no means cocksure — surely the greatest weakness in detective or doctor alike? In *Green for Danger*, out of his depth in the world of anesthetics and operating theaters, he has some bad moments. "Cockrill could not bear to look. His mind, usually so keen and clear, was a dark confusion of terror and self-questioning and a hideous anxiety. He had made an experiment, thinking it all so safe: had taken a terrible gamble with a man's life and suddenly everything was going wrong." He wipes his damp hands down the sides of the theater gown, fighting off a black panic.

He is sufficiently sure, however, to work without the somewhat inevitable sergeant, a uniformed Dr. Watson to whom he can confide, as he goes along, the workings of his mind — that is, perhaps, why we know so comparatively little of them, until at the end he makes them clear. No doubt some splendid, reliable chap will be at his beck and call in the regular way, to take instructions and see things carried out; but no complacent underling sits at Inspector Cockrill's side, interrupting interrogations with chirpy questions of his own. (I once asked a way-up policeman if a sergeant would really act like this when his superior was present. He replied in a deep voice: "*Not* if he ever hoped for promotion.")

With Mr. Charlesworth, when he becomes involved in cases where that young gentleman is in charge, the inspector maintains an armed neutrality. "Oh, yes!" Charlesworth remarked in his guileless way on their first introduction, "You're the chap that made such a muck of that hospital case down in Kent?" Infiltrating into his cases on behalf of his friends (always with the most generous welcome — Cockie is scrupulous in sharing information and deduction, only very, very slightly obscuring this little point or that — if the silly young fool can't take a hint, too bad!) he pursues his own somewhat Machiavellian way. And Charlesworth is a little inclined to Kindly Pity. He can hardly keep back a grin as he listens to the inspector's great build-up of a highly elaborate case — against the wrong suspect — at the end of the Jezebel affair. A bit past it, poor old boy — these dear old duffers are all the same! Cockie observes the grin and his blood boils; but — "*You're* a clever little man," says the real murderer, inveigled by the fantasy into confession at last. And with a single look into Mr. Charlesworth's face, off goes the inspector, *clopin-clopant* into the night.

My father-in-law was a small man, white haired already when I knew him. An old mac trailed over his shoulder as he stumped off on his short legs into the veil of fine rain that hangs incessantly over the valleys of South Wales; visiting twenty or thirty patients in a day, he had a rich choice of hats. But nobody thought of *him* as a figure of fun! His mind was keen, his glance was bright with a sort of mischievous glee. His surgery was an old converted stable; from it he dispensed a little medicine and a great deal of down-to-earth advice, and patients have seriously told me that he could raise the dead. To me, when I write about Inspector Cockrill, it seems that I also for a little while raise the dead, and live again a few hours in the company of one whom I deeply admired and respected and deeply loved. Louli was wrong when she thought of my inspector as a funny little man. "Do you think that the truth really mattered so much?" asks the saddest and best — in the sense of intrinsic goodness — of my murderers; and, "Yes," says Cockie. "It's something sacred. If you're a doctor — you have only one idea, to preserve life. If you're a policeman, ditto — to preserve the truth." Nothing small or funny, it seems to me — about *that?*

Two thousand words, he said. Or thereabouts.

Captain
José Da Silva

Robert L. Fish

Most of the great writers of mystery fiction are English or American, and it is therefore hardly surprising that most of literature's great detectives are English or American. Although Robert L. Fish is no exception to this long-established tradition, Captain José Maria Carvalho Santos Da Silva is. As the pride of the Brazilian law enforcement establishment, Da Silva has been a policeman for some fifteen years (though still in his late thirties).

Fish lived in Brazil for more than a decade as a consultant to that country's plastics industry, acquiring a familiarity with Brazilian life that lends authenticity to the Da Silva series.

The first book about the courageous police captain, The Fugitive, *earned Fish an Edgar Allan Poe Award from the Mystery Writers of America for best first novel of the year, in 1962. But Da Silva is not the only memorable character created by the prolific Fish. A series of police procedural novels and short stories (written under the pseudonym Robert L. Pike) features Lieutenant Clancy of the N.Y.P.D., whose name was changed to Bullitt when Steve McQueen portrayed him as a San Francisco cop in the film version of* Mute Witness, *and later became Lieutenant Reardon of San Francisco.*

A long cycle of parody-pastiches published in Ellery Queen's Mystery Magazine *involves Schlock Homes of 221B Bagel Street and his assistant, Dr. Watney. One of the great crooks of recent years is also a Fish character: Kek Huygens, a Polish-born smuggler with a Dutch name, who carries a valid American passport. And in 1963, Fish completed* The Assassination Bureau, *a crime novel left unfinished by Jack London at the time of his death. The resemblance of the book to the film made from it (starring Diana Rigg and Telly Savalas) ends with its title. The 65-year-old author lives with his wife in Trumbull, Connecticut.*

Captain José Da Silva

by Robert L. Fish

THE FIRST TIME I met Captain José Da Silva — Zé Da Silva, I later learned, to his friends — was at Mario's, that great restaurant with its world-famous brandy bar located in Leme, that short cul-de-sac portion of Copacabana beach in Rio de Janeiro that runs north from the Avenida Princesa Isabel to deadend in rock and ocean, barring further passage. I was living in the section called Leblon at the time, rather a distance from Leme and Mario's, but I had gotten into the pleasant habit of dropping in there for a drink or two on my way home each evening. It was very relaxing to sit at one of the small outdoor tables in that quiet backwater on the otherwise busy beach and watch the shadows darken on the ocean while they lightened on the glass in your hand. The vast endlessness of the Atlantic, stretching to the dimming horizon, was soothing; it seemed to put a person into a more proper perspective after a day in the city battling small people for small rewards and somehow thinking it important.

This particular day I had seated myself and was waiting for a waiter to appear. Two men began to pass me, edging their way toward an unoccupied table, when the one in the lead suddenly stopped and bent toward me, smiling, his hand outstretched.

"You're Robert Fish, aren't you? The writer?"

I made my living as an engineer in those days, and the writing was almost a hobby, but I cannot imagine a writer failing to respond to such an implied suggestion that his work had been read. It took me several moments, though, even while shaking the man's hand, to realize he was a Mr. Wilson I had met several times at the American embassy, the first time when I had gone there to register as an American living permanently in Brazil. Wilson — to my shame I cannot recall his first name to this day — was the type of person, not only whose first name could easily be forgotten, but whose face could elude one as well. This must have been the third or fourth time I had seen the man, and it was only now that his nondescript personality was impressing itself upon me to the extent that allowed me to recognize him.

"Mr. Wilson. Sit down. Please!" I said, somehow happy with the interruption. It had been a dull day and Wilson's companion appeared to be a rather interesting type. Not, certainly, a man one would forget as easily as one did Mr. Wilson.

The two men seated themselves and Wilson introduced his friend to me as a Captain José Da Silva, of the Rio Police. (It was only later I learned the full extent of his rather effulgent name, or the fact that he was the Brazilian representative to Interpol — even as I later learned that Wilson was his American counterpart in Brazil . . .)

I must say that my first reaction was one of complete surprise. At first glance, Da Silva seemed much more the type the police might pursue, rather than the type to be the pursuer. He was a bit taller than myself, which would make him about six foot, or six foot, one inch in height; he had an athletic build with, I judged, between one-eighty and one-ninety pounds in weight. He had wide shoulders, narrow waist and hips, and while his face was well structured, some early childhood disease had covered it with pockmarks. He wore a brigand mustache almost as a challenge, and both it and his wild black shock of unruly hair could have stood a barber's attention. There was a saturnine look on his Indian-like face, a humorous glint in his black eyes, as if he were reading my thoughts and being amused by them. As for his dress — and one must remember this was in a day when Brazilian functionaries wore jackets and neckties as regulation, regardless of the insufferable heat — Da Silva was dressed carelessly and comfortably in an open-necked sport shirt, and I later realized the only reason he wore a jacket at all was to conceal his belt holster and the gun he carried.

There were several things that impressed me about the man, though, that first evening we met. First was the fact that he was no sooner seated than a waiter appeared, as if by magic, carrying a drink for both him and Wilson. At Mario's, this is no small recognition! I have seen ministers of the state wait as long as I have before a waiter would deign to notice them. The second thing that impressed me was that, as if by magnet, every feminine eye in the place swung around to study him with obvious approval, as well as several women merely walking pets in the area. Although Da Silva gave no indication that he was aware of the inspection, I was sure he not only knew of it, but enjoyed it thoroughly. Since in my opinion he was not, and is not, a particularly handsome man, I could only concede some magnetism on his part that is, frankly, beyond my understanding.

Still, I found Captain Da Silva quite interesting that first evening, and remarkably well informed. His English was perfect, which was just as well since my Portuguese at that time was rather sketchy. I knew for a certainty as we spoke that the captain's many adventures could well prove excel-lent grist for the mill of my restless typewriter. But it was only after we had bade each other good-evening and I was driving home that I realized that while the captain had been quite gregarious — one might even say garrulous — he had managed to reveal remarkably little about himself.

The next day, by now thoroughly intrigued by the idea of putting Captain Da Silva on paper, I called the American embassy and was fortunate in finding Wilson free for lunch. I felt sure I could discover far more about the captain from his friend than I could from his own lips. Wilson and I met at the upper-deck restaurant in the Santos Dumont Airport terminal, a place I later learned was a favorite of Da Silva himself. Over our first drink I mentioned my thought of doing some fiction based on Da Silva, and added that I would like to include Wilson in the stories as well, being positive that such flattery to a man as prosaic as Wilson was sure to guarantee me his complete cooperation. "But," I added, "I'm afraid I will need your help. Captain Da Silva seems rather — well, possibly modest isn't the exact word . . ."

Wilson laughed delightedly. "Yes, I must agree with you on that. Modest is not the exact word for Zé."

"What I mean is," I went on doggedly, "is that he talks a lot, but he says so little about himself."

"Count your blessings," Wilson said in the tone of one giving valuable advice. "You only met him last night." He saw the look on my face, and smiled. "Tell me, as a writer how do you see Da Silva? As what type of character?"

I gave the matter some thought. "I see him as an adventurer," I said at last. "The captain of a ship running contraband — well, chasing contraband, then — or the pilot of a fighter plane, swooping down on the enemy, guns blazing —"

Wilson laughed again. "Da Silva hates airplanes with a passion! He nearly swoons with fear every time he has to climb into one. He is utterly convinced of the theory of gravity, and he is positive every time he gets into one that he is signing his own death warrant. He is sure it will crash."

I stared at the man, by now convinced that Wilson was merely jealous of the captain's exploits. "Are you saying that Captain Da Silva is a coward?" I asked coldly.

Wilson's smile disappeared instantly. He looked at me with a touch of disappointment, as if wondering how anyone as dense as myself could ever aspire to becoming a writer.

"I am saying quite the contrary," he said evenly. "I am saying that Zé Da Silva is the bravest man I know. He hates and fears airplanes, but he flies in them. He has an almost pathological fear of snakes, but he once went to an island that was literally covered with them, in order to solve a case. He hates fat women in slacks, but he once —" His smile returned and with it his previous lightness of tone. "Well, I don't know if his bravery went quite that far. You'll have to ask him that one yourself." He raised a hand for a waiter. "Look, I've been invited to his mother's home on Sunday for cocktails; I imagine she feels much as you apparently do, that she can get more information on her son and his doings from me than from him. Why don't you come along? I'm sure you'll find it interesting . . ."

So Sunday found me at the home of Dona Beatriz Carvalho Santos Da Silva, in the suburb of Santa Teresa, high in the wooded hills above Rio. The home was quite a surprise; I had no idea that policemen's families ran to such luxury. But his mother was equally surprising. I'm not sure exactly what I had been expecting, but certainly not this small, delicate woman with beautiful eyes that seemed to read my thoughts. Wilson was there when I arrived and apparently he had briefed Dona Beatriz on my mission, so I wasted little time.

"How did it happen that your son took up police work?" I asked. "It doesn't seem to be — well, I mean the majority of police I've seen here — as well as in most places — well, they aren't particularly educated, and it doesn't seem to be the type of profession — what I mean is —"

She saved me in my floundering. "José Maria" — she never referred to her son in any other way, I discovered — "José Maria is rather stubborn, as you'll discover if you get to know him better." (Her English was as good as her son's — or as mine. It was only later I learned her mother had been American, and that English was the home language.) "José Maria became interested in criminology when he was studying in the United States, and fortunately our family can afford to let him indulge in his hobbies. I'm afraid I spoil both José Maria and his sister, but they are all I have. Their father died when they were children."

I had so many questions I didn't know where to begin. "You consider his work merely a hobby? Does he?"

"I hope so," she said calmly. "Any work properly done must be a hobby if it isn't to become boring. But if you're thinking of a hobby as something to be dropped when one is tired of it, then we are at odds. José Maria will never drop police work. He likes it, which is all that counts." She smiled at me. "He is also very good at it."

There was little I could say to that, so I plowed on. "You say he studied in the United States?"

"Only his last two years of university. He had been studying law here at the University of Rio, but he was

thrown out after he put a knife through his cousin's hand."
I'm afraid I stared, but Dona Beatriz was not at all per-
turbed. "Nestor had taken something without José Maria's
permission, which was very foolish of the boy. But Nestor
was always doing foolish things. Poor Nestor! He was
killed in a foolish way not too long ago. Fortunately, José
Maria was able to find the people responsible."

There was the sound of the bell, and a moment later a
group came in. Apparently Sunday was a get-together day
at Dona Beatriz's home, and our hostess had to excuse herself and take charge of her other guests. Wilson walked to
the sideboard, refreshed our drinks, and sat down beside me.

"Are you sure you want to write about Zé Da Silva?" he
asked. "He's quite a bit different from most fictional policemen, or private-eye detectives, you know."

"In what way?" I asked.

"Well," Wilson said, "to begin with, most fictional policemen — official policemen — are stupid, and their cases are
solved either by brilliant amateurs or by private-eye detectives. Zé is far from stupid, and I pity the brilliant amateur who
gets in his way on a case. And as for the private-eye detectives, the Mike Hammers and their ilk, if they're hit on
the head with a sledgehammer, they merely scramble themselves some eggs (why always eggs?), wash them down
with whiskey — a sickening thought in itself — take a cold
shower, and are as good as new, ready to get right back to
criminal-chasing. Well, first of all, Zé hates cold showers,
although I do admit he's fond of eggs. And when he's hit on
the head — which has happened several times to my knowledge — he bleeds, and gets to a doctor as fast as he can. Zé
recognizes the danger of infection from dirty sledgeham-
mers, which most fictional detectives apparently do not."

"What else?"

"He laughs when he's happy and weeps when he's sad. And complains like the devil if he hurts. He also has a nasty temper, which the cold, calculating investigators in fiction are not supposed to have. When his cousin Nestor was killed, I recall watching him interrogate a waiter at the restaurant where the killing took place. The waiter had some information that Zé wanted, but he was a little slow in giving it. Zé damn near beat his head off."

"You mean," I said, "that he's human."

"Unfortunately," Wilson said, and drained his drink.

Well, that conversation at Dona Beatriz's lovely home in Santa Teresa took place many years ago. Since that time the beach at Copacabana has been doubled in size and the Avenida Atlantica more than doubled, and Mario's now has room for more tables before it on the patterned sidewalk. The capital of the country has been moved to Brasília, and Wilson is now working out of the American consulate rather than the embassy, a step down in rank, perhaps, but I am sure he would never have been happy very far from his apartment on the Lagoa. Captain Da Silva remains a captain, although he is now attached to the federal police rather than to the local police; he, too, remains in his beloved Rio de Janeiro, and the price of his remaining has been the promotions he has refused.

But the captain still has his same battered, souped-up taxi with the two-way radio in the horn ring, and the engine under the dented hood that is capable of over one hundred fifty miles an hour. And the little exercise he takes — because Da Silva still abhors exercise — is still in the form of *capoeira*, that form of fighting with the feet that is considered hooliganism by the upper classes in Brazilian society.

Both Wilson and Da Silva are getting older, but they are still far from through. I still manage to see them from time to time, either at Mario's or the Santos Dumont restaurant for lunch, and between the two they have given me the plots of ten books covering their joint adventures. Da Silva has suggested I stop before I report his tottering into the old-folks' home, but I know eventually there will have to be at least one more. I was accused of murdering one of my best friends, and the fact that I wasn't even in Rio at the time — or even in the country — did little to convince the local police of my innocence. Were it not for Zé Da Silva, I might well have been in serious trouble, for Zé found the real criminal.

We sit around Mario's at times and laugh at the idiocy of the first detectives assigned to the case, but for me it was no laughing matter. And Captain José Maria Carvalho Santos Da Silva took on a new dimension for me in that affair. Someday I hope to be able to properly translate the captain's skill in that case for his reading fans . . .

Nancy
Drew

Carolyn Keene

Aside from all the other inconveniences, it must be an acute embarrassment for the many master criminals of literature to be caught by the inspired genius of the amateur detective, or by the methodical attention to detail of the stodgy policeman. But consider the ego-shattering plight of the archvillain who is unmasked by a slender teenage girl. Still, it happens with regularity. Nancy Drew, the most successful of adolescent sleuths, has solved fifty-five cases and shows no sign of slowing down. Although she appears younger, Nancy is, in fact, 18 — and has been for nearly a half-century.

Carolyn Keene is one of the many pseudonyms of Edward Stratemeyer, founder of the Stratemeyer Syndicate in 1906. He created virtually every popular series of children's books in America, personally writing about 400 books and supplying plots for an additional 700. When he died in 1930, the Syndicate was run by his two daughters until one retired in 1942; since then, it has been headed by Harriet Stratemeyer Adams. Mrs. Adams, now 84 has rewritten or updated the early Nancy Drew books, the first three of which were written by her father. Among the other popular series characters created by Stratemeyer and subsequently produced by the Syndicate are Tom Swift, the Hardy Boys, the Bobbsey Twins, and the Rover Boys. No one can accurately compute the total number of books sold by the Syndicate, but estimates place the number in excess of 100 million copies since 1930. A new television anthology series featuring Nancy Drew or the Hardy Boys in four of every five episodes made its debut on ABC on January 30, 1977. Mrs. Adams claims that many story incidents in her books are based on personal experiences. Small wonder! The resident of New Jersey has four children, eleven grandchildren, and a great-grandson.

Nancy Drew

by Carolyn Keene

PERHAPS IT WAS BECAUSE Nancy Drew was created by someone who understood but did not admire weepy women, 'fraidy cats, and overfeminine girls, that she became a levelheaded, logical-thinking teenage detective. Perhaps her readers were drawn to her with a subconscious sympathy because Nancy had been motherless since she was three years old. But this omission in her growing up period was well filled by her father, a prosperous lawyer, and Mrs. Hannah Gruen, the lovable housekeeper. With Mr. Drew giving Nancy the mystery end of some of his cases and Hannah worrying about the young sleuth's exploits, Nancy is kept busy, and protected most of the time. As her fame spread, people with strange mysteries began to request the girl sleuth to solve them. Right now she is working on her fifty-fifth case.

Nancy remains eighteen, though a humorous reporter came out with the headline, "Nancy Drew, eighteen going on forty." Physiologically this is no doubt true, but the wonderful world of science fiction has permitted me to keep her and her friends at a static age. Nancy has a boyfriend but I do not intend to have them marry. Why? Immediately her fans will put their beloved sleuth in a class with their parents. And what little girl wants to read about mommy's and daddy's problems when she can become engrossed in a mystery her teenage Nancy is solving?

Although there are now three generations of readers, among whom is a large sprinkling of boys, I continually update or rewrite any stories which no longer are in line with customs and language of today, but rather of some twenty-five or thirty years ago. Nancy's little blue roadster had to go when everyone else's had to. Dialects had to be removed so Nancy Drew stories would not offend any ethnic group. The ethnic groups of subteen and teenage children are now fans of Nancy Drew. Overenthusiastic artists from time to time picture the characters in the stories as black, Indian, or Asiatic. Fortunately I see these sketches and insist that Nancy and her family and friends be pictured as they always have been.

That is, with one exception. Nancy was always described as a blonde. To my consternation an artist had given her bright red hair! When I asked why, he told me that the book cover called for three girls. Two were blondes, one a brunette. He felt that a contrast would help the picture. I finally compromised and let him make her a strawberry blonde. I think a hairdresser could have done better, but unfortunately such coiffeurs are not permitted to tamper with book-cover hair.

Minor changes have taken place in Nancy's acquaintanceship with Ned Nickerson during the past twenty years. In the early stories about her adventures there was no romance. Her life was strictly the business of solving mysteries. Gradually Ned and his college friends have appeared more often "with affectionate greetings" and *au revoirs* that included some hugs and kisses. Now the boys often help solve the mysteries. Their visits to Nancy and her two chums include at least one hair-raising adventure for them and of course they come through manfully. Critics used to complain that

Ned was an ineffectual partner, so I have made him more virile and at times he rescues Nancy just in time from a near fatal predicament. Yes, in her zeal to get a clue or track down a suspect, she tries to be cautious but inadvertently throws caution to the wind and becomes trapped. On the other hand, she often manages to extricate herself, proving she is a real and very well informed and quick-thinking detective, as she did when locked up with a poisonous spider.

Nancy has great respect for the truly supernatural, but none for man-made ghosts, masks, spooks, superstitions, phantoms, or haunted castles and ships. She delves persistently into these mysteries until she uncovers the instigator or the natural cause of the rumor. Most of her adversaries are human, but in *The Crooked Banister* story there is an incredibly strong robot programmed to attack or to embrace, whichever the occasion calls for. But its embraces are never the result of admiration or affection; rather they are of the boa constrictor type. Nancy was a near-victim and it took all her ingenuity and some help to extricate herself from the situation. From the experience, however, she picked up a valuable clue to the mystery of a strange house whose owner was missing.

Like me, Nancy enjoys traveling and she is rarely out of my mind when I am on a trip. From the notes and photographs I have taken all over the world, episodes are woven into Nancy's adventures. Of course many of them are exaggerated for dramatic reasons. In Africa I saw a baboon about to pluck off a woman's wig and yelled to stop him. In *The Spider Sapphire Mystery* I let the baboon lift the wig from an unpleasant and annoying, appearance-conscious young woman. Through this adventure Nancy and her two girl companions were able to change the young woman's whole outlook on life. Suddenly she became attractive without the excessive use of makeup and a wig, and began to have dates at once.

Probably the most challenging puzzles that come to Nancy are the seemingly unfathomable code messages upon which she often stumbles. For instance, what should she do with "Blue bells will be singing horses?" When the young sleuth finally deciphers the message, she is able to make a daring rescue of victims held illegally in a nursing home. A puzzling note and the sketch of an oversized eye with Greek letters under it send Nancy after a bizarre scientific criminal. Of course, after some harrowing experiences she catches him! Once she communicated with a ghostlike intruder by tap dancing in Morse Code.

In *The Secret of the Forgotten City* the girl detective is shown an ancient stone tablet with petroglyphs on it. After deciphering them, she joins a dig to hunt for gold reputed to be buried under the Nevada desert. My favorite of Nancy's clever deductions of decoding appears in *The Clue in the Crossword Cipher*, which I consider the most ingenious of all her mystery solving. It takes her to romantic Peru, from sea level to the mountain where Machu Picchu stands in sky-line ruins, to the unexplained Nascan site lines, those gigantic figures of beasts and birds carved into the mammoth gravelly plain. The monkey clue, in Spanish, gives Nancy the key.

Nancy has no illusions about the superiority of the police over her work as an amateur, and consults and confides in them at all times. Naturally, she never asks them to solve her cases, but is delighted to alert them to be present at the denouement and make the arrests. Captain McGinnis of River Heights, her hometown, is one of her best friends. The officer has sung the praises of the lawyer Drew and his daughter over a wide area so that they are well known and if in need of assistance in other towns or cities are recognized at once from their exploits. Nancy, however, has been stopped in her car and at airports and steamship docks with a possibility of arrest before proving her innocence to some charge spread by the very people she is accusing of a crime. Tense moments probably start the young reader biting her nails for a few minutes — for which I am apologetically sorry.

I am often asked how I regard slender, attractive Nancy Drew — just as a fictional character or as someone alive and vibrant. Actually I think of her as a third lovely daughter. The two who are mine by birth have advanced in age, married, and have children. Being forthright individuals, we had our moments of disagreement. I adopted Nancy, who, unlike them, does and says exactly what I tell her to, or rather let her do. She never disagrees and together we get the job accomplished and the mystery solved. Nancy is a believable type of girl, even though she is independent and much admired for her perspicacity. Nancy is a blue-eyed sportswoman, proficient in horsemanship, even to circus bareback stunt riding. She plays tennis, and used her golf game to help solve the mystery of *The Haunted Bridge* from which superstitious caddies stayed away. To solve the *Mystery at the Ski Jump* Nancy uses her ability as a skier and a skater. Incidentally, my children and grandchildren are proficient at all these sports. (This includes a son.) They could not let Nancy Drew beat them in the athletic line, even though Mother can do what she wishes with her pen and dictating machine.

Nancy has many friends, but confides her mysteries to only a few. Bess Marvin and George Fayne (a girl) are her constant companions and often are a great help when Nancy is trying to extricate herself from a tight spot like the one in *The Moonstone Castle Mystery*. The powerful muscles of the footballers Ned, Burt, and Dave come in handy when Nancy is dangling on one-half of a broken bridge. Incidentally, all of them lend humor to the conversations, and there is a lot of good-natured teasing.

While Nancy does her share of this, she is more apt to be figuring out how she can crack the case on which she is working. One thought is never out of her mind — to help other people, but never to ask others to help her just for herself. I am a graduate of Wellesley College, whose motto is *Non ministrari sed ministrare*, which has become my own motto also and which I have instilled into Nancy Drew's character.

Librarians and teachers wonder why the impact of this series is so great. I believe that basically young people want to admire their fictional heroes and heroines. They look forward to reading another and yet another adventure *ad infinitum* about a character or group of characters whose exploits are exciting but where the contents of the story are safe and sane in any analysis — moral, correct, and geared to the reader's age, not the character's age. Nancy remains a lovable girl, somewhat above the average in ability and acumen, but why not?

Carolyn Keene

The
87th Precinct

Ed McBain

Pity Ed McBain. It must be tough for a writer to accept the fact that his readers think they know more about his books than he does. McBain, for example, writes about Isola, a fictional city which he states is not — emphatically not — New York City. But everyone knows the action takes place in Manhattan. McBain succeeded in making a series character — and one of the most successful in the history of detective fiction — out of a squad. Not a man, not a woman, but an entire police precinct squad. And he knew that no single member of that squad was essential to its success; no one was indispensable. So he killed Steve Carella. Who, naturally, refused to stay dead and was immediately resurrected from his premature grave. That miraculous event has delighted the many fans of the Eight-Seven ever since. Carella is healthy and still strong after thirty-two books, several films, and a television series (which ran for the 1961 and 1962 seasons, starring Robert Lansing as Carella and Gena Rowlands as Teddy, his wife).

McBain is both prolific and versatile, his voluminous police procedural novels and other crime books ranging from stark terror to frenzied slapstick. He has also written books under the pseudonyms Curt Cannon, Hunt Collins, and Richard Marsten, but his most famous, The Blackboard Jungle, *appeared under his real name: Evan Hunter. He has also written screenplays for television and motion pictures, most notably* Fuzz *(based on his own book) and* The Birds, *Alfred Hitchcock's classic thriller. A native New Yorker, McBain, 51, now lives in Connecticut.*

The 87th Precinct

by Ed McBain

THEY KEEP TELLING ME Carella is the hero of the series.

I keep telling them it isn't supposed to be that way. In fact, and hardly anyone will believe this, I actually *killed* Carella in the third book of the series. Not I, personally, but someone named Gonzo who, on page 116 of Permabooks' edition of *The Pusher* (in 1956, the series was published only in paperback), had the audacity to shoot Carella three times in the chest:

The only warning was the tightening of Gonzo's eyes. Carella saw them squinch up, and he tried to move sideways, but the gun was already speaking. He did not see it buck in the boy's fist. He felt searing pain lash at his chest, and he heard the shocking declaration of three explosions and then he was falling, and he felt very warm, and he also felt very ridiculous because his legs simply would not hold him up, how silly, how very silly, and his chest was on fire, and the sky was tilting to meet the earth... He opened his mouth, but no sound came from it. And then the waves of blackness came at him, and he fought to keep them away, unaware that Gonzo was running off through the trees, aware only of the engulfing blackness, and suddenly sure that he was about to die.

There is no self-respecting mystery writer who would dare write those words — "and suddenly sure that he was

about to die" — unless he was using them to foreshadow an
event in the pages ahead. Those words almost constituted
a contract with the reader; and so (of course) I paid off
the marker at the end of the book. At least, at the end of the
book as it was delivered to my publishers.

The original scene took place in the hospital where Carella
had been on the critical list since the shooting. Lieutenant
Byrnes was there to visit him. Teddy Carella was coming
down the corridor toward Byrnes.

At first she was only a small figure at the end of the corridor,
and then she walked closer and he watched her. Her hands
were wrung together at her waist, and her head was bent, and
Byrnes watched her and felt a new dread, a dread that attacked
his stomach and his mind. There was defeat in the curve of
her body, defeat in the droop of her head.

Carella, he thought. *Oh God, Steve, no* . . .

He rushed to her, and she looked up at him, and her face was
streaked with tears, and when he saw the tears on the face of
Steve Carella's wife, he was suddenly barren inside, barren and
cold, and he wanted to break from her and run down the corridor, break from her and escape the pain in her eyes.

Outside the hospital, the church bells tolled.

It was Christmas day, and all was right with the world.

But Steve Carella was dead.

Now, I thought that was pretty classy. The original concept of the series as I'd outlined it to Herb Alexander, my
editor at Pocket Books, was to use a squadroom full of
detectives as a conglomerate hero. I would try to portray
accurately the working day of a big-city cop, but I would
do so in terms of a handful of men whose diverse personalities and character traits, when combined, would form a

single hero — the 87th Squad. To my knowledge, this had never been done before, and I felt it was unique. I felt, further, that the concept would enable me to bring new men into the squadroom as needed, adding their particular qualities or defects to the already existing mix, while at the same time disposing of characters who no longer seemed essential to the mix. The squad was the hero, and no man on the squad was indispensable or irreplaceable. In real life, detectives got shot and killed. So, in *The Pusher*, Detective Stephen Louis Carella got shot, and on Christmas Day he died.

Ha.

The call came almost at once from Herb Alexander. He said, "You're not serious, are you?"

I said, "About what?"

He said, "You can't kill Carella."

"Why not?" I said.

"He's the hero," Herb said. "He's the star of the series."

(Carella thus far had appeared in only one book, *Cop Hater*, the first book in the series. In the second book, *The Mugger*, he was off on his honeymoon for 158 of 160 pages, returning to the squadroom only on page 159. But all at once, he was the hero, he was the star.)

"Who says?" I said. "The concept is . . ."

Herb said, "Yes, I know the concept. But you can't kill Carella. He's the hero."

We argued back and forth. I finally yielded, and brought Carella back to life by adding three short paragraphs to the original ending, and by cutting the last line that would have sent Carella to an early grave. I *still* did not believe he was the hero. The concept of a conglomerate protagonist was firmly entrenched in my mind — a splintered hero, if you will, a man of many parts because he was in actuality many men, the men of the 87th Squad.

Years later, in a conversation about successful television series, Mel Brooks said to me that the essential ingredients of any hit show were a family and a house. The family could be doctors, in which case their house was a hospital. The family could be teachers and students, in which case their house was a school. The family could be interplanetary travelers, in which case their house was a spaceship. Well, *my* family, in *my* series, was then (and is now) a family of working cops. Their house is the squadroom; their backyard is the precinct territory; their world is the city.

In this family, Lieutenant Peter Byrnes is the father. Detective Meyer Meyer is the patient older brother. Detective Steve Carella is next in succession, perhaps closest in age and temperament to the man who was presented with a double-barreled monicker at birth. Bert Kling is the youngest brother, learning constantly from his more experienced siblings — and by the way, you should have heard the *geschrei* that went up when, in *Lady, Lady, I Did It!* (the fourteenth book in the series), I killed off the girl who'd been Kling's fiancée since the second book in the series. But, damn it, they could try to tell me Steve Carella was the "hero," but they could not convince me Claire Townsend was the "heroine" — so dead she remained (you should pardon the pun), causing all sorts of later character mutations in Kling. Redheaded Cotton Hawes, the detective with the frightening white streak in his hair, is a cousin who came from the provinces (actually another precinct) to become an adopted brother. There are other members of this tight-knit clan — Hal Willis, with the diminutive size of a jockey and the hands of a judo expert; hard-luck Bob O'Brien who keeps getting into deadly shootouts he neither encourages nor desires; Arthur Brown, a huge black cop who fights prejudice in his own steady, unruffled manner; Captain Frick, in charge of the precinct and nominally the squad, the titular head of the family, going a bit senile in his most recent appearance. And, to stretch the metaphor to its outer limits, we can even consider stool pigeons like Danny Gimp or Fats Donner or Gaucho Palacios part of the family, like distant uncles on the outer fringes.

In this family, there is also a black sheep, a bad cop, a lousy cop, a rotten cop necessary to the balance of the squad. His name used to be Roger Havilland. In *Killer's Choice* (the fifth book in the series), in keeping with my concept of cops coming and going, and perhaps because I'd earlier been prevented from killing off Carella and still resented it, I killed off Havilland in a spectacularly satisfying way:

Havilland knew only that he was flying backwards, off balance. He knew only that he collided with the plate glass window, and that the window shattered around him in a thousand flying fragments of sharp splinters. He felt sudden pain, and he yelled, with something close to tears in his voice, "You bastard! You dirty bastard! You can go and . . ." but that was all he said. He never said another word.

One of the shards of glass had pierced his jugular vein and another had pierced his windpipe, and that was the end of Roger Havilland.

Much to my regret.

A family *has* to have a ne'er-do-well brother or uncle or cousin in it. If there are good cops, there have to be bad cops (as in real life) and they can't be bad cops working in some faraway precinct, they have to be bad cops in your own bailiwick. In a later book (and I can't honestly remember which one), I reincarnated Roger Havilland in the shape and form of Andy Parker. I promise (maybe) that I will never kill Andy Parker. He is too necessary to the mix. Similarly, Fat Ollie Weeks of the 83rd Precinct is another bad cop, a recent addition to the family, without whom the squad could not properly function. I'm not sure whether he'll ever succeed in getting transferred to the Eight-Seven, as he is constantly promising (or rather threatening) to do. He may be more effective where he is, a country cousin who causes the immediate family to wince, or sigh, or both, whenever he puts in an appearance.

That is the family, and this is their house, as described in *Cop Hater* in 1956; the house hasn't changed much over the years, but neither do real-life detective squadrooms:

Where you were was a narrow, dimly-lighted corridor. There were two doors on the right of the open stairway, and a sign labeled them LOCKERS. If you turned left and walked down the corridor, you passed a wooden slatted bench on your left, a bench without a back on your right (set into a narrow alcove before the sealed doors of what had once been an elevator shaft), a door on your right marked MEN'S LAVATORY, and a door on your left over which a small sign hung, and the sign simply read CLERICAL.

At the end of the corridor was the detective squadroom.

You saw first a slatted rail divider. Beyond that, you saw desks and telephones, and a bulletin board with various photographs and notices on it, and a hanging light globe and beyond that more desks and the grilled windows that opened on the front of the building. You couldn't see very much that went on beyond the railing on your right because two huge metal filing cabinets blocked the desks on that side of the room.

This is where the men of the 87th spend part of their working day. The rest of their day is spent in the city. The city is a character in these books. As any reader of the series already knows (and as any *new* reader is promptly informed at once), the city is imaginary. This has not stopped a great many people from remarking on the fact that it strongly resembles New York City. It does. The similarity may be due to the fact that it *is* New York City — with a liberal dash of geographical license. When I began writing the series (and please remember that I *knew* from go that this was going to be a series, or at least I knew there were going to be three books about these cops because that's how many books were contracted for, the future being in the hands of the gods, who — thank God — smiled), I came to a decision about real cities as opposed to imaginary cities. I had done a lot of research on cops and police departments, and I knew they changed their rules and regulations as often as they changed their underwear — say once a year (come on, guys, you know I'm kidding). I knew that a series needed a familiar sameness to it, not only of character and of place, but also circumscribing the rules within which the hero (my squad) had to work while solving a mystery. (There *are* no mysteries, my cops are fond of repeating; there are only crimes with motives.) I recognized at once that I could not change *my* police working procedure each time the cops in New York City changed *theirs*. Keeping up with the departmental or interdepartmental memos or directives would have been a full-time job that left me no time for writing. So I froze the procedure (except for scientific techniques, which are constantly changing, and which I keep up with and incorporate to the best of my ability) and I made my city imaginary because, Harold, the procedure here in this here city is *this* way, and it never changes, dig? And these are the rules of the game in this city, the same rules for the reader as for the cops. A cop can't search an apartment without a court order, and he can't interrogate a prisoner in custody without first reading off Miranda-Escobedo, and he can't expect the lab (which is run by former Lieutenant, now Captain, Sam Grossman, another member of the family) to come up with the identity of a murderer on the basis of a smudged fingerprint of the left thumb — and neither can the reader. Those are the rules. We play the game fair here. We're sometimes frustrated by this damn city with its complicated bureaucratic machinery and its geographical complexity, but it's there, as imaginary as it may be — and out there are killers.

Take a look at this city.

How can you possibly hate her?

She is all walls, true, she flings up buildings like army stockades designed for protection against an Indian population long since cheated and departed. She hides the sky. She blocks her rivers from view. (Never perhaps in the history of mankind has a city so neglected the beauty of her waterways or treated them so casually. Were her rivers lovers, they would surely be unfaithful.) She forces you to catch glimpses of her in quick takes, through chinks in long canyons, here a wedge of water, there a slice of sky, never a panoramic view, always walls enclosing, constricting, yet how can you hate her, this flirtatious bitch with smoky hair?

There are half a dozen *real* cities in this world, and this is one of them, and it's impossible to hate her when she comes to you with a suppressed female giggle about to burst on her silly face, bubbling up from some secret adolescent well to erupt in merriment on her unpredictable mouth. (If you can't personalize a city, you have never lived in one. If you can't get romantic and sentimental about her, you're a foreigner still learning the language. Try Philadelphia, you'll love it there.) To know a real city, you've got to hold her close, or not at all. You've got to breathe her.

That's from *Let's Hear It for the Deaf Man*, published in 1973. (The Deaf Man is my Moriarty, but also a member of the family, so to speak. Without him, the cops in my precinct would never be made to look like fools, and all families must appear foolish at times.) But take a look again at the city paragraphs above. Somebody there is talking about this "imaginary" city as if it were "real." Who is that person talking? Is it Carella? Is it Kling? Is it Meyer or Hawes? I'm glad you asked that question. It is the voice of another character in the series. The character is omnipresent, like the characters that are the city and the weather. The character has no right to be there at all, because every writing instructor in the world will tell you author-intrusion is the cardinal sin. That character is Ed McBain. He likes to put his two cents in. I sometimes feel he is speaking for the reader as well as himself.

So how can anyone possibly say Carella is the hero of this series when there are so many other characters that go into its realization? Nobody can. But I'll tell you something. Sometimes, when somebody yells at me, or when I've had the oil burner repaired unsuccessfully twelve times, or when I've had to write six letters trying to get a change of address on a credit card, I find myself wondering what Carella would do in such a situation.

Does that make him a hero?

Ed McBain

Fred
Fellows

Hillary Waugh

Just as locked-room puzzles, "Had-I-But-Known" stories, and private-eye novels have had their vogue, the police procedural enjoys enormous popularity today. Ed McBain writes about the 87th Precinct squad, John Ball chronicles the adventures of Virgil Tibbs, Elizabeth Linington's books feature Lieutenant Luis Mendoza, and Michael Gilbert has given the world Patrick Petrella. What separates Chief Fred C. Fellows from his fellow cops is that his police work takes place in and around the small town of Stockford, Connecticut, while most sleuths pursue criminals in the world's great cities. Fellows may not have all the latest technological equipment at his command, as he would in an urban police department, but his keen eye, attention to detail, and active mind make him more than a match for the local bad guys. His office is located in a tiny room in the basement of the town's city hall.

Hillary Waugh's first police procedural novel is an early milestone in the development of that subgenre of detective fiction. Last Seen Wearing . . . , published in 1952, introduced Frank W. Ford, who did not become a series detective. Later, Frank Sessions began to appear regularly in police novels set in New York City, starting with "30" Manhattan East, in 1968. Sessions is more brutal than Fellows, perhaps reflecting the tougher environment in which he works.

Most of Hillary Waugh's 57-year-long life has been spent in New England, where he was elected first selectman of Guilford, Connecticut, as a Republican in 1971. He did not seek reelection two years later because it took too much time away from his writing.

Fred Fellows

by Hillary Waugh

IT IS NOT EASY to reconstruct the genes and genealogy of a character of fiction twenty years after his birth, especially when the decade of his heyday is already a decade gone. Unless one keeps a diary account of the pangs of creation, any number of relevancies become lost to memory. This is not to say that the origin of Stockford, Connecticut's Chief of Police Fred C. Fellows is not well remembered, for it is. Rather, it is to remark that the more I think back upon his career, the more the fragments that contributed to his makeup are recalled to mind.

To get a picture of Fred and what he's like, it's necessary to trace his heredity through an almost forgotten father to a vividly remembered grandfather. Mostly it is the grandfather we must consider, for his influence was probably the stronger on Fred and certainly he had a great influence on me.

Frank W. Ford was the grandfather (note the similarity of the FF initials. That's undoubtedly Ford's influence) and, unlike grandson Fred, who was built up piece by piece like Frankenstein's monster (but with happier results), Frank Ford sprang, Athena-like, from his creator's head, fully clothed and armed, already in command of all he surveyed.

It started very innocently. I was writing my first police procedural, a book ultimately titled *Last Seen Wearing*

. . . . The year was 1950 and my goal was to show how the disappearance and murder of a college girl would be handled, as in real life, by the local police of the town involved. The technique was to report the case in the manner of those fact-crime writers who filled the pages of the pulps with their write-ups of real-life murders. The only differences were that my case was to be of novel, rather than short story, length, and it was to be fiction rather than fact.

So far, so good. The book was started, the scene was set: a girl is discovered missing from her college, the efforts of the school authorities to locate her fail, and the police have to be called in.

Up to this point, I had given no thought to the police themselves. I only knew that the chief was a gray-haired, bullet-headed man of 58 who had a crew cut and whose name was Frank Ford; and that his second in command was a taller, thinner, younger detective sergeant named Burton K. Cameron. They were scheduled to be the main investigators of the case and I did not expect anything more from them than professional competence. I did not, in fact, *want* anything more from them than that.

They started out in proper fashion. The chief, upon learning of the disappearance, assigned Cameron and plainclothesman Donald C. Lassiter to the case and they went to the campus to begin their investigation. Fine and dandy; everybody was doing his job and behaving properly.

But then Cameron returned to headquarters and what happened there turned everything around. It was quarter to five Saturday afternoon and Ford had not yet gone home. He was sitting on a table waiting for the detective sergeant to show up and when he got off the table, he said, "About time you got in —"

I stopped him in mid-sentence. "Wait a minute, Chief," I

told him. "You can't say that. That's not an appropriate remark. Let's take it from the top again."

Cameron repeated his entrance and Ford got off the table. "About time you got in," he grumbled.

"Hold it, hold it," I said. "Listen, Frank. You have to understand something. A girl has disappeared from the campus. This is a serious matter. Your first concern is the welfare of this girl. Your opening remark should be 'What'd you find?' or 'Is there any trace?' or something. You can say it your own way, of course. I'm not trying to put words in your mouth, but that's the gist of what your response should be. Realize it, Frank. You shouldn't be griping because you've been hanging around headquarters an extra three-quarters of an hour. First things first. Now, let's try it again. You get off the table and you say —?"

"About time you got in."

I went around with him a couple of more times and then gave up. "All right, Frank," I said, "if you insist on using that line, I'm going to let you. But I'm warning you: I think you're going to lose reader sympathy. I think you're going to be wrong for the role. I'm going to give you the reins and let you show me what you can do, but don't be surprised if you get jettisoned and I put a new man in as chief."

I gave in to him, as you see, and that was all he needed. From that point on, the book became his book rather than mine. I managed to adhere to the format I had laid out — that it would be the story of a police investigation into a crime. The rest of the book went his way and, in fact, he even encroached on my preserve, for the book isn't really so much the story of "a" police investigation into a crime as it is "his" investigation into a crime.

What is interesting is that he pulled all of this off without

being a soft-hearted, gentle, sympathetic, caring type of
guy. He did care, that is true, but you'd have to look
damned hard to find any signs of it. Most of the time he was
irascible and he was dogged. He had an inferiority complex
because he'd never gone past high school (in a girl's college
town yet!) and Cameron had had some higher education
(either a minor college or a junior college). He and Cameron bantered, but it wasn't always good-natured. Only
Cameron dared talk back to Ford and, as a result, their barbs
were sometimes sharp. In fact, at one point, as the pressures
grew great, Ford really blew his stack at Cameron and it is
to Cameron's credit that he knew how to handle it.

Thus came into being the prototype of my sequence of
procedural detectives. One small aside might be made here.
Ford was the father of a 16-year-old daughter, which is
interesting since he was 58 himself. His wife was younger
but, though I don't know her age, I doubt that she was much
younger. This means they produced their only offspring
late in life. I don't know why they had no other children
nor had their child earlier. It's a subject I never sought to,
nor thought to, explore. I wasn't doing Ford's biography,
after all, and it wasn't relevant to the matter at hand.

For the next few years I explored other forms of the
mystery, but eventually I returned to the small-town police
procedural and, when I did, I was naturally drawn to the
same type of detective team. I found myself in the market
for another chief of police with another detective sergeant
as legman and alter ego.

Why couldn't Frank Ford have done the job himself?
Granted, eight years had gone by, but that wouldn't mean
Ford would be eight years older. Fictional series characters
don't age at the same pace as their readers.

Frank Ford was, in fact, considered for the job, but not seriously. He was too obviously a one-shot hero. I feared that trying to use him in a sequel, or in a series, would dilute and alter him. His charm was the fact that he wouldn't be manipulated and I was afraid that if I forced him to go the series route, he would no longer be his own man and thus would cease to be the same man. Besides, he was best in that one case and I was loath to sully his image. A calculated, small-town police procedural would require a new man for the new role.

The result was the very brief appearance (one book, which appeared only in England) of an interim police chief, the offspring of Frank Ford, you might say, and father of Fred Fellows, though his presence was so fleeting that his impact upon Fellows is slight, and more physical than anything else.

This chief's name was Amos G. Camp and he held forth in the small community of Marshton, which is the definite forerunner of Fred Fellows's Stockford. The town has the same traits and, for all I know, might even have had much the same map — my recollection of Marshton is too vague to give any assurances on that score.

To get back to Camp, who had a couple of cohorts in a Lieutenant Willis and a promising officer named Ken Shevlin, he was notably different from Frank Ford in appearance. While Frank was on the short side, no more than 5'9" or 5'10", Amos Camp stood 6'4" and "tipped the scales in the neighborhood of two hundred and fifty pounds, all of it muscle." He had sandy hair, slate-gray eyes, smoked acrid cigars, and was in his forties. This physical difference was inspired, I now remember, by the actor, whose name I do not recall, who played a sympathetic sheriff in the movie

The Defiant Ones. It was that man, and the kind of sheriff he played, who came to mind when I set about contriving Ford's successor.

Unfortunately, neither Camp nor his circumstances had what it took to survive in the world of mystery fiction and a replacement was needed. Here, at last, came Fred Fellows, and we can now begin to identify the structure of his being.

His physical appearance can be traced more to Camp than to Ford. He's over six feet, just under 6'2", I'd guess. He doesn't weigh 250, but would be more in the 225 area, some of it flab, though not as much as he's afraid of. He could balloon without any trouble, though, so while he's a quixotic dieter, the kind who worries about calories all the time, drinks coffee black and avoids sweets, but never systematically goes about the problem of weight control, this probably keeps his weight reasonable.

Fellows is between Camp and Ford in age, too, totaling about fifty-three years at the beginning of the series, but aging year by year as the series progresses. The aging, however, is more applied to his children than to him. It is desirable, in other words, not to think of Fred in terms of his age.

As for children, there are four: Larry, Shirley, Katie, and, three years behind Katie, Peter. Fellows is a family man and though the period of his active work was late Fifties to mid-Sixties, he and his gently plump, bland wife, Cessie, do not suffer from a generation gap. In fact, when Larry marries a cute young girl named Denise, who calls him "Pops," he's delighted with the addition.

What else can we say about Fred Fellows? He chews tobacco. He had nude calendar art on the wall over his desk at a time when the only nudes were on calendars. He has a close relationship with Sid Wilks, his detective sergeant.

They are good friends as well as co-workers and if they don't banter the way Ford and Cameron did, there are no knife-edges in their relationship either.

Fellows is also mellower in manner than Ford, quieter, less animated, more relaxed, certainly more philosophical. There was something of the bantam rooster about Ford. He was a doer, not stopping to reflect, but getting the job done. Fellows shows the influence of Camp and the movie sheriff. He's of the opinion that if one pauses to reflect, one is less apt to make mistakes. He also has a sense of humor, something totally lacking in Ford. Fellows's humor usually illumines itself in a Lincolnesque tendency to illustrate his views or make his points with homely little stories. As a sample, one time he says: "I'm just reminded of this guy who had a BB gun he liked to play with. So one day he fired a shot into the ceiling and the whole ceiling fell in on him. At the hospital, one of the doctors asked him why he did it and he said he didn't think the ceiling would fall in, he'd been shooting BBs into it for three years and it never happened before."

This trait of Fellows is totally his own. There's no trace of it in any of his forebears. In fact, I have no idea where he got it unless from Lincoln himself.

Lastly, Fred Fellows is an imaginative thinker whose flights of fancy often take him into what Sid Wilks calls "stratosphere stuff." This quality was bred into Fred to enable him to cope with those problems that would resist all the scientific know-how and manpower available to him.

Unlike Ford, who exploded on the scene with all his warts and moles, virtues and vices firmly in place, Fellows was carefully groomed to fit the town he worked in and fulfill the needs of a cop who must solve a great many difficult crimes over a good many years without running out of resources or wearing the readers' patience thin.

He seemed to thrive as a result and, at last reports, is still thriving.

Hillary Waugh

Inspector Ghote

H. R. F. Keating

Ganesh V. Ghote, pronounced GO-tay, is not the sort of arrogant, brilliant, infallible detective who fills the majority of volumes devoted to mystery fiction. Although he is good at his job as inspector in the Crime Branch of the Bombay Police Department, he gets pushed around a good deal — by his superiors and even at home by his forceful wife. But it would be a mistake to think of Ghote as a weakling. He is intelligent and, just as important, wily. Furthermore, he has a toughness which makes him able to cope with his superiors, his wife, Protima, and the villains who always seem intent upon figuratively sitting on him.

The books about Ghote are unusual in that each is based upon a philosophical theme. The first Ghote novel, for instance, is about perfectionism. Explains Keating, the question is "whether you should strive to be perfect, or whether you should settle for the halfway, which applies in even the smallest things of life. You're typing a sheet of paper and make one mistake; do you rip it out of the typewriter, and retype it, or do you erase the error?" The novel, called The Perfect Murder, is about — naturally — an imperfect murder; it won the British Crime Writers' Association Gold Dagger as best novel of the year in 1964.

H. R. F. Keating, 51, began his career as a journalist and keeps his hand in as a free-lance, often book reviewing for The Times of London, where he lives with his wife, Sheila Mitchell, an accomplished actress.

Inspector Ghote

by H. R. F. Keating

IT IS BIO-DATA you are wanting? Bio-data on Inspector Ghote? Well, well, no one here at Bombay Crime Branch is knowing all that much about the fellow. Not at all. He is meant to be working here, but all the time no one is ever seeing him. Only from those books which that writerwallah in England is always publishing am I at all knowing that Ghote is a colleague of mine only.

They are saying that one time they are making a TV film about the fellow here, and he is supposed to be seen in that. But no one in Bombay has witnessed any such film, so what I am always wondering is: is the fellow a real top-notch CID inspector at all? Sometimes I am thinking he must be no more than an idea in that writer fellow's head. And I was reading in *Times of India* that this Mr. Keating had not been to India even, not until he came here in 1975 only. But he had begun to put out those books in 1964. Well then, I am asking you: how could he know what like was the life of a CIDwallah? Was he for ever reading books about India? And watching films and television also? Did he obtain even such magazines as *Illustrated Weekly of India* on regular basis? Well, I am unable to say. But there can be no doubt at all that all this constitutes suspicious circumstances. Isn't it?

And I am not at all sure how much this Mr. Keating is knowing about Ghote even. Why, in the first books he was

writing — I have gone through them all because I am wanting to find out just exactly what this fellow Ghote is doing
in Crime Branch when there are questions of relative senior-
ity arising — well, in those first books it is altogether clear
that this Mr. Keating is not even knowing what are Ghote's
forenames. He is called "Inspector Ghote" all the time. And
then one day all of a sudden we are learning that he is named
Ganesh, and not until Case No. 10, wherein he investigates
certain nefarious activities in the Bombay film studios, do
we find that the "V" of his second name is standing for
Vinayak. Well, well, Ganesha is the god of wisdom, but I
am often wondering just how much of wisdom this fellow
Ghote has. And, please to remember, Ganesha is the god
of success also. Well, I am telling you, a lot of bloody help
from above this Ghote seems to be needing in his cases. A
lot of bloody help.

But, I am telling you also, I am thinking that this notable
British author is not knowing what Ghote looks like any
more than any of his fellow inspectors in Crime Branch,
who are always just missing seeing him round some corner
or other. If what I am all along suspecting is right, Mr. Keating in the beginning saw a pair of shoulders only, thin and
bony shoulders with a burden always upon them. I am believing he saw no more than that, and even now when we
have nine-ten of Ghote's cases I do not believe the fellow
altogether knows what like are Ghote's feet. And sometimes
Ghote is having a mustache and looking very like that Pakis-
tani actor known by the name of Zia Mohyeddin, and sometimes he is not having a mustache at all.

Well, I am hearing that this notable British Mr. Keating
when he was coming to Bombay at last is saying that one
day a fellow is asking to see him at Taj Hotel where he is
then resident and he is saying that he is a private inquiry

agent and former Sub-Inspector of the Bombay Force. And Mr. Keating is alleging that when he saw this fellow he said to himself, "He is the spitting image of Inspector Ghote." Well, well. That is as may be. But there are still matters to be cleared up.

For example, how old is this fellow Ghote? There is a great deal of conflicting evidence on that. He is reported to have a son known by the name of Ved who seems now to be about twelve years of age. But he has grown from five years to twelve only during the whole eleven-twelve years of Ghote's cases. And I am asking: where is the arithmetic in that? And, after conducting scrupulous examination of every part and parcel of the evidence, I am still not at all in a position to give an accurate account of Ghote's physical characteristics in accordance with the methods of Dr. Hans Gross, the German criminologist who is frequently referred to as a be-all and end-all by Ghote himself. If you are asking me, I am believing that there are as many pictures of Ghote and as many ages for him as there are readers of those books of Mr. Keating. And I am wondering: is this a plot only? Is the said Mr. Keating deliberately withholding information? And, if so, is there a case to be brought under Indian Penal Code Section 179 "Refusing to answer a public servant authorised to question" or under Section 202 "Concealing evidence"?

And there is the question of Ghote's wife also. With her name of Protima. Well, that is a very beautiful name, I am granting, and altogether suitable for a beautiful and elegant woman. But it seems to me that Mr. Keating could not at all have been knowing that this is a Bengali name. But then all of a sudden he is making out that Ghote after all married a Bengali lady. Well, I am wondering only how that came to happen. No explanation have we had.

So is it after all true what I am hearing that Mr. Keating once said that while he was sitting there in his armchair in his house in London thinking about how he would write a book about India since he was not able to write any that were thoroughly pleasing to American publishers but were altogether too English, that while he was sitting there, and perhaps chewing a *paan* which his servant had brought, I am not knowing, suddenly there came strolling into the room — or was it into his head only? — this fellow Ghote. Only, if what I am hearing is true, then the fellow's name was not then at all Ghote but Ghosh only. Well, as everybody who is at all understanding India must know, that is a Bengali name only. It would be like saying that that so famous Commissaire Maigret of the Paris police force was called all the time Boris Ivanovich. Well, well, I am not at all knowing.

But, if you are asking me, Ghote was not at all intended to have a career in our Branch. No, no. Just one case only this Mr. Keating intended to describe. But then some sort of prize was given to Ghote, some sort of a Crime Writers' Association Golden Dagger. And that was the year that I myself was having my promotion to inspector rank when I had nabbed the gang responsible for the theft of seven hundred and twenty-six bicycles. And not a word was written by Mr. Keating about that.

But he is altogether a damn cautious fellow about what he is writing about Ghote also. What I am suspecting is that he does not want anybody to meet with Inspector Ghote or otherwise they might be discovering that the fellow is a fraud only. So he is never telling just where his office is and just where is his house or anything like that. I mean, first of all Ghote was said to be living in a Government Quarter house. Well, it is well known that for the Bombay police there are no such houses. In Delhi there are. But in Bombay, no. But then, after this notable writer from U.K. visits Bombay, all of a sudden he is seeming to say that Ghote after all stays in a flat like every other inspector in the Branch. Yet he is cunning also. He is never quite saying it is flat. "Home" only he is saying. And that could be flat or it could be house. And that, I am saying, is altogether unfair when an officer is attempting to make investigation into this chap Ghote's present whereabouts. I am after all wanting to give the fellow a clean chit only. I have absolutely no malafide intent in the matter, I am assuring you. But all the same I am wondering whether the fellow is persistently doing the bunk in office hours. Otherwise why is it I have not found?

Sometimes I am wondering even if the fellow has obtained extended leave for the purpose of visiting America. He is already U.K.-returned, you know. And that was a very very bad business. There are a great many officers senior in rank to Ghote, but he is the fellow who is sent to investigate some sort of a case of missing peacocks in London. Well, I am certain he is planning to make a trip to U.S.A. also. And that is another thing. I am having a cousin of a cousin in U.K., and he is telling that he has heard on the radio there a certain Inspector Ghote visiting the country to act against smugglers of immigrants. Yet nothing whatsoever has been put about that in these books that Mr. Keating has written. So what I am asking now is: are there two of this chap Ghote? Is it that one of them does what is written in the books and another altogether is carrying out those activities that are reported on the wireless waves only? One thing is certain: it is all a damn mysterious business.

And this is something else. Why is it, I am always considering, that whether it is on the radio or whether it is in these books, the chap Ghote always and invariably has a hundred percent success? I am having a very good record myself, none better among any of the inspectors of Crime Branch, but I have had cases where in the end I have had to admit total and utter defeat. "Left open upon the file." That is the best I have been able to do.

But this Ghote fellow, never one single failure. But it is not as if he appears to have very very good qualifications of a personal nature to be solving cases. Not at all. He is most persistent, that I am admitting. And he has learnt his police procedures. He is shrewd sometimes also, agreed. But nevertheless he is always being exploited and put upon by rascals and miscreants of all sorts. And he seems also to be in a state of holy terror of his superior officers. And they themselves have an attitude of altogether very little trust in Ghote, and I am sure that such views are very much justified. They are after all senior officers. So why is it then that despite all and sundry Ghote ends up every time successful? Why is that? Is it because he has to do so for the purposes of literature only? Or is it because the gods are wishing to show us that Good always in the end must triumph? Well, if that is the case, it is frankly bloody damn unfair.

It is all very well for Commissioner Kulkarni, Head of Crime Branch, to state in that television film the BBCwallahs were making — if this is what he did state, because I for one have never seen sight or sound of that film — it is all very well for Kulkarni Sahib to state that he himself is wishing and wishing to have a sensitive fellow like Ghote on his staff and that he would make an altogether fine detective officer. But what I am asking is this: there is such a matter as a question of politeness, and if you are being interviewed by the chap who is writing all these books, well then, what more polite can you be saying than that you have a high opinion of the chap he is writing about? Isn't it? Isn't it? Isn't it?

And there is one other thing I can tell you also. However many cases this Ghote fellow tucks under his belt only, he would never rise above inspector rank. Never. Never.

H. R. F. Keating

Matt
Helm

Donald Hamilton

There is more than a touch of James Bond in Matt Helm. Both work for their respective governments, the United Kingdom and the United States, performing heroic feats of counterespionage in a variety of locales, generally assisted by beautiful young women. Bond takes his orders from "M"; Helm takes them from "Mac." Both men are physically violent when the situation demands it, and neither shows hesitation or remorse if he is forced to eliminate an enemy. They do have their differences, however. While Bond drives a classic Bentley, Helm is most comfortable at the wheel of his battered old pickup truck. Bond prefers vintage champagne or gimlets; Helm drinks beer or martinis. Bond's environment is the supper club and the gambling casino; Helm prefers the outdoors and made his living as a free-lance writer of Western novels and a wildlife photographer until his country asked for his services.

Just as the James Bond novels served as the basis for a successful series of motion pictures (notably with Sean Connery as agent 007), Matt Helm is the hero of four major films (starring Dean Martin). The character was somewhat altered — some might say distorted — for the films, as was the case with the 1975 television series with Tony Franciosa, to make Helm appear even more like Bond. The extensive Helm saga, published as paperback originals, has enjoyed the rare distinction of critical praise and enormous popular appeal.

Born in Sweden, the 61-year-old Donald Hamilton now lives in Santa Fe, New Mexico. He is the successful author of many books, among them such Westerns as The Big Country, *which became a renowned film starring Gregory Peck, Charlton Heston, Jean Simmons, and Burl Ives.*

Matt Helm

by Donald Hamilton

"LOOK," SAID MY EDITOR, calling from New York back in
the late 1950s, "look, you really can't call that guy George,
you know."

"What guy?" I asked.

"The guy in your last book. The one we're working on."

"Oh, that guy." I was already busy with another book,
a Western as I recall. "What's the matter with George?"

"It's too damned anti-hero."

I said, "General George Patton would hate you for that.
Not to mention old George Washington himself. And what
about George Armstrong Custer? No anti-hero, he, although I guess you couldn't call him much of a hero, either,
after the way he let himself get clobbered at the Little Big
Horn." The phone was silent. I gathered I wasn't making a
tremendous impression at the other end. I sighed. Maybe
he was right. He often was, damn him. "Okay, if you insist,
I'll give it some thought and write you . . ."

"I've got to have it now. We're just wrapping it up."

I said, "Well, it's your dime. Hold on." I thought for a
while. I frowned and scratched my head. I looked around
the room. The family Bible on the bookcase caught my
eye. Aha! Matthew, Mark, Luke, and John. Luke? It didn't
have quite the right feel to it. "Hell, call him Matthew," I
said, and so Matt Helm was born, but not quite. It took
another long-distance telephone call to finish the job.

"About *Death of a Citizen*," said my editor some months later, after discussing other business.

"About what?"

"*Death of a Citizen*. That's what we're calling it now, remember?" I'd originally entitled the book something else, never mind what. He went on. "You know, Don, I've been thinking, if you take that guy, and kill off his wife, you might have a great series character . . ."

Well, I didn't kill off the wife, I just arranged a bloodless divorce, but the basic idea was sound. The editor in question isn't editing anymore; he's turned agent. It's too bad, because he was a good editor, with a good editor's knack of seeing not only what was wrong with a book or character — although he was never bashful about pointing that out — but what was right with it. He saw what was right with Matt Helm before I did: that he was *not* an anti-hero, and that the time was ripe for him. We'd had too many anti-heroes.

Matt Helm wasn't the gentle civilian protagonist, long fashionable in suspense fiction, who gets involved in mysterious undercover shenanigans against his will, takes a hell of a beating, and finally pulls up his socks, musters his feeble and amateurish resources, turns the tables on his tormentors, and walks off with the girl, swearing he'll never, never get mixed up in anything like *that* again, so help him. I'd written about anti-heroes, both eastern and western, with reasonable success; in fact you might say that my writing career, such as it was, had been built on anti-heroes. Now, however, it seemed that the time of the hero had come, both for me and for those who were kind enough to read my books.

I found Helm a refreshing change from the pacific citizens whom I'd been arranging to get reluctantly enmeshed in sinister spiderwebs of intrigue. Here, for Pete's sake, was a man who went looking for trouble, a tough professional deliberately sticking his neck out as required in the line of duty. After all the peaceful patsies I'd written about, a guy like that was a revelation, from the author's angle. He opened up a whole new field of writing — but I'll admit it didn't occur to me at the time that it was a field I'd still be cultivating eighteen years later. That was my editor's contribution.

I had, as I've already indicated, planned only one novel about this stimulating but — for me and for the times — somewhat unorthodox character. Encouraged to bring him back, I went to a retired manuscript that hadn't turned out very well: another gentle-anti-hero yarn set in Scandinavia, where I'd recently spent a year. I thought I might, perhaps, be able to salvage the basic plot and the fine Nordic settings. To my surprise, the whole previously unsuccessful story (*The Wrecking Crew*) came to vibrant — and violent — life when I switched the polarity, so to speak, and used a decisive hero who acted, for a change, instead of an irresolute anti-hero who sat around waiting to be acted upon.

Apparently most readers found him as much fun to read about as I found him fun to write about, and Matt Helm was on his way. However, there were some who disapproved.

"I'm sorry, I simply can't *stand* them," a fellow-writer's very frank intellectual-type wife told me at a cocktail party, referring to my Helm books. "That man, the one who kills people, he's so *unpleasant* . . ."

I poked and pried a bit. If there was something basically wrong with my newly established character, something that turned readers off, I certainly wanted to know about it. I discovered that what the lady considered unpleasant about Matt Helm was that he wasn't unpleasant at all. She was morally offended by the notion of a relatively nice guy running around with a gun. Great. She'd got the idea. She just didn't like the idea. People who killed people ought to be obviously horrible monsters all the time, in her opinion, and my writing about a homicidal character who wasn't wasn't cricket.

She had, of course, put her finger on the fundamental conflict that, I feel, makes Matt Helm Matt Helm; a conflict I set up deliberately for one book, that still seems to intrigue people as I now tackle the nineteenth volume in the series. It can be stated very simply:

a. He's actually a pretty good guy.

b. He kills.

Well, let's leave that for a moment, while we consider other attributes of Helm. He's six foot four and he weighs around two hundred pounds. He's not particularly handsome and he's always wary of women who claim to find him irresistible — as an experienced professional agent, he can't help suspecting them of ulterior motives. Sometimes he's right, but sometimes he isn't. He's not particularly concerned about male clothes; he does, however, have an old-fashioned prejudice against female trousers, although he'll admit ruefully that this crusade is now a lost cause. Where food is concerned, he's pretty much a meat-and-potatoes man, although he does prefer good meat and well-prepared potatoes. His drink is the martini but he's not rabid on the subject; he'll drink whiskey if he has to. He has also been known to partake of wine and beer. He quit smoking back when he was a peacetime photographer — the smoke interfered with good, sharp darkroom work — and he's never gone back to the habit although he has no strong feelings about it. He finds that his photographic experience provides him with a convenient and convincing cover upon occasion.

Professionally, he's knowledgeable about automobiles, and

a good wheelman. He's never mastered flying, however, and airplanes make him a bit apprehensive, although he did manage to get a small one down once without killing himself, after the pilot had suffered a sudden demise at 5000 feet. He's picked up a little seamanship during the course of his career — he's had to — but he doesn't consider himself a very good boatman.

On the other hand, he does admit to a certain expertise where firearms are concerned. He's a very good marksman with a rifle, and competent with a pistol, although he doesn't have much faith in quick-draw techniques or equipment. Like many pros, he feels a smart operative ought to know enough about any developing situation to have his gun ready in his hand when he needs it, without having to indulge in any risky, last-minute, sleight-of-hand tricks. He likes edged weapons and knows fencing, a knowledge that has stood him in good stead with instruments varying from sticks to machetes. He has a number of unarmed-combat tricks, enough to get by on. He thinks fist-fighting is stupid. As a pro, he either fights to kill or he doesn't fight.

As for his background, he comes from Scandinavian parentage, and acquired a college education on the second try, having been thrown out of the first school he attended for reacting too violently to upperclass hazing. After college, he put in time as a newspaper photographer, and had a brief army experience, but was soon selected for the special, nameless, government organization of which he is still a member. Released from active duty at one point, he married and had three children while making his living for several years with camera and typewriter. The violent past caught up with him, however, the marriage broke up, and he went back to work for the man in Washington known only as Mac. . . .

Would I have put together this character this way if I'd known from the start that I'd be spending a couple of decades with him? That's a stupid question. I didn't put Matt Helm together, he put himself together. In the first book, particularly, but also in subsequent volumes, he simply revealed himself to me with a ruthless logic any writer knows. A good character runs the show. All the author can do is chase along behind him with a typewriter.

Which brings us back to the basic question: what makes this a good character — from the fictional, not the moral, viewpoint? I believe close to twenty million people have now bought the books. They must like something about Matt Helm; something beyond the entertainment value I try to provide in the action stories in which he figures.

What makes people want to read about a pretty nice guy who kills people? Do they, perhaps, find him a refreshing antidote to the sentimental hypocrisies currently fashionable?

You tell me.

Donald Hamilton

Duncan
Maclain

Baynard H. Kendrick

In the search for a new twist, mystery writers have created detectives with every imaginable intellectual or psychological idiosyncrasy or, as a variation on that search for uniqueness, physical deformity. When these distortions are invented purely as a gimmick, they frequently serve only to demonstrate the author's lack of imagination. Occasionally, however, a deviation from normality is either a logical development of personality or powerfully informs it. That is when an immortal is born. Duncan Maclain is such a character.

Tall, dark, handsome, a superb dresser and extremely personable, Maclain was blinded totally in World War I while serving as an intelligence officer. Instead of withdrawing from the world, he worked tirelessly to develop his other senses, and was so successful that he is able to function as well as most men with eyesight. He moves gracefully, is a deadly shot (locating his target by sound), reads voraciously, in Braille, enjoys music, and assembles massive jigsaw puzzles. Kendrick is not fantasizing Maclain's accomplishments; everything his hero does has been done by real people who are blind.

Upon his release from the military, Maclain established a private detective agency in New York City. He is assisted by his best friend and partner, Spud Savage; by Rena, Spud's wife, who is his secretary; and by his Seeing Eye dogs: Schnucke, who is gentle, and Dreist, who is not. Longstreet, a blind insurance investigator on a recent ABC television series starring James Franciscus, is based on Maclain.

A founder of the Mystery Writers of America, Kendrick carried membership card number one. Exactly one hour after Canada entered World War I, he became the first American to enlist in the Canadian army. From his research on Maclain grew the Blinded Veterans Association. He lived in Leesburg, Florida, until his death early in 1977.

Duncan Maclain

by Baynard H. Kendrick

THE FIRST SHORT STORY ever written about my blind detective character, Captain Duncan Maclain, appeared in *Ellery Queen's Mystery Magazine* in January 1953 (there has only been one other, which also appeared in *Ellery Queen's*). That was more than fifteen years after the first full-length mystery, *The Last Express*, about Captain Maclain, who was a fictional U.S. Army officer blinded at Messines in World War I. It was published by the Crime Club in 1937. Following is the introduction to this short story, written by Frederic Dannay, co-writer with his cousin, Manfred B. Lee, under the pseudonym "Ellery Queen," who, like this writer, is one of the Grand Masters of the Mystery Writers of America, Inc.:

Ernest Bramah is generally credited with having invented the first modern blind detective, Max Carrados, but the most famous exponent in the contemporary field of blind detection is, without doubt, Captain Duncan Maclain, created by Baynard Kendrick. Mr. Kendrick acknowledges that it was the earlier blind detective who started him writing about Maclain —but for curious reasons . . . in Mr. Kendrick's opinion, Max Carrados had very strange powers that went far beyond the limits of credibility. For example, Carrados could run his fingertips along the surface of a newspaper, feel the infinitesimal height

of the printer's ink over the paper itself, and "read" any type
larger than long primer. Mr. Kendrick questions that feat, and we
must say we are inclined to side with Mr. Kendrick. . . .

Indeed, Mr. Kendrick found it so difficult to swallow Max
Carrados's supersensory accomplishments that he determined to
create a blind detective of his own — a completely believable
sleuth who could deduce by touch, hearing, taste, and smell,
with no reliance whatever either on sight or sixth sense. And
the simple truth of the matter is that while Baynard Kendrick
has spent fifteen years of his life unearthing extraordinary
things done by the totally blind, he has never had his blind
detective do anything which he, Kendrick, had not actually
seen done by a living blind man, or had fully authenticated.

When it came to developing the character of Duncan Maclain, Mr. Kendrick again went to the highest authority — real
life. He patterned the character of Maclain on that of a real
person — a young blind soldier in St. Dunstan's Home in London, who by touching the emblems on Kendrick's own uniform, accurately traced four years of Kendrick's Army career.

Canada declared war on Germany on August 8, 1914,
four days after Great Britain. I was living in a boarding-
house in Windsor, Ontario, across the river from Detroit,
and left a lunch table to go downtown to the Armory and
enlist. So far as can be ascertained, I was the first American
to join up with the Canadian forces in World War I. After
a few weeks' training at Valcartier, Quebec, I became No.
6468, Private Kendrick, B.H., 1st Battalion, 1st Brigade, No.
1 Company in No. 1 Section. Since even then I was six feet,
two inches, I was the tallest man in my company and became flank man on the line. This was a hair-raising experience inasmuch as I was forced to pace 33,000 men in a
review before Sir Sam Hughes, of whom the Canadians glee-

fully sang, to the tune of "John Peel": "Do you ken Sam Hughes, the enemy of booze. The first champeen of the dry canteen. And the camp so dead you have to go to bed, but you won't have a head in the morning."

The first expeditionary force sailed from Gaspé Bay on the twenty-first of September and the 1st Battalion of 1200 men was on board the White Star liner *Laurentic*. Thirty-three ocean liners crossed in that convoy in three rows of eleven each — the largest convoy to that date that the world had ever dreamed of or seen. There was certainly no tinge of patriotic fervor in my enlistment. I was 20 years old and the idea of putting an ocean between me and Detroit, where I had once been arrested for vagrancy for sleeping out in Grand Circuit Park, and drawing $1.10 a day plus food and clothes and medical expenses looked like paradise.

If this autobiographical prologue seems prolix and redundant I will have to plead guilty as I put it here for just one purpose — to make the point that not until 1917 when I was 23 and blindness confronted me face to face, had I ever given it a passing thought. By that time I had served in France, Egypt, and Salonica and had spent over two years in army hospitals. Subconsciously, I believe, like 99 percent of the people in the world, I blotted the condition from my mind beyond relegating it to the shadowy realm of the tin cup, pencil, and street-corner school.

In the winter of 1917, when I had been marked "C-3" by a medical board (light duty), I was stationed in London working as a pay sergeant in the Canadian Pay Office at 7 Millbank. There, quite by accident, I learned that a boy with whom I had gone to school in Philadelphia had joined up with the Canadians a year after I did. I'll call him Paul Henderson, which was not his name. He had been blinded at Vimy Ridge several months before and at that moment was in St. Dunstan's Lodge, the hospital for blinded soldiers in London.

I took to visiting St. Dunstan's in Regents Park regularly on Saturday afternoons to have tea and play the piano. Once having overcome my initial ingrained fear of the blind, I continued these visits for many months after Paul Henderson had been invalided back to Canada and resumed his U.S. citizenship — as I did later, in December 1918. It was on one such visit that Captain Duncan Maclain was born, although I had no inkling of it at the moment and it was twenty years later — in 1937 — before he came to life in print in *The Last Express*. The conditions at St. Dunstan's for the training and welfare of the blind — while modern for World War I — seemed antiquated when compared to Valley Forge, Dibble, or Avon Old Farms. Mobility was given little thought and the grounds of St. Regents Park were festooned with strings for the blinded veterans to follow, and knots marked the benches. When I was visiting there the lodge was so overcrowded with veterans and personnel that it had been necessary to move the piano out in the hall. There was little amusement since radio and talking books were unheard of — the big moments came when some noted entertainer, such as Sir Harry Lauder, Sir George Robey, or Alfred Lester, dropped in for an evening from one of the music halls.

It was on a blustery, freezing December afternoon in 1917 when I first became conscious of the fact that while a blind man might have lost his sight, he hadn't necessarily lost his mind. I had seated myself at the piano and given my usual introduction by leading off with "Tipperary" and the coterie of blinded British Tommies quickly gathered around me. There was just one straightback chair to the right of the piano next to double doors in the vestibule (always closed since a rear entrance was used) that led out onto the grounds. I had shed my cap and greatcoat and put them on that chair.

The Tommies were packed in almost solidly around me and one British Tommy was standing with his hands lightly on my shoulders while I went through half a dozen pieces. When I had finished and some requests were made, he moved around to the right of the piano, picked up my cap and greatcoat from the chair, sat down and laid them across his knees. I noticed while I was playing that he was giving them a thorough going-over with his fingertips ("brailling," although it turns a noun into a verb, has become the common term today).

A bell rang and I was suddenly deserted by my captive audience as they poured into an adjoining lounge for afternoon tea. Only the Tommy to the right of the piano remained. He stood up, replacing my cap and greatcoat on the chair, and started in with a preamble, as though something had been burned into his brain.

Then he said: "You certainly have been around in the Canadian army, haven't you? You've been in nearly every bleeding outfit in it. You came over here in nineteen fourteen with the First Battalion, went out to France with them, were invalided back here to England and then joined up with the Fourth General Hospital from Toronto and went out to Salonica with them. You were invalided back from Salonica through Egypt and landed back here at Netley Fever Hospital at Southamption — that big pile of bricks with the corridors a quarter of a mile long.

"When you were discharged from Netley you went to

Shorncliffe to the C.C.A.C. [Canadian Casualty Assembly Center]. There you faced another medical board which marked you 'C-3' and transferred you to the Canadian Army Service Corps on light duty instead of sending you back to Canada as you had hoped. When they found out that you couldn't even lift a Ford motor, let alone carry one around on each shoulder, the sergeant in charge of the machine shop kicked to the C.O. that he was tired of being sent walking corpses marked 'C-3.' So they sent you up to this cushy job with the Canadian Army Pay Corps here in London where you will stay for the duration of the war."

I stood with my mouth hanging open, staring at him intently until I was positive that I had never seen him before. Then I blurted out, "I suppose you got all this dope from Paul Henderson who was invalided back to Canada from here a couple of months ago."

"Never heard of him," he said smugly. "He was before my time. I have only been in here just over a couple of weeks. I was blinded in the big tank push at Cambrai."

"Then where the hell did you know me and get all my army history? You sound like you had taken it from a sheet in the Canadian Record Office."

"I don't know you, never saw you, and never will," he grinned delightedly. "Sir Arthur Pearson spoke to us here last week about how much a blind man can really see. I decided to try it out on you. Your army history that I just gave you is written all over your uniform."

I took a closer look at his heavily bandaged eyes and decided that even if he had some vision left, it was obvious that he couldn't see. "Okay," I said. "Start at the beginning and spell it out. I'm certainly listening."

"Well, first," he said, "you have blue shoulder straps sewed on the khaki ones on your tunic."

"Blue?"

"Sure, you're wearing brass C-1's — that is a 'C' with a bar under it and a '1' attached underneath. That was your original unit, the First Battalion of Infantry, and all the infantry in the first contingent in nineteen fourteen wears those blue shoulder straps. The Medical Corps wears red. You were invalided back from France because you have a gold perpendicular wound stripe on your sleeve. Right?"

"Right! Go on."

"Well, the metal bars on each of those blue shoulder straps just read Canada in raised letters so the infantry was your original unit. Now, take your greatcoat. It has just the regular khaki shoulder straps but the bars on each shoulder are cut out CAMC, running from back to front, and easy to feel. Over them you have 'four' with a small bar over a 'G' in brass. That shows you were overseas with the Fourth General Hospital. It came from Toronto and was the only unit from the Canadian Army which was out in Salonica. I'm no wizard but I happened to have had a cousin who was with the same outfit, the Fourth General Hospital, and most of the men from Salonica were invalided back with fever through Egypt. So I took a guess that the same thing happened to you. All the men invalided back to England from anywhere with fevers end up in Netley and then at the C.C.A.C. at Shorncliffe. But the badge on the front of your cap is Canadian Army Service Corps, indicating that was the last unit you were transferred to here in England. My cousin went through that light duty routine, only they sent him out to France again driving a lorry. Now, I know you're stationed up here in London with a permanent pass since you are up here nearly every Saturday afternoon, playing the piano. You have sergeant's stripes on your greatcoat so I imagine you're working as a pay sergeant in the Canadian Pay Office. They have no emblem of their own."

Just then, an orderly stopped in from somewhere to collect him for tea, leaving me too dumbfounded even to inquire his name. He left me with a happy smile and a wave of his hand saying, "I'll be seeing you." He never did, of course, and I never saw him again. It was after New Year's of 1918 the next time I went up to St. Dunstan's and my blind detective had gone.

It was ten years later (1927) before I came in contact with Paul Henderson again.

My father died in Philadelphia in January 1927. Banks had already closed in Florida and our family savings were going fast while I fiddled around without much success at writing. But I had tasted blood because *Field and Stream* had bought my first short story, "The Captain's Lost Lake," in 1926 for $60. I hastened up to Philadelphia from Florida to see what could be salvaged from my father's business and the day after his funeral, Mrs. Henderson, Paul's mother, phoned me to say that she had seen the notice of my father's death in the newspapers. She told me her own husband had died five years before. She and Paul were still living in the old family house on Queen Lane in Germantown, and could I come to dinner. I sensed desperation in her voice and went out to see them the following evening — a filthy snowy night.

The house was a mausoleum, housing a frail invalid already feeling the effects of a cancer which killed her in 1930, and her blind, 31-year-old son, who hadn't been out of the house since his father's death, five years before. The dinner was meager but by the time it was served none of us much cared — the bootlegger had made a delivery earlier and the orange blossom cocktails had flowed freely.

Paul's mother, through ignorance, fear, and too much love, did practically everything for him except take him to the toilet. It helped turn Paul into an alcohol-soaked cabbage with nothing to do but sit and look at the back of his eyes and curse at the fictional Max Carrados and his fictional supernatural powers. Paul was too frightened to move from the house that had become the only world he knew — and his mother, through misdirected love, encouraged his indolence.

I sold out the Trades Publish Company that belonged to my father and went to New York, where I obtained a job as general manager of Bing & Bing Hotels. Within three months after his mother died in 1930, Paul Henderson sold the heavily mortgaged house in Germantown and sobered up long enough to catch a train to New York — purely because I was there. He hoped that I could get him a job — at anything, even making brooms. God knows I tried! But I soon realized that Paul had lost all interest in life, and I dreaded the tenth of every month when his small pension check would arrive. He'd disappear from the room I had gotten for him on Bank Street in Greenwich Village and make the rounds of speakeasies where kindly but misguided customers would buy him drinks when his money ran out. I started to think it might be better for him if he were a troublemaker and created a disturbance so the police could pick him up and tuck him safely away long enough to get off the booze. It took me more than a year to enlist the aid of enough friendly bartenders who would call me as soon as he came in.

The Depression caught me full in 1932 and I was laid off with twenty other administrative office workers a week before Christmas — facing a world that seemed utterly jobless. I determined at that moment that I'd never work for a

corporation again and I'd succeed at writing or starve to
death trying. I rented an apartment for $25 a month in a
basement in Astoria and started my first full-length book —
a Florida mystery called *Blood on Lake Louisa*. Paul moved
in with me two months later and on and off for a year we
existed on what short unsigned pieces I could sell to *The
New Yorker* and *Liberty*. I established a moderate credit
rating at a nearby friendly Italian grocery and ate so much
spaghetti that I finally broke out with a wheat rash. During
this time, I sought out a great deal of material regarding
famous blind people and read about them to Paul. I hoped
that some of their accomplishments would inspire him, but I
eventually realized that Paul had slipped into his own private
paranoiac world — identifying with Max Carrados, using
liquor to bolster confidence that he could duplicate the impossible feats of Ernest Bramah's overdrawn character. Paul
would also challenge the accomplishments of blind persons
with a negative approach that defied argument, such as
claiming that John Milton "was educated at Cambridge, besides being an established poet before he went blind at
forty-four."

By 1932 I had reached the point of utter desperation with
Paul and made an attempt to convince him that someone
with even more severe handicaps than his could do something productive. I finally succeeded, through my agent, in
getting in touch with Mr. John A. Macy, whose wife was
the famous Anne Mansfield Sullivan who had trained Helen
Keller. Mr. Macy was quite ill and died several months
later, in August 1932, but the lengthy letter I wrote his wife
interested her enough to furnish me with a list of famous
blind people — and in reply to my complaints about Max
Carrados, she wrote me: "You're a mystery writer . . .

so why not draw on the knowledge that you've accumulated and create a blind detective of your own — one who would be the antithesis of Max Carrados, who would never perform any feat in his detection or deduction that couldn't be duplicated by someone totally blind — presuming they had the necessary brains and willpower to train themselves to try it."

Thus the idea of Captain Duncan Maclain was born. It was in 1937 that the Crime Club published the first of the books about him, *The Last Express.* For forty years he has served me well — in serialization, syndication, movies, and foreign editions. He's responsible for the organization of the Mystery Writers of America, Inc., and for the Blinded Veterans Association — formed at Avon Old Farms Army Schools of the Blind at Avon, Connecticut, in 1945, in which I hold honorary life membership Card No. 1. Even today, if you sit up late enough and watch the third repeat of *Longstreet* on ABC, you can see that the series is based on "Characters Created by Baynard Kendrick."

Speaking to the B.V.A. on the occasion of their twenty-first annual convention at the Deauville Hotel, Miami Beach, Florida, on August 20, 1966, I was asked by one of the members if I happened to remember the name of that young blind soldier in St. Dunstan's Home in London who through his perspicacity had quite unwittingly been the progenitor of the B.V.A. I was forced to say no — I hadn't forgotten his name for I never knew it; he was merely one of a number of blinded British Tommies ensconced for the time being in St. Dunstan's.

I intended to call this piece "The Birth of a Blind Detective" because, to me, Captain Duncan Maclain was really born — and I hope will live forever — showing to sighted people that although the blind of the world may have lost their eyes, their brains and their work live on.

Baynard Kendrick

Mark
McPherson

Vera Caspary

Vera Caspary's Laura *is one of the rarest of literary gems — a classic recognized as such from the first by its readers. Curiously, critics gave it lukewarm or mixed reviews upon publication, but quickly reversed themselves to applaud it.*

Three characters dominate the action of the novel, which is presented largely from their points of view: Laura, the enigmatic and romantic beauty of the title; Waldo Lydecker, the epicene columnist who loves her; and Mark McPherson, the unusual, sensitive detective who falls in love with the ethereal Laura as he investigates her murder. His eerie, haunting passion marks him as a character destined for immortality but doomed to a single volume. Vera Caspary chose to write no more of his pursuits. Indeed, after Laura, *any further case would have been anticlimactic.*

Vera Caspary has written dozens of original screenplays and stories on which motion pictures have been based, notably Les Girls, Letter to Three Wives, I Can Get It for You Wholesale, The Night of June 13, Easy Living, *and the excellent Fritz Lang thriller,* The Blue Gardenia. *Among her eighteen novels are* Bedelia, Evvie, Stranger Than Truth, The Husband, The Weeping and the Laughter, The Dreamers, The Rosecrest Cell, *and* Elizabeth X.

In addition to Dana Andrews's memorable portrayal of Mark McPherson in the 1944 film, the romantic and idealistic hero has challenged other actors. Hugh Marlowe appeared in the 1947 Broadway drama (which had a modest run), and Robert Stack was McPherson in Truman Capote's television adaptation, in 1968. Miss Caspary remembers that production as "an abortion."

Born in Chicago in 1899, Vera Caspary Goldsmith now lives in New York City's Greenwich Village. She married producer I. G. Goldsmith during her long stay in California.

Mark McPherson

by Vera Caspary

MARK MCPHERSON IS HONORED to be included in this catalog of distinguished detectives. He is the only one, I believe, who has not appeared in a series of murder stories, but became a hero only once.

McPherson was conceived of necessity, born of prejudice. In my first draft of *Laura* (in play form) the detective had no special quality. He was simply a device. Later, when the novel was started, the detective was the only character who failed to come alive. The other characters were fashioned in the forms of people I'd known, not prototypes but combinations of friends and acquaintances.

There were no detectives in my working or social life. As editor of *Fingerprint Magazine* I had interviewed a number of professionals in the trade, including J. Edgar Hoover in the early days of his career and mine. None had the dash and wit of the reporters and advertising executives I flirted and danced with in the great jazz days of Chicago.

I cannot say when or how the idea for the story of *Laura* came into my mind, but do recall that a murder-romance about a detective who falls in love with a murder victim kept me awake many nights. The idea was not new. Several writers had tried unsuccessfully to solve the problem. I can't remember what triggered my solution: that the girl was not dead but mistakenly identified. This gave shape to the story of the man who, investigating her murder, is fascinated by the dead woman; comes to know her as he has never known a living girl; discovers her charm through intimacy with what she has left behind, her apartment, her wardrobe, her scents and cosmetics, her checkbook and diary, her taste in books, music, and sports, the bottles on her bar, the friends she entertained, the men who loved her. It was to be the tale of a man yearning for a woman he has never met and believes he can never know.

What sort of man would he be? Not psychotic certainly, nor the swaggering hard-boiled private eye of popular mystery stories. Quick, easy satisfaction would be that fellow's dish, pushovers with large exposed breasts his ideals. He would never waste time in daydreams. (If he did his creators neglected to mention the fact.) Nor would my romantic detective fit the pattern of the persevering, stolid public servant, nor the impassive genius of deduction.

This is where the prejudice came in. I did not like detectives. I knew they were necessary in modern society, but I loathed men who spied for money. It seemed preposterous for me to make a hero out of such a fellow. In few, if any, of the early "originals" I wrote for the movies was the murder solved by a professional sleuth. Until the problem arose in the writing of *Laura*, I had never glorified a detective. In the first two drafts the character remained a dummy. It was only when I made notes for the following dialogue between Laura and McPherson that he came alive:

She said, "You don't seem at all like a detective."

"Have you ever known any detectives?"

"In detective stories there are two kinds, the hard-boiled ones who are always drunk and talk out of the corners of their mouths and do it all by instinct; and the cold, dry, scientific kind who split hairs under a microscope."

"Which do you prefer?"

"Neither," she said, "I don't like people who make their livings out of spying and poking into people's lives. Detectives aren't heros to me, they're detestable."

Thus I purged myself of prejudice and Mark McPherson was born. Like the rest of us he came into the world naked. To fulfill his destiny he had to be clothed with certain attributes which could not merely be draped upon him, but which had to be part of his bearing. In several editions of the book, the blurb calls him "the toughest detective in town." This is sales talk. Mark is tough-minded but warmhearted. Toughness is required in his job but he is too imaginative, too intelligent to play the roughneck.

At the outset he is sullen about his job. The search for Laura's killer seems a waste of time to a man who has investigated the perpetrators of social crime, been demoted to the Homicide Squad because of a private feud with one of his superiors. He is angry and cynical. He despises the chic world which Laura inhabited, is scornful of her smart circle, contemptuous of luxury, also charmed by these things. Native wit is his weapon. He loathes pretense but can be awed by pretentious persons whose culture he envies. His lower-middle-class Scotch Presbyterian morality is rigid but a burden to him. He is ambivalent, therefore human.

Such qualities were developed in him by the demands of the story. The detective has to be a foil for the brilliant, malicious columnist, Waldo Lydecker. As a hero Mark is obliged to top Waldo in repartee. He does. And having fallen in love with a dead girl, he is compelled to adjust his emotions when she returns alive, yet he must conceal his ardor when it becomes his job to investigate her as the possible killer of her rival.

Mark is defensive, almost bitter about an almost imperceptible limp. Although reported to have been the result of a wound during a gangster gun battle, it was caused by (but not in) World War II. The book was written in that grim time when every able-bodied young man was in service. Why was Mark investigating a murder on the home front? The hero could show no visible defect. The "silver shinbone" had a certain romantic aura. That he had acquired it in police work gave credibility to his job. It was also a symbolic characteristic. Mark does not tread heavily, he walks carefully.

Much of the tale is told by Mark himself. His style contrasts with Waldo's florid prose and Laura's feminine confessions. Since style expresses point of view, Mark writes in direct unadorned sentences that reveal as much about his own character as about the people he describes.

Having come alive, he took over the drama, influencing not only the mood but the movement of the story, asserting his personality in a way never contemplated in early drafts and outlines. I have been asked to write other books about him and would very much have liked to; I had become fond of the man. The only trouble is that I am not a real mystery writer and have never been able to think of a plot.

Vera Caspary

Lieutenant
Luis Mendoza

Dell Shannon

It is not unusual for professors, writers, lawyers, doctors, and professionals of every imaginable vocation to turn up in the pages of detective novels as amateurs of crime, helping to solve cases because they cannot resist the lure of the chase or because they are inextricably drawn into a nefarious tangle. It is more unexpected for an independently wealthy policeman to continue to combat crime as a matter of principle — because of a desire to bring some order to the frightening chaos in his city. Luis Mendoza's grandfather left him a substantial estate, but the Los Angeles police officer's devotion to his ideals and career remains unchanged.

Dell Shannon — chronicler of Lieutenant Mendoza's cases — is one of the pseudonyms of Elizabeth Linington, the prolific author of police procedurals which have appeared steadily since 1960. As Lesley Egan, she also writes about Andrew Clock of the L.A.P.D., lawyer Jesse Falkenstein, an amateur detective who quotes extensively from the Talmud, and Vic Varallo, a Glendale police captain. Under her own name, she writes about the squad at Hollywood precinct of the L.A.P.D. She has also written several historical novels and, as Anne Blaisdell, a suspense thriller (Nightmare). In addition to producing at least three books a year, the 56-year-old Californian devotes considerable time and energy to politics as an active member of the John Birch Society.

She views the detective story as a philosophical statement, calling it "the morality play of our time . . . it deals with basics; with truth versus lie, law and order versus anarchy, a moral code versus amorality."

Lieutenant Luis Mendoza

by Dell Shannon

MENDOZA, Lieutenant Luis Rodolfo Vicente, Bureau of Robbery-Homicide, Los Angeles Police Department. A rather unlikely professional police officer, Mendoza was born sometime between the wars. His parents killed in an accident shortly afterward, he grew up in the east L.A. slums, devoted to his resolute grandmother, Teresa Maria Sanchez y Mendoza, and hating and fearing his miserly grandfather. A naturally brilliant cardplayer, he was mastering the art of the stacked deck and crooked shuffle in his teens, possibly revealing a latent kinship with his grandfather who was amassing a fortune probably by means of crooked gambling at the time. To this day Mendoza "thinks better with the cards in his hands," and though domesticity has ruined his poker game, is given to practicing the art of stacked decks as he ruminates on problems.

Some dim but obstinate conviction about principles of justice prompted him to join the force at the age of twenty-one, and he became a sufficiently dedicated L.A.P.D. officer that he stayed on at the job even when his grandfather's death brought him a modest fortune. As a ranking detective, he served his apprenticeship in the Vice Squad, where his talents were chiefly utilized in pursuit of crooked gamblers and con men — a genus he still retains much sympathy for (*Double Bluff*). Probably his early poverty is responsible for his well-known penchant for expensive tailoring, the discreet but elegant jewelry; but his fanatic fastidiousness is a built-in idiosyncrasy. Although he is not a physically impressive figure, slender and under six feet, Mendoza's smooth and often sarcastic charm makes its own impression; and when the occasion arises (*The Ace of Spades*) he can give a good account of himself.

An utter cynic and egotist, Mendoza was a casual chaser and catcher of females up to the age of forty, when a combination of circumstances (*Knave of Hearts*) led him to marriage with his redhaired Scots-Irish girl, Alison Weir. Subsequently they became the parents of twins, John Luis and Teresa Maria. Mendoza is a fanatic cat lover, which offers another clue to his essential personality; any extroverted idiot can love a dog, but as Mr. Gallico has remarked, it requires a very stable and subtle character fully to appreciate and understand cats. As of the moment the Mendoza ménage includes four cats and, rather grudgingly on Mendoza's part, an Old English sheepdog acquired by accident (*Schooled to Kill*). Since the advent of the twins, also of the household is Mairí MacTaggart, the staunch and devoutly Catholic Scots nanny.

As a matter of fact, it can be inferred that the cynicism, egotism, and sardonic humor are camouflage on Mendoza's part for a large and sentimental heart, though he is inclined to prefer animals to humans. And though he seems at all times to be master of his household, the probability is that it just looks that way. He made quite a fuss about the dog Cedric, but we notice that the dog stayed to become a member of the family. It can also be inferred that everybody who knows Mendoza really well is quite aware of this, and that all the affectation of the hardened cynic is merely a mannerism somewhat fondly accepted by his friends.

In the last few years he has become an avid Kiplingphile:

stumbling late upon the master storyteller, his conversion was sudden and fanatic. It is one facet of his character neither his men nor Alison quite understands — but unfortunately this inner circle of the discerning few is a relatively small one.

Mendoza's occasional uncanny intuition has earned him the reputation of having a crystal ball. Perhaps surprisingly, his money, brilliance, and refusal to suffer fools gladly have not antagonized the men under his orders; on the contrary, he is a popular and well-liked officer. The other men in his office — formerly Homicide, recently merged into Robbery-Homicide — are much more usual types of working detectives, from his two senior sergeants Hackett and Higgins to ingenuous-looking Tom Landers, handsome Palliser, the earnest fundamentalist Piggott, the phlegmatic Glasser, the deceptively bright Jason Grace, et al. They have all experienced some interesting occasions together, aside from the monotonous run-of-the-mill cases turning up day by day in any big-city police bureau. Over the years, they have shared changes and troubles, laughs and surprises: the murder of Sergeant Dwyer (*The Death-Bringers*), the humble pursuit of his widow by Higgins, the astonishing charge against Landers (*The Ringer*), the macabre antics of *Coffin Corner* — the grim chase of all the thieves and killers and lunatics and fools which makes up the working day of the professional police officer. At the same time, they are only human, with human problems and foibles even as the rest of us: Hackett on his perennial diet, Landers frustrated by his too-youthful looks, Piggott seeing the devil on all sides.

A lapsed Catholic since his not-so-tender youth, Mendoza had resisted all the cunning efforts of his grandmother and, latterly, Mrs. MacTaggart, to woo him back to the church; but recently the rather suspenseful affair of the kidnapping of the twins (*Deuces Wild*) accomplished even that. Most recently, also subsequent to that occurrence, the Mendozas are anticipating another addition to the family. As he has over the years, Mendoza is continually threatening to quit the thankless job, but it is unlikely he ever will. As Alison says, he wouldn't know what to do with himself; and as he says, *Mañana sera otro día* — Tomorrow is also a day.

I don't know where Mendoza came from. There was no gestation period, as it were. At the time I was still feeling quite annoyed at various publishers who were rejecting my latest historical novel in spite of the fact that the others had sold very well; but being fond of eating I had to write something. I had a small, rather interesting idea for a suspense novel, and sat down to start it; the plot was all the interest to me, and it was quite casually — led on by the exigency of the developing plot — that I introduced a police officer on the scene on page eleven of the thing (*Case Pending*). Almost instantly he rose up off the page, captured me alive, and dismayingly refused to let me stop writing about him. Of course he is an egotist. Willy-nilly I was kept writing about Mendoza, and over the next four books all the various aspects of his character emerged. At this point I managed to stop myself temporarily, and as it appeared I would be writing about Mendoza and police work for some time, I began some intensive research on police techniques, apparatus, regulations, and the L.A.P.D. in particular. As a historical novelist I was accustomed to extensive research, and the mere mechanics of it made me feel rather less uneasy about this strange and sudden enthrallment — put Mendoza at one remove, so to speak. At the first stirring, again, of the impulse to write about Mendoza, I hastily concocted another plot and wrote a book, and then another, about some very different people (both of these turned into series too, purely as a device to keep Mendoza at bay). But when I was ruthlessly captured again and set to writing about Mendoza, although I was deliberately (and I hope plausibly and authentically) producing the police-procedural novel, Mendoza was still in charge and dominating the scene. My other detectives were all acquired, somewhat desperately, to keep him from forcing me to write about him every time I picked up my pen to write *something*.

It can be argued, I suppose, that the various productions of a reasonably prolific writer always have much in common: a writer tends to write about the same kind of people in book after book. Doubtless the Freudians would have glib explanations; having a simple mind (like Jason Grace) I am inclined to think that any given writer's protagonists tend to similarity just because the writer finds something attractive, admirable, or amusing about that kind of character. Many of the people in my other books are "larger than life" people — as Mendoza certainly is (and that is the sole reason I might advance even to myself to explain why I once wrote one entire thick book about that less than admirable creature Oliver Cromwell). Curiously, a majority of my other protagonists have also been shrewd cardplayers, though it is a pastime I personally detest.

Aside from that — no, I don't know where Mendoza came from, or why. Just, there he was — and there he is.

Dell Shannon

Mr. and Mrs. North

Richard Lockridge

There is an irresistible appeal in those scatterbrained young women of fiction who find themselves in the unlikeliest situations, never quite knowing how they got there and only miraculously escaping some horrible fate at the last moment. While they are as exasperating as real-life women, they still have a mad charm that squeezes affection out of the grumpiest reader. No one better exemplifies this personality than Pamela North, the delightful albatross around Jerry North's neck. Perhaps the most likable couple in mystery fiction (along with Nick and Nora Charles), the Norths made their investigative debut in The Norths Meet Murder. *They had previously been the central characters in a 1936 collection of sketches, originally published in* The New Yorker, *titled* Mr. and Mrs. North, *and were in time the subjects of a popular Broadway play, a radio series, and a television series.*

Richard Lockridge had created the couple for those humorous sketches and, when his wife Frances decided to write a mystery, he suggested the already established characters for her novel. They appeared in a total of twenty-seven books (twenty-six of them mystery novels), all co-authored by Frances and Richard, until 1963, when Frances died and the series ended.

Richard Lockridge also wrote of the adventures of Nathan Shapiro, a New York City police detective plagued with self-doubts, and Merton Heimrich of the New York State Police. After his wife's death, Lockridge continued those detective series alone. He also created Bernie Simmons of the New York District Attorney's office in 1965. The 79-year-old Richard Lockridge is now married to another mystery writer, Hildegarde Dolson; they live in Tryon, North Carolina.

Mr. and Mrs. North

by Richard Lockridge

MR. AND MRS. NORTH had been fictional, or semifictional, characters for several years before they first met murder. I paraphrase the title of the first mystery novel about them — *The Norths Meet Murder*. I had written pieces about them for *The New Yorker* — not short stories, precisely, but what *The New Yorker* then called "casuals." Brief domestic comedies, I suppose they were. And they were based, sometimes closely, on things which had happened to my wife, Frances, and me.

I wrote, and the magazine bought, a good many of those pieces, and eventually they were collected in a book called *Mr. and Mrs. North.* The publisher, rather ill-advisedly, called this collection a "novel." Several reviewers snorted and so, in a mild way, did I. Novels, like short stories, require plots, and I, then, was plotless. And the Norths, in the early *New Yorker* pieces, were without first names.

The surname was easy. It was merely lifted from the somewhat amorphous, and frequently inept, people who played the North hands in bridge problems. In *The New Yorker*, in their early appearances they were merely "Mr." and "Mrs." But midway of one piece, it became necessary for Mr. North to call to his wife in another room of their apartment. It seemed unlikely that he would call out, "Hey, Mrs. North." So, on the spur of the moment, he called for

"Fran." I do not remember that I had ever called Frances that, although, among other things, I did call her "Francie."

When proofs — *The New Yorker* always sent proofs — came back the "Fran" stuck out. The spur of the moment had, clearly, struck too close to home. As a one-time printer I could count spaces, so that only one line would have to be reset. (I had been, a few years earlier, the printer in the Kansas City, Missouri, post office. I had learned to set type in a "journalism" course at Kansas City Junior College, where journalism certainly started with the fundamentals. I was taught to run a job press at the post office by an elderly man, who really was a printer and was retiring. He lacked two fingers on his right hand, which was conventional for long-time operators of job presses. I did manage to retain mine.)

Anyway, I counted spaces, and "Pam" came close enough, and Mrs. North became Pamela, "Pam" for that line of type. I have no idea how her husband became "Jerry" or, for that matter, how he became a publisher. In *The New Yorker* stories, he had no occupation, so far as I can remember. Except, of course, that of being foil, straight man, to his wife.

Actually, I suppose the Norths did not first appear in *The New Yorker*, although that was the first time they had names.

When we first went to New York to stay, the *New York Sun* devoted that part of its back page not occupied by John Wanamaker to a department called The Sun Rays. It consisted of very short, preferably humorous pieces, and fragments of verse. We were broke; *flat* broke is not excessive. Frances got a job reckoning payments due from people who were buying on time — buying electric generators, as I recall. She was paid twenty-five dollars a week. It was a job for which she was totally unsuited, and which she did very well. We paid twenty dollars a week for a large room with a bath and a gas plate at one end. I, for some months, had no job at all, although I kept applying to all the city's newspapers, which then were numerous. So I started submitting pieces to The Sun Rays.

Most of them were about the "babes in the studio apartment." In retrospect, the "babes" seems to me unbearably cute. It was also inaccurate. We were both experienced newspaper reporters, Frances much more experienced than I. But we *were* babes in Manhattan and had fallen into the habit of eating. The Sun Rays pieces helped us sustain the habit. They also helped me, finally, to get a job on the city staff of the *Sun*.

The "babes" were the Norths in embryo. And the time was fifty years ago. You could buy twenty-five cents' worth of stew meat and make it do for two dinners. If, of course, the stew didn't spoil between meals: we had no refrigeration in the studio.

I kept on writing North stories while I was doing rewrite, and covering murder trials, on the *Sun*. We seemed to spend more than our combined salaries, although by then Frances had found a job more suited to her skills, and somewhat better paid. *The New Yorker* kept on buying. And we both, from time to time, read detective stories — mystery novels, novels of suspense, whatever publishers care to call them. (My own preference is for "detective stories," or the variants which I think of as "chases." Chases are more likely to become one-shots in magazines, or did before general magazines shrank so drastically in size and, of course, in number.)

It was Frances who first decided to write a detective story of her own. For several days her typewriter clicked happily. Then it stopped clicking. Then she came to me. There was one point with which she was having a little trouble, and perhaps I could help.

I read the dozen or so pages and it seemed to me to start very well. Then there was a scene, obviously crucial. A rowboat, apparently with nobody in it, was crossing a lake in the moonlight. I recognized the lake; we were renting a summer weekend cabin on just such a lake.

The rowboat came ashore. There was a body lying in it. "Fine," I said. "Very good scene. Foreboding. Only, with only this dead man in it, what made the boat move? You say it was a still night; no wind to blow it ashore. So?"

"Yes," she said, "that's the point I'm having trouble with. I thought maybe you could help. After all, you were in the navy."

I had been. On a battleship which had spent most of 1918 in what was then the Brooklyn Navy Yard. New engines were being installed. With new engines she could move herself. In fact, she did move while I was still aboard. Across water in the yard and, with a considerable bang, into a pier. U.S.S. *North Dakota* managed, later, to steam to a drydock for junking.

None of this seemed to have much to do with a rowboat, occupied only by the dead, moving across a quiet lake under a full moon.

Frances was disappointed. I promised her we would work on it.

We did work on it. And we got nowhere. I still think about it now and then. I still get nowhere.

But then we got the idea of collaborating on a mystery,

without the magical boat, but with Mr. and Mrs. North, already established characters.

The way we worked together, on that and subsequent books in what became a series, was to have story conferences. Who will we kill this time? Male or female? And who will do the killing, and why?

We would talk things out, making notes, coming up — usually slowly — with ideas, each of us accepting or rejecting the other's notions.

After some hours of this, each of us would type up a synopsis of the book and of individual scenes in it. We would name the characters, which is often a tricky business. We would, finally, jumble it all together. Then I would write the story, drawing on our outlines and my experience, not very extensive, as a police reporter. And also my experience in covering murder trials, which was much greater. (Hall-Mills, Snyder-Gray and others celebrated in the now-distant past. Newspapers went all out for trials in those days. Some rented houses to lodge their covering staffs. The *Sun* made do with three of us and now and then, as in the Browning separation suit, with only two.)

I did all the writing on all our books. Frances summed it up neatly in one speaking appearance we made together: "I think up interesting characters and Dick kills them off."

(The Norths themselves almost got killed off before, as detectives, they were ever born. Somebody, and I am afraid it was the late George Bye, my agent and close friend, suggested that they be renamed — perhaps become the Souths, or maybe the Wests.

It would be too much to say that by then the Norths had a following. But they were known to *New Yorker* readers. The suggestion that this perhaps minimal advantage be thrown away was hooted down, mostly by me, but also by the editors.)

When Frances died very suddenly and I kept on writing, several reviewers searched diligently for change in our style. One or two found it, which I thought very astute of them.

I wrote no more North stories after Frances's death, partly because, in my mind, she had always been Pamela North; partly because the spontaneity seemed to be ebbing out of them.

People used to ask me what Pam and Jerry looked like. I could never tell them. I have always avoided detailed physical descriptions of characters. It is better, it seems to me, to let readers form their own conceptions. (This attitude of mine may stem from the days when I was a boy and my mother read Dickens to me. She read from heavy volumes of an edition set two columns to the page in six-point type. There were sketches of the characters. None of them ever looked remotely like the people I had learned to know so intimately from Dickens's words.)

So Inspector Heimrich is a big man, who thinks he looks like a hippopotamus; Lieutenant Shapiro is tall and thin. He wears gray suits which need pressing and has a long sad face. Readers can take it from there.

They have taken Pam North a good many places. Nobody ever seemed to care much about what Jerry looked like. When the collection of North stories was published in England, the publishers decided they needed to be sketched as chapter headings. They were stolid-looking characters. Pam was matronly; Jerry smoked a pipe. Neither was in the least what I had, vaguely, imagined.

I suppose I had thought, insofar as I thought of it at all, that Pam was small and quick and blond. I had no quarrel with the casting of her in either the play or the television series. Either Peggy Conklin in the play or Barbara Britton in the TV series was all right with me. (During rehearsals of Owen Davis's play, Miss Conklin used to crouch in the wings, for all the world like a runner preparing for the hundred-yard dash, and make her entrances at a runner's speed. Which was, to my mind, entirely appropriate.) Gracie Allen, in the movie, seemed to me a triumph of miscasting.

Pam's mind is another matter. It seemed to me to glint. Its logic was darting, now and then bewildering but always acute. The female mind is often like that. Owen Davis once told me that Pam North was what every well-married man likes to think his wife is.

I have been most lucky to be twice married to women with minds like that, which is obviously more than any man deserves. Men plod their ways on paths of logic, and laboriously reach conclusions to find women sitting on them, patient as they wait for laggards.

Men like to call this superior mental alacrity "womanly intuition."

Richard Lockridge

Patrick
Petrella

Michael Gilbert

It is difficult to write espionage fiction with any degree of authenticity, but when Michael Gilbert chronicled the adventures of counterintelligence agents Daniel Calder and Samuel Behrens in Game Without Rules *(1967),* Ellery Queen *selected it for* Queen's Quorum — *the list of the 125 most important books of detective/crime short stories. Queen thought it, after Somerset Maugham's* Ashenden, *the best volume of spy stories ever written.*

It is perhaps only slightly less difficult to write police procedurals with any degree of authenticity (the N.Y.P.D., for example, being a tiny bit more open than the CIA). But when Michael Gilbert wrote Blood and Judgment, *in 1959, his first novel about Patrick Petrella, it was selected as one of the year's best mysteries by Anthony Boucher.*

It is not easy to create a memorable series character, but Michael Gilbert is the creator of novels about Inspector Hazelrigg, as well as the gentlemen noted above.

The versatile and accomplished Gilbert, 65, writes while commuting from his home and family in Kent to his full-time legal practice in Lincoln's Inn. At one time the legal adviser to Raymond Chandler, the English solicitor/author drew up the will of the great mystery writer. Michael Gilbert's daughter, Harriett, has also published highly acclaimed mystery novels in recent years.

Patrick Petrella

by Michael Gilbert

WHEN LIEUTENANT OF POLICE Gregorio Petrella married Mirabel Trentham-Foster, their acquaintances were more than surprised, they were positively aghast. They predicted disaster; and if not disaster, rapid disillusionment and separation. The two persons concerned confounded these prophets. They lived together in love and amity, and have continued to do so until this day.

The use, in the previous sentence, of the word "acquaintances" rather than "friends" was deliberate. Both of them were solitary by nature. This may have helped to cement their happiness. When two solitary-minded people find each other their union can be very firm.

At the time of his marriage Gregorio was a lieutenant in the political branch of the Spanish police, the equivalent, in England, of the Special Branch. It would scarcely be an exaggeration to say that he spent most of his working life keeping General Franco alive. He carried out his duties efficiently, not out of any love of *El Caudillo*, or even of any particular sympathy with his policies, but because it was his job, and one which he was technically well equipped to do.

For one of Gregorio's particular accomplishments, uncommon in a Spaniard, was that he was a linguist, bilingual in Spanish and French, competent in Arabic and English. This was useful since most of the hopeful conspiracies aimed at the removal of the head of the Spanish state had their origins abroad. A lot of his work took him into the country of the Basques and across the Pyrenees into Southern France. Sometimes he went further afield: to Tangiers, to Sicily and to Beirut. It was in Egypt that he found Miss Trentham-Foster. She was attempting a painting of the pyramids.

She had already torn up three versions in disgust, and said ᵗo the friendly young Spaniard who had been watching her, "They all look so damnably conventional." Gregorio considered the matter, and said, "Might it improve them, if you painted the pyramids lying on their sides? Or even upside down?"

They were married three months later. Patrick was their only son. His upbringing accorded with his parentage. For the first eight years of his life in Spain (a country democratic with children, rigidly autocratic with adults) he spent his time running around with other boys of his own age from all classes of the community, learning things which horrified his mother as much as they amused his father. On his eighth birthday she put her small foot down. Coming as she did from an English professional family she had irreversible ideas about the proper education of male children. Capitán Gregorio saw that Mirabel's mind was made up and gave way. His pay was not large, but fortunately there was family money on both sides. Prospectuses were sent for. The rival claims of different preparatory schools were carefully examined and the small Patrick was launched into the traditional educational system of the English middle and upper classes.

With such an upbringing he might have found it difficult to adapt himself to boarding-school life, and it is reasonable to suppose that he was, to start with, fairly miserable; but there were factors in his favor. His temperament was, for the most part, sunny and equable. On the other hand, when he lost his temper, he lost it thoroughly; and he knew how to fight. He had not altogether wasted his time with the small banditti of the slums of Madrid. His methods might be unorthodox, but they were effective.

By the time that he stepped off the other end of the educational escalator at the age of seventeen there was nothing except the jet blackness of his hair and a slight darkness of his skin to distinguish him from any other public schoolboy.

At this point his father took a hand, and Patrick went, first, to the American University in Beirut, where he learned to speak and read Arabic; then to a college of rather peculiar Further Education in Cairo, where he learned, among other things, how to pick locks.

His own ambitions had hardly changed since the age of eight. On his twenty-first birthday he joined the ranks of the Metropolitan Police as a constable. A slight difficulty, arising out of the question of his nationality, was overcome through Colonel Gregorio's personal friendship with the then assistant commissioner. After he had completed his training at Peel House, Patrick's first posting was to the North London Division of Highside, and it was about his experiences here that the first stories were written.

It will be appreciated that the protagonist of a fictional series differs in a number of respects from his counterpart in real life. He is not born; he springs into being, mature, competent, and armed at all points to deal with the first problem his creator has seen fit to face him with. ("Oh, damn!" said Lord Peter Wimsey at Piccadilly Circus. "Hi! driver.") Such autogenesis has its dangers, even for so meticulous a plotter as Miss Sayers. A whole literature has sprung up in an attempt to reconcile the details of the earlier life of Sherlock Holmes and Doctor Watson.

There is an equally important matter, which afflicts real and fictional characters alike, the matter of growing older. If Hercule Poirot really had retired from the Belgian Police Force in 1904, how old was he on his last appearance?

It may be true that readers, on the whole, care little for these niceties. For them their favorite characters live forever in a fifth dimension where time does not wither nor custom stale. It is, however, worth noticing one point. Just as people believe that exterior circumstances occurring at the time of a child's conception (a period of happiness, a sudden shock, the conjunction of the planets or the phases of the moon) can affect the infant's whole character thereafter, so can quite trivial occurrences on the occasion of his first public appearance affect, for better or for worse, a character destined for a long fictional life.

The fictional Patrick Petrella was conceived in church. The moment of his conception is as clearly fixed in my mind as though it had happened yesterday, not twenty-five years ago. It was a drowsy summer evening and the preacher had reached what appeared to be only the midpoint of his sermon. It was not an inspired address, and I turned, as I sometimes do in such circumstances, to the hymn book for relief. It opened on the lines of Christina Rosetti, *"Who has seen the wind? Neither you nor I. But when the trees bow down their heads, the wind is passing by."* A commonplace thought, given great effect by the rhythm and placing of the words. Then — *"Who has seen the wind? Neither I nor you. But when the leaves hang trembling, the wind is passing through."*

And there, quite suddenly, it was. A scene, complete in every last detail. A working-class family, composed of wife and children, sitting in their front room, being talked to by a visitor (parson? social worker? policeman?) but remaining totally unresponsive to his efforts. Answering in monosyllables. Trembling. Heads bowed down. Why? Because they know, but their visitor does not, that there is a monster in the back room. Their father, a violent criminal, had escaped that day from prison and is hiding there. Certainly heads would hang and limbs be trembling. It is at that moment that their visitor (he is now quite definitely a policeman, and a youngster at that) recalls the lines of the poem and realizes the truth. He bursts into the back room, and tackles the intruder, who gets the better of him, and escapes. Pursuit. Final capture.

In that short sequence, which cannot have lasted for more than a few seconds, a complete character was encapsulated. A young policeman, in his first posting (this was automatically North London, since we had lived in Highgate before migrating to rural Kent), sufficiently interested in his job, and in the people involved in it, to visit the wife of a man who was serving a prison sentence; sufficiently acute to notice the unnatural behavior of the woman and her normally rowdy children; sufficiently imaginative to deduce the reason for a single, furtive glance in the direction of the kitchen door. Courageous enough to go for the man, not nearly strong enough to overpower him, but with sufficient tenacity to continue the chase after he had been roughly handled; above all, an unusual young man, who read and could quote poetry.

Most police work was knowledge; knowledge of an infinity of small, everyday facts, unimportant by themselves, deadly when taken together. Nevertheless, Petrella retained an obstinate conviction that there were other things as well, deeper things and finer things; colours, shapes and sounds of absolute beauty, unconnected with the world of small people in small houses in grey streets. And while in one pocket of his old raincoat he might carry Moriarty's *Police Law*, in the other would lie, dog-eared with use, the Golden Treasury of Palgrave.

"*She walks in beauty, like the night of cloudless climes and starry skies*" said Petrella, and "That car's been there a long time. If it's still there when I come back it might be worth looking into."

Almost everything that happened afterwards was as traceable to that first conception as is the character of a real person to the vagaries of his parents and the accidents of the nursery and the schoolroom.

Other things were added later, of course.

Why was he called Petrella? A foolish question. Why are you called Gubbins? Because it was your father's name. Why such an odd name? Because his father was a foreigner. Then why Patrick? Because his mother was an Englishwoman.

It was this dichotomy which produced the two opposite strands in his character. His father was a professional policeman, who carried out a job which was not always agreeable in a totally professional manner. In such a situation, the end might be held to justify the means. At the same time, since he was a political policeman, it was inevitable that he would, from time to time, question the motives and the character of the people who gave him his orders.

From his mother, the daughter of an architect and the granddaughter of a judge who was also an accomplished painter, he derived the cultural heritage of the English upper middle class, together with something else: an abstract notion of what was fair and what was unfair. It is a notion which is unfashionable in the materialistic win-at-any-price atmosphere of today. But curious that it should be sneered at when one considers the state in which the world now finds itself.

A Spanish temper and an English sense of equity. Such dangerous opposites were capable, from time to time, of combining into an explosive mixture capable of blowing Patrick Petrella clean out of the carefully regulated ranks of the Metropolitan Police.

At the moment of writing he is a detective chief inspector, in charge of one of the three stations in a rowdy but colorful South London Division.

His position dictates both the types of wrongdoing he will encounter and the general method of their solution. (Incidentally, it also overcomes an initial difficulty. A purely amateur detective who is also a series character has somehow to account plausibly for the extraordinary sequence of crimes with which he becomes involved. If a corpse is found in the library every time he happens to visit a country house, people will soon stop asking him down for the weekend.)

To a member of the C.I.D. crime is his daily portion. It will certainly not be an undiluted diet of murder. The crimes which come his way will cover innumerable variations on the general themes of theft and violence, of arson, blackmail, intimidation, forgery and fraud.

For the most part such crimes will be solved by the well-tried methods of the police. The asking of questions; the taking of statements; the analysis of physical evidence; the use of the Criminal Record Office, the Fingerprint Bank, and the Forensic Science Laboratory. It is routine stuff for the most part, more perspiration than inspiration, but maybe none the less intriguing for that.

Petrella has the good fortune to belong, at a particular

stage in its development, to what is, without question, the finest police force in the world. Whether he will rise any higher in it depends in part on his own efforts, in part on whether he can get along without unduly upsetting the top brass, and in part on a number of imponderables about which it is pointless to conjecture.

I can only wish him well.

Michael Gilbert

Superintendent
Pibble

Peter Dickinson

It was surely as happy a circumstance for the criminal element of London as it was melancholy for Scotland Yard when Superintendent Pibble was forced to retire in 1970. Although not without a dossier of unsolved cases, Pibble was a dogged and generally successful policeman, especially if one considers the difficult and thankless investigations with which he somehow managed to saddle himself. The loss of his crafty mind and determined energy in solving exotic crimes was a blow to readers, too. For Pibble's exploits are set down in but five books, in the last two of which he is already retired but nonetheless rendering invaluable service.

Peter Dickinson almost resumed writing about Pibble in 1976, after an abstinence of several years. "But," says Dickinson, "Pibble's getting on, you see. I'd have to check, but I think he's sixty-four. I can't say definitely that I shan't write about him again, but if I had to bet on it, I would say it wasn't likely."

It is disappointing to think that we may hear no more of the rather ordinary fellow who has enjoyed so much success as a detective, both in his own profession and in print. (The first two adventures of the already-aging Pibble, The Glass-Sided Ants' Nest *and* The Old English Peep Show, *won the Gold Dagger Award for best novel, presented by the British Crime Writers' Association in 1968 and 1969.) Born in Zambia, educated in England, Peter Dickinson was for seventeen years an editor of Punch. At 50, acclaimed for his children's stories as well as his mysteries, he lives with his family in London.*

Superintendent Pibble

by Peter Dickinson

PIBBLE, James Willoughby. b. 1915. Educated Clapham Academy and Hendon Police College. Joined Metropolitan Police Force 1933. Served with Hammersmith Division until outbreak of war. War Service in Intelligence. Reached rank of Major. Returned to Metropolitan Police 1946, Vice Squad, New Scotland Yard. Chief Prosecution Witness in Smith Machine case, 1948, in which Chief Superintendent Richard Foyle was convicted on corruption charges. Retired as Detective Superintendent 1970.

MC WRITES: I worked with Jimmy Pibble for three years in the late sixties. In some ways I'd have liked to stay with him longer, but in other ways it was a bit of a relief when he had to "retire" after the Francis Francis affair in 1970. He was a copper's copper all right, and a cracking good one, but there wasn't much chance of early promotion if I hitched myself on to Jimmy too firmly. From the point of view of an ambitious sergeant, he was a walking dead end. He always got himself landed with the wrong jobs, the ones that were likely to turn out messy if they went wrong but where there wasn't much by way of kudos if they went right. Like a lot of us he'd really have been happier working in a much smaller machine.

I don't know much about his early career. His father had been a lab assistant to Francis Francis at the Cavendish Laboratory before the First World War, and I gather had done a lot of the work building the gadgets with which FF won his first Nobel Prize. Jimmy Pibble was born while his dad was in the trenches — invalided out, gassed, in 1917. Pibble Senior never went back to lab work, but worked for Southern Railways until his death in the mid-twenties. Jimmy's early life was spent in Clapham. His mother had been something of a beauty, but later became a stalwart of a body called the Revised Chapter of Saints. Jimmy himself was never very religious when I knew him.

His war service was much less romantic than it looks, mainly concerned with the investigation of enemy alien internees prior to their release. At some point during the war he met his wife, Mary, socially a cut or two above him, I think. Though unfailingly loyal, he often gave the impression that life with her was a strain, though on the few occasions I met her I found her a lovely lady, very intelligent and sprightly.

To my mind the turning point of Jimmy's career came, not as some of his friends will tell you with the Herryngs scandal, but with a funny little case in the Shepherds Bush area of London about a year earlier. This happened on the fringes of the great Furlough case in which Jimmy's friend Ned Rickard was killed, but typically Jimmy didn't get any of the credit for providing the piece of gen which enabled us to bust the Furlough gang. Instead he finished up with a complicated little affair involving a weird New Guinea tribe and, in the end, two corpses. I had flu at the time and so only heard about it all fifth hand. Jimmy wouldn't tell me a thing.

He was very shaken up about Rickard, but I have always thought he knew exactly what had happened and for some reason wasn't letting on.

The big schemozzle came with the case at Herryngs, in which the Clavering Brothers, heroes of the St. Quentin Raid, both managed to get killed. Jimmy too was almost for it once or twice, but he sorted it out in the end. You would have thought no one could ask for better publicity than that, but of course it didn't come Jimmy's way. Instead A. N. Other was sent barging in when it was all over, picked up all the medals and at the same time managed to make it seem as though Jimmy had caused the whole mess.

After that he only had to put a foot wrong and he'd be for it. And being Jimmy, he did. I've met one or two of his friends who say that but for him Sir Francis Francis would have been a dead man seven years ago, instead of all of us sitting round waiting to toast the old villain's hundredth birthday, and from what I know of Jimmy that's probably right. He certainly exposed a pretty scary religious setup out on that Hebridean isle. But in the process — he was supposed to be on leave, but he overstayed it — he broke pretty well every rule in the book, and a lot of sacred cows came home to roost on him. So, from a police point of view, curtains for Jimmy.

Naturally after that I rather lost touch with him. He got, somehow, into the ambit of the shipping millionaire Athanasius Thanatos, and was even present at the assassination attempt that so nearly succeeded on Hyos. Before that there'd been something about a rum little charity hospital in South East London. I didn't hear much about that, but I rather gather that Jimmy managed to tread on a lot of toes at the time. If I know him, he finished up knowing quite a lot more about what had happened than went into the official reports.

What was he like? I don't know why I say "was," because he's still going strong, last I heard. But it's "was" as far as work is concerned.

Well, I've said he was a copper's copper, and that's almost true. He was very good at his paperwork, for instance. He had a darn quick memory, especially for faces and places. He had a nose, too — I don't mean he was an intuitive copper — there wasn't much of the Maigret about him — but he was especially good about which areas of a case to bear down on. He didn't neglect the others, and he was damn quick to change his tack if something new cropped up to shed a fresh light on things; in fact the best part about working with him was that he had no vanity at all — he'd never impose his own view on a case because it was his. For himself, he was a worrier, but he was easygoing about other people. One or two of his colleagues put his back up for no reason that I could see, but on the whole practically everybody liked him.

So what went wrong? Was it just a case of his being unlucky, a sort of Jonah? No, I don't think so. In fact, if you compared his record of cleared cases with those of some of the prima donnas I think you'd find he had a surprisingly good average. But there was something else. To my mind Jimmy lacked . . . I don't know the right word . . . he had plenty of character in his quiet way. He had fiber, if that means sticking to your guns against odds. But he did allow himself to be done down. In a way he almost asked for it. I sometimes used to think that he got a weird satisfaction out of being bullied or used, as if he was continually needing to prove to himself that he was so dead honest and incorruptible that even when he was being cheated he wasn't going to cheat back.

Come to think of it, that Foyle affair, back in the forties, must have been a bit of a shaker for a copper trying to settle back into business after the war. From all I hear Foyle was a pretty charismatic figure, and the Smith machine was quite as nasty as anything that we've come up with since. When something like that happens to you, when you're actually in the middle of it, having to say, "Yes, my boss whom I thought was some kind of God turns out to have been a villain too, and I'm the only one who can prove it," then you're going to be a bit obsessive about honesty for the rest of your days.

It seems funny to be writing about him like this. I suppose I'm lucky to have begun with Jimmy, and not with Foyle. He taught me a lot, so good luck to him, wherever he is now.

PETER DICKINSON WRITES: That was Mike Crewe, Pibble's missing sergeant in *The Glass-Sided Ants' Nest*. It seems funny to me, too, to be writing about old Pibble like this, as if he were real. I don't think many writers — perhaps only the great ones — start with totally solid characters in their heads. Usually, with a major character, you have certain ideas about him/her which you embody in characteristics. Then you find yourself adding twiddly bits, sometimes for fun, sometimes for plot, judging what to say by a vague notion of "rightness" for that particular person. If your invention is of a piece you finish up with a real-seeming character. That's how Pibble evolved. I simply wanted a detective who was not at all James Bondish, was unsexy, easily browbeaten, intelligent, fallible. Then he became real-seeming. That, I suppose, is why I stopped writing about him.

You can't go on creating somebody when he's already created. Five books is a lot to live through. If he wasn't solid by then he never would be.

Peter Dickinson

Quiller

Adam Hall

Mystery, detective, and espionage stories have changed a good deal since their initial popularity. The day of the eccentric genius, quietly solving puzzles from his armchair, has passed. No longer can Hercule Poirot point to his "little grey cells" as the ultimate crime-solving device. The technocrat, the faceless operative employed by a great corporation, institution, or government, is the new hero of mystery novels. The villain is no longer a simple murderer or thief but often another faceless operative, or his employer.

The quintessential corporate operator, the best-known and most professional of them all, is Quiller. In Quiller's world events unfold with a chilling efficiency, as colorless as a corpse and as inexorable as death.

Adam Hall is a pseudonym of Elleston Trevor, a prolific writer of novels, adventure tales, and espionage stories. The best known of his many books is The Quiller Memorandum, which introduced his distinguished agent. It won the coveted Edgar Allan Poe Award of the Mystery Writers of America, the French Grand Prix de Littérature Policière, and was made into a memorable motion picture starring George Segal. The Quiller character served as the basis for a British television series in 1975.

Trevor, a former RAF pilot, began writing after his World War II service. The English-born author was described by Time magazine as "the most successful literary double agent now in the business." The 57-year-old novelist and screenwriter lives in Fountain Hills, Arizona, with his wife, Jonquil Trevor.

Quiller

by Adam Hall

IN LONDON, there is a Bureau, notable mainly for its lack of features. It doesn't exist, officially, because it is empowered to do things that couldn't be countenanced by any other government department. Nobody among the shadow executives of the Bureau has ever heard of the man who runs it; he is nameless. It is known only that he is directly responsible to the prime minister. No mission is ever set up by the Bureau at lower than prime minister level; if other departments like Scotland Yard, Special Branch, or M.I.5 could handle the operation, it wouldn't be sent to the Bureau.

There have to be names for people at the Bureau so that they can be identified, but nobody on the staff has anything but a code name. Their real names are known only to the hierarchy (whoever the hierarchy may be) and their personal dossiers are held in files with autodestruct mechanisms, so that any attempt at unauthorized opening will result in the automatic obliteration of the material inside.

The work of the Bureau is not espionage, nor is it counter-espionage, otherwise it would be done by D.I.6 and M.I.5, respectively. Sometimes a mission will overlap the work of these and other branches, but when it does it is because they've elected not to do it or because the operation is too sensitive, or too specialized, or too hazardous. In a less physical sense, the executives of the Bureau can be likened to the commandos of an army at war: dedicated men, self-committed to tasks that are more exacting than normal. There is no political aspect to a mission. An executive normally has a single simple job to do and he does it without consideration of the consequences.

One of these executives is Quiller. That, of course, is his code name; his real name is unknown.

About his past there are various rumors: that he was someone in the professional category of lawyer or doctor, denied his license; that he once served a prison term, undeservedly (hence his bitterness, which is never far below the skin); that he is a man on the run who has found a perfect cover in the Bureau.

In his forties, he is as fit as an alley cat and his whole makeup is tense, edgy and bitten-eared. Without the imagination to see that life is wide open to any man's need for self-expression, Quiller seems to have to synthesize drama for himself, to invite danger and privation and bitter challenge so that his life can have significance. He needs to live close to the crunch. Like bullfighters and racing drivers, he is a professional neurotic, half in love with death.

Obviously antisocial, shy of people and human contact, he is wary of giving anything of himself to others. But, on rare occasions when the pressures of a mission have forced him into a position where he must consider other people — sometimes a deadly opponent — he reveals compassion, surprising himself.

His last will and testament is revealing: "Nothing of value, no dependents, next of kin unknown." This nihilistic aspect of his character, his isolationism, suits perfectly the atmosphere of the Bureau, where anonymity and facelessness are virtues. If all the requirements of the Bureau were put through a computer to synthesize the ideal executive, they would result in Quiller.

Fiercely professional, he is contemptuous of the amateur and of people who refuse to take things to the limit before they give up. This critical attitude extends to the Bureau itself. Like many a competent ship's officer with ambition and talent, he thinks he could run things better than the skipper. As a mission heats up, he begins to curse "London" for what they're doing to him. Still, he respects the Bureau and its hierarchy. In talking of the executive-Bureau relationship, he says, "Sometimes I suppose we'd get the hell out of this trade if it wasn't for the bruised, lopsided sense of loyalty to the Bureau that's always there in front of us like a scarecrow wherever we go." At other times, other thoughts come to his mind: "Those bloody people in London won't ever give you a break. They'd grind a blind dog into the ground; they'll drive you till you drop and then step on your face."

Quiller has completed thirty-five missions — a tribute to his professionalism in a trade where life is cheap. He doesn't drink because it would affect his reaction time, and for the same reason he doesn't smoke. He refuses to carry a gun. Ever. He puts his reasons this way: "If a man has to carry a gun it means he's got no better resources. A gun can be more dangerous to you than to the other man, if you carry one. It gives you a false feeling of power, superiority, and you get the fatal idea that, with this thing in your hand, you don't have to make any effort because the conflict's already been won. And for Christ's sake watch it if you find you've left the safety catch on or forgot to load or there's a dud in the clip or the other man gets time to kick the thing out of your hand — then you've really had it. Better to use your brain because your brain won't stop working for you till you're dead. Guns are for amateurs, and anyway . . . I don't like the bang they make."

Quiller is often introspective, and likely to conclude that
"In this trade you grow a protective shell, the years of de-
ceits and betrayals adding to it layer by layer till the day
comes when you feel trapped and want to break out and it's
too late, because you know it's yourself you've been betray-
ing and deceiving over all those years. The shell is a part of
you; it grows from the inside outwards, like your finger-
nails."

Also, "You don't do what you do for the sake of your
country or world peace, though you kid yourself. You do
it to scratch an itch. I'm not talking about the people who
do it for the money — they're just whores. Most of us do
it because we don't get a big enough kick out of pushing a
pen or punching the clock or washing the car on Sundays.
We want to get outside of all that and live on our own so
we can work off our scabby neuroses without getting arrested for it. We want to scratch the itch till it bleeds."

Quiller and four other executives at the Bureau have the
suffix 9 to their code names. It means they've proved themselves reliable under torture. It's not an award of any kind,
but an indication to directors that a man with the 9 suffix is
suitable for sending into an area (behind the Iron Curtain,
for example) where "implemented interrogation" will be
made if he is captured. Quiller's reaction to this ability to
stand torture is straightforward. "Within a couple of hours,"
he says, "an efficient interrogator and his team can turn any
man into a raving animal if they use the full technique. But
they can't; there's a breakoff point because the whole idea
is that they want information out of you and they know
they won't get it if they've gone too far and wrecked the
psyche. What you've got to do is try not to talk this side
of consciousness, because once you've flaked out you're safe

till they start again. And if you can do it once, you can do it a dozen times."

Quiller is at home with wild animals. He feels a brother to them and knows their ways, their fears. What he calls "mission feel" — the sixth sense of the working executive — is closely related to the instincts of the animal. "Mission feel is never wrong," he says. "It's the instinct we develop as we go forward into the dark like an old fox sniffing the wind and catching the scent of things it has smelled before and learned to distrust. The forefoot is sensitive, poised and held still above the patch of unknown ground where the next flicker of a nerve can spring a trap."

His attitude toward women stems from his fear of people, his need to feel cut off and isolated. He chooses women who are themselves solitary, reserved, each in her own way a lone wolverine with some hurt to heal, a past to forget, or a lie to live. Some of them are seeking their own identity, as Quiller himself may be, and he finds himself attracted to them as reflections of his own enigma. They are lean and have quietness, are watchful, talking little, turning their heads slowly to appraise a newcomer, withdrawing with the speed of a spring if their approach is too immediate.

Quiller is versed in psychology, sleep dynamics, the nervous system and its behavior under stress. His fast-driving technique is based squarely on a knowledge of what happens to a car when it's pushed to the limit. He is aware of the target-finding values of positive and negative feedback as he makes his way through a mission. He is good enough at code-breaking sometimes to intercept a signal from an opposition cell without having to ask London.

Knowing Quiller to be difficult, obstinate, obdurate, and perverse, the directors at the Bureau handle him in the most appropriate way. They seldom offer him a mission outright, because it would give him the chance of refusing it out of sheer bloody-mindedness. They lead him into it with a carrot, working up his interest indirectly. "I understand," they'll say, for example, "they've landed Smythe with a real stinker, and frankly I don't think he can handle it." Or they'll just tell him this one "isn't for him" without saying why, so that he feels deprived of an important mission.

"Of course, this kind of job isn't really in your field."

"Why not?"

"It's not much of a mission. Everyone else has refused it."

"Oh, have they?"

Quiller understands this technique. "They know," he says, "they've got to look for the man who stands facing the wrong way in a bus queue to show he doesn't really want a bus, the man who always wants the window open when everyone else wants it shut, the awkward fellow who's going to kill himself one day trying to prove he's bullet-proof. And if they want him for a dirty, rotten, stinking job that he'd normally throw back in their faces, all they've got to do is tell him that everyone else has refused it."

An executive can refuse to accept a mission for any one of a dozen reasons: it doesn't seem to fit his particular talents, it means working in extreme heat (Africa, say) and he prefers extreme cold (or vice versa), he doesn't get along well with this particular director or director in the field, he's too well known behind the Iron Curtain, and so forth. But if he accepts a mission, he's totally committed, even to the point of using a cyanide capsule.

The executive is told as little as possible about the background to a mission. He needs to go in with a clear head, uncluttered by minor details or major (often political) considerations.

Quiller is aware of this. "You can always refuse a mission," he says, "it's in the contract. But you can't ever judge the odds against coming out alive and you can't even tell whether you're due for a rough ride or a great big routine yawn because they won't give you any information. We accept that. We know we'd be scared stiff by the size and scope of a big operation if we could see the overall picture, and all we want is our own little box of matches to play with in the corner while the boys at the top work out how to stop the whole house from going up if we make a mistake."

Most missions require a cover for the executive, with a cover name. During his clearance, therefore, from the Bureau, he is given his cover name when he departs on an operation. Quiller seldom carries out a mission under his code name; he becomes Mr. Gage, or Mr. Longstreet, and so on. The cover name is even used in signals from Control (the London office) to Local Control (the operational base in the field) unless absolute secrecy can be relied on. Thus, any shadow executive working on a mission is already two removes from his true identity. Although this is mere formal security, he is bound to feel nameless, rootless, and his identity tends to become associated with the mission in hand rather than with his past as a person. This is reflected in most executives' attitude toward the Bureau. Despite the grandiose title of "shadow executives" (probably coined by the hierarchy at the time when rat catchers became "rodent operatives") these men know what they really are. As Quiller puts it: "We're ferrets, to be put down a hole."

Quiller prefers working alone, on solo missions, accepting a director in the field where necessary but never working alongside other executives.

Once he has left his base and begins work in the field, he is usually at risk. If he is captured and interrogated, or if he is exposed to the opposition's view (perhaps holed up in a building or on a ship and unable to leave), or if there is the slightest risk of his giving away his base and his director in the field, he will cut himself loose and take the consequences — just as any other executive would. If he is slow to do this, the director will do it for him.

Quiller once had to brief a recruited agent: "You've got to learn to cross the line and live your life outside society, shut yourself away from people, cut yourself off. Values are different out there. Let a man show friendship for you and you've got to deny him, mistrust him, suspect him, and nine times out of ten you'll be wrong but it's the tenth time that'll save you from a dirty death in a cheap hotel because you'd opened the door to a man you thought was a friend. Out there you'll be alone and you'll have no one you can trust, not even the people who are running you. Not even me. If you make the wrong kind of mistake at the wrong time in the wrong place, and it looks like you're fouling up the mission or exposing the Bureau, they'll throw you to the dogs. And so will I."

This situation is accepted by the executives. So is the fact that they are expendable if the crunch comes or a wheel falls off. The executive is cut loose the instant he presents a risk to the network, to the Bureau. The working phrase is: "The mission is more important than the man."

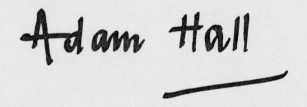

Inspector
Schmidt

George Bagby

*Some detectives have difficulty keeping pace with their prey
because they lack physical strength, or prowess, or even basic
fitness. Some are prisoners to precise police procedure and
never deviate from it, either because of lack of imagination or
unwillingness to break the rules. Some are lazy; others prefer
to chase women or drink or gamble. Some detectives blunder
into solutions because they are not smart enough to resolve a
case logically; others run the risk of eggs Benedict on their faces
because of unchecked arrogance. None of these shortcomings
afflicts Inspector Schmidt, Chief of Homicide of the New York
City Police Department. He has one flaw, and one only: his
feet. Just as Nero Wolfe has the most famous girth in mystery
fiction, and Hercule Poirot the most illustrious grey cells,
Schmidt has the most notable feet.*

*George Bagby is a pseudonym of the prolific and erudite
Aaron Marc Stein, author of more than ninety detective novels.
As Hampton Stone, he also writes about Jeremiah A. "Gibby"
Gibson. Under his own name, he tells about Tim Mulligan and
Elsie Mae Hunt in one series and about Matt Erridge in another.*

*After graduating from Princeton with a degree in classics
and archaeology, Stein worked as a journalist for more than a
decade. During World War II, he served as a cryptanalyst of
Chinese and Japanese codes. Born in New York in 1906, he still
resides in Manhattan.*

Inspector Schmidt

by George Bagby

IN RECOUNTING THE FACTS of Inspector Schmidt's birth, I
might be happier if I could say they were ordinary. That,
however, would be to tamper with the truth. So, if any
reader concludes from the circumstances of the birth of the
chief of homicide that the inspector is an exotic, it is only
to be hoped that the rest of this account may serve to erase
that erroneous impression.

In this century most people who are born into an urban
environment are born in hospitals. Inspector Schmidt was
not. He was conceived in a hospital, but he was born in my
bathroom. The year was 1934 and I was hospitalized. Kind
friends came to call and, since people I know always do the
correct thing, each of them brought me a detective story. It
must have been that their kindness and goodwill far exceeded their knowledge of the literature because none of
the books they brought me was much good. With appalling
unanimity they had missed the masterworks of the genre.

As a result, in the space of three hospital days I read a
dozen or more indifferent to unconscionable detective
stories. Naturally enough I came up for air muttering: "I
could write a better one with both my mind and my imagination tied behind my back." I was not prepared to say I
could do better with both hands tied behind my back since
I have always found pencils, pens, and typewriters quite
difficult enough to manipulate even with unfettered hands.

Since in actuality both my mind and my imagination were
far too vigorous to be tied down and I was too indulgent of
them to attempt it, Inspector Schmidt was conceived at a
time when both were being given full play. After a period
of gestation — not nearly so long as the customary nine
months — one morning when I was only a few months out
of the hospital I was shaving and there he was in full occupation of my theretofore empty mind. Lest anyone think
that this term of less than nine months is too peculiar, it is
well to remember that for a great man there is a classical
precedent for such haste. Was not Macduff untimely ripped
from his mother's womb?

My bathroom was familiar territory. I can vouch for it.
There was no mother about, not even a womb. Inspector
Schmidt, nevertheless, was born that morning in my bathroom. I don't know where he came from and he insists that
he doesn't know either.

"How would I know?" he says. "You were there before
I arrived and I wasn't. If you don't know, who should? Is
it my fault that you're a lousy witness?"

This, by the way, is one of Inspector Schmidt's characteristics. He's a master of the affectionate insult. As his closest
friend, I can testify to that. I bear the scars. But back we go
to his birth. I was working up a nice lather and he wasn't
there. I applied the lather to my whiskers and there he was,
fully grown and fully panoplied. He resembled no one I
had ever known. He was *sui generis.*

Again if this mode of birth should seem odd, remember
that here, too, there is the classical precedent. The goddess
Athena's birth was much the same. She sprang fully grown
and fully panoplied out of the forehead of Zeus, so why not
Inspector Schmidt, although no goddess he, out of a cloud
of lather?

If the inspector has a given name, he has never made me privy to it. I can only assume that it may be something like Percy or Obadiah and as a schoolboy he had suffered such tortures because of it that by the time he appeared in my bathroom he was permanently traumatized into keeping it well concealed. On army records a man might be listed as John NMI Doe. That doesn't stand for John Nehemiah Murgatroyd Ichabod Doe. It stands for John No Middle Initial Doe. If the inspector had ever been in the army, they would have had him listed as NFI NMI Schmidt — No First Initial No Middle Initial Schmidt.

In dealing with the inspector's history, one is confronted with insuperable metaphysical problems. When a man is born fully grown and at the moment of his birth he has already risen through the ranks from rookie patrolman to the exalted station of inspector, chief of homicide, N.Y.P.D., he has obviously had a history and it cannot be more than that mere pre-parturition fetal history that is common to all the rest of us.

Furthermore at that place and time of his birth — my bathroom in 1934 — he was already in the prime of life. In all the years that have passed since 1934, however, he has not aged by even a single gray hair or even one arterial plaque. Since he has never been to Florida, it cannot be said that he succeeded where Ponce de León failed and that he found the Fountain of Eternal Youth. I don't know where he found it and he is adamant in his refusal to share the secret, but it is obvious that he did find the Fountain of Eternal Prime of Life.

The inspector is a native New Yorker. We can narrow it down even closer than that. He is a native of Manhattan Island and on Manhattan Island he grew up and went to school. Do not assume from this that he is any pale and puny city flower. He is able-bodied, well muscled, and physically tough. He earned his splendid physical development playing in the city streets where a ball that breaks a window is an automatic home run and the runner needs to be very fast if he's not to have that broken window taken out of his hide. In football season the city-street quarterback cannot worry about any quarter-ton of defensive linebackers bearing down on him. He has to watch out for the ten-ton truck. Playing against that kind of opposition toughens a kid. He grows into a man who can handle himself.

Physically, however, the inspector does have one weakness and he has never made a secret of it. His feet hurt. The pain is not unremitting. He can gain relief any time he is in a situation that permits him to shed his shoes. He never misses an opportunity. Inspector Schmidt goes shod only when he must. He attributes this problem of his to the beat-pounding he did at the beginning of his departmental career when he was a rookie patrolman. He served his patrolman time back in those dark ages when the policeman was a pedestrian presence in the streets. He walked his beat. He didn't ride around in a squad car. He met the citizenry, lawful and unlawful, face to face and toe to toe. It was then that he learned to know people and to judge human character. It was then that he learned how to deal with people.

It was then also that he did permanent damage to his feet. Here, too, you must be reminded, there is a classical precedent to be cited. Had not Achilles the one area in which he was vulnerable and, like the inspector's, was not his problem pedal? The resemblance ends there. Achilles had his temper on a short fuse. Inspector Schmidt is a patient man. He is implacable in his pursuit of killers, but he never flies off the handle.

Early in our association he was on a case where a fleeing fiend took advantage of one of those times when the inspector had his shoes off. As the dastardly sadist fled, he sprinkled carpet tacks in his wake and with the aid of that vicious device made his escape. It was, of course, only a temporary escape. Inspector Schmidt eventually did catch up with him.

I cannot say that, so far as I have been able to observe, the inspector ever since has been more cautious about watching where he is putting his feet down, but for one reason or another it has never happened again. It may be that the word has been passed among the ungodly that it's not worth the cost of the carpet tacks. It will stop Inspector Schmidt only temporarily.

One might think the inspector would envy those young patrolmen of this latter day who can cover their beats sitting down as they ride about in the squad cars. He doesn't. In the first place he is incapable of envy. There's never been any of that in the man. Also he is equipped with a mind that in all things moves straight from cause to effect. He foresees the day when those young patrolmen are young patrolmen no longer and in the prime of life they will find it painful to sit down. The inspector believes in the law and for him that includes the Second Law of Thermodynamics. Everything wears out. Everything breaks down. Something's got to give.

There are, of course, those who say that walking a beat had nothing to do with it. The world, they say, is full of fuzz and former fuzz, men who have nevertheless gone through life with their shoes on. These detractors would have it believed that it is a simple matter of Inspector Schmidt's being too big for his boots. This silly canard, however, must be considered in terms of the source from whence it comes. Are you prepared to take as authoritative the word of some killer the inspector has brought to book?

Schmidt is a man of sensibility but he has never been sentimental. He has at least never fallen into sentimentality when I've been around. On one occasion when he wandered into the television tubes where I didn't follow him, he handled an investigation in what seemed to me a grossly and shamefully sentimental fashion. Every scrap of evidence lay against a teenage boy and for no reason either logical or evidential the inspector pinned the rap on a mature man.

He stoutly denies, however, that even then he was moved by sentiment. He says he was merely adapting to the exigencies of the milieu in which he was forced to operate.

"In a mere thirty minutes of air time," he said, "and with all those minutes they take away for the commercials, there isn't the elbow room for building a solid, logical proof of guilt. You have to move on instinct and intuition. My instincts are solid and my intuition is infallible. The guy was guilty, wasn't he? So what if there wasn't a scrap of evidence against him?"

It's a good defense, but I still think Inspector Schmidt was temporarily affected by cathode-ray poisoning. He's had no relapses since, but it may be because he's been staying out of the tube.

As any detective must, the inspector uses informants, but he has never left it to them to do his job for him. He is a firm believer in the presumption of innocence but an even firmer believer in the all-pervading prevalence of mendacity. He listens carefully to what people tell him, be they witnesses, victims, informants, or suspects, but he takes what they tell him just as he takes any material clues that come his way. He examines either with searching skepticism, evaluating it in terms of its relevance and of the way it fits when juxtaposed to the other available evidence.

Growing up in New York, the inspector was educated in the New York public schools. They taught him to read. Back in his day they were doing that. Departmental reports shower down on his desk and I've never known him to experience even the slightest difficulty in assimilating them. They taught him to write. He produces his own reports and they are never less than lucid and grammatical. The more colorful treatments he leaves in my hands. They taught him arithmetic. No matter how multitudinous the suspects he must keep in mind, he's never been known to lose count of even one of them.

They taught him some Latin. I've heard him quote from Caesar's Gallic Wars, but only the opening sentence. If they took him beyond "All Gaul is divided in three parts," no more of it has gone with him into adult life.

He is a brilliant logician, but through the quality of his mind and not through learning. I can remember a case when in the course of the investigations I came up with a complicated theory of what had occurred. The inspector rejected it out of hand and he explained that in any situation where you are confronted with a choice of theories you take on the simplest one that will contain the evidence.

When he heard me mutter "Occam's razor," he thought my mind was wandering as it often will — his never does — and that I was talking about some throat-slashing episode that had nothing to do with the case in hand. I had to explain to him that this was a razor that was employed neither for shaving nor for throat slitting, but that it was a cutting edge of philosophical thought, a principle of logic enunciated early in the fourteenth century by a Franciscan friar

named William of Occam. If a man has a mind like Inspector
Schmidt's, he can be totally ignorant of the jargon of the
logicians and, nonetheless, be brilliantly logical in his pursuit
of proof.

Since he went to school in Manhattan, he profited greatly
from the extracurricular aspects of his education. Early on,
before chin or lip showed even the faintest sprouting of the
down of an adolescent's beard, the youthful NFI NMI
Schmidt achieved a profound understanding of the ways of
crime and a sympathetic penetration into the tortuous complexities of the criminal mind. He learned through observation of his schoolfellows. He learned then and he has never
forgotten that no crime is committed without reason. It
need not be a good reason, but there always is a reason and
one that seemed good to the perpetrator.

The inspector has no hobbies. Chasing killers gives him
all the exercise needed by any man unless perhaps he is a
professional athlete. Schmidt is a professional cop and he is
all cop. If it should be argued that a man must do something
for relaxation, Schmitty does do something. He takes his
shoes off and he wiggles his toes.

The inspector might be described as insular, but only insofar as he is almost always confined to the one island — Manhattan. I do recall one case which did take him as far afield
as Brooklyn. He was dealing with a freshly sunburned
corpse. It became necessary that he extend his investigation
to a beach, and, true Manhattanite that he is, he immediately
thought of Coney Island.

Otherwise, on those few occasions when he has left town
it has been on my account. I have suburban friends and
exurban friends and there have been times when murder
has intruded on one of these. Out of friendship Inspector

Schmidt comes to the rescue. On at least two occasions he has gone even farther afield on my account. There was the time when I was doing a term as writer in residence at a jerkwater college way up in New England. I came down with a bad case of freshly murdered corpse. It was on my doorstep. Schmitty came up and coped. Happily he was fully as effective among the meadows and woodlots as he is in the city streets.

The other time was even farther afield. I was in Madrid and likewise afflicted with a freshly murdered corpse. It was a disastrously sticky situation since it happened to be the corpse of a member of the Guardia Civil. There is no police force anywhere that takes kindly to cop killers, but if you know anything at all about the Guardia Civil, you must know that no presumption of innocence has ever taken lodgment under their shiny patent-leather hats.

The inspector came to the rescue. Through the exercise of exquisite tact, even past the language barrier, he managed to insert himself into the investigation and save my neck.

Inspector Schmidt enjoys his food and drink, but unlike his great French colleague, Inspector Maigret, he never drinks on the job. As other men take aspirin for headache, Maigret takes beer. Schmidt, however, takes neither. He doesn't have headaches and beer does nothing for his feet. Again unlike Maigret, he does not, when hot on the trail of a killer, take time out for the leisurely ingestion and appreciation of a superb meal. Many's the time when I have been with him on one of his killer hunts that I have wished he could be different. Logic and pursuit anesthetize his taste buds and generate in him digestive juices fully up to the job of dealing with the execrable ham sandwiches, the soggy wedges of apple pie, and the corrosive coffee he finds in the nearest quick-and-dirty when lull in the pursuit gives him a moment to take on something he needs for keeping up his strength.

A French friend has expostulated with me on this subject. "Your Inspector Schmidt," he said, "drinks too much coffee and he eats the wrong food. It is a wonder that it has not already done irreparable damage to his tripes, but it will. It must. You should use your influence with him. Persuade him to eat properly. Induce him to take a glass of good wine or even a cognac instead of another of those too numerous bad coffees. All work and no *cuisine* makes Jacques a dull *flic*."

My French friend doesn't know the inspector as I do. He underestimates the man. Inspector Schmidt is a latter-day Achilles. North of the feet he is invulnerable.

George Bagby

The
Shadow

Maxwell Grant

"Who knows what evil lurks in the hearts of men? The Shadow knows!"

Probably no lines in the history of radio, or perhaps in the history of detective fiction, are more famous. And no character stalked the perpetrators of evil more relentlessly than the almost supernatural phantom known only as The Shadow.

In the spring of 1931, Street & Smith published the first issue of The Shadow *magazine, which contained a novel written by Walter B. Gibson, under the pen name of Maxwell Grant. The character was instantly successful and the magazine ran for 325 issues, each with a short novel about the spectral personage sometimes known as Lamont Cranston. Under the Grant pseudonym, Gibson personally wrote 282 of those novels (and later wrote one for book publication under his own name), while the famous nom de plume was also used by the other writers who produced the remaining 43 novels in the series. For fifteen years Gibson wrote a million words a year, yet still found enough free time to create another popular pulp detective hero: Norgil the Magician, who used his knowledge of stage magic in the solution of crimes. A student of Houdini, Gibson ghostwrote books for him and Thurston, and became a premier stage magician himself.*

The radio program chronicling the adventures of The Shadow began on the Mutual Network in 1936, as a spin-off from the magazine. The anonymous narrator, played for a time by Orson Welles, introduced each weekly melodrama with the unforgettable lines, followed by a mirthful, if sinister, laugh.

The 80-year-old Gibson, still a prolific author of books and articles on magic, lives in Eddyville, New York.

The Shadow

by Maxwell Grant

IF EVER A MYSTERY CHARACTER created himself in his own image, that character was The Shadow. From a nebulous nothing, he materialized into a substantial something, then merged with enshrouding darkness like a figment of the night itself — terms that were to be used to describe his comings and goings in nearly three hundred novels that were dedicated exclusively to his adventures over a span of more than fifteen consecutive years.

To say that The Shadow sprang spontaneously into being would be putting it not only mildly, but exactly. As a factual writer, with an eye toward fiction, I had been thinking in terms of a mysterious personage who would inject himself into the affairs of lesser folk, aiding friends who would do his bidding and balking foemen who tried to thwart his aims. So when I learned that an editor was looking for a writer to do a story about a so-far undefined character to be known as The Shadow, it marked a meeting of the minds.

From then on, The Shadow took over, both in a literal and a literary sense. In order to assure his own evolution and give it plausibility, The Shadow needed an amanuensis to transcribe his annals into a palatable, popular form. That, of course, demanded The Shadow's own official sanction, hence the opening paragraph was attributed to the leading character himself. It ran:

This is to certify that I have made careful examination of the manuscript known as *The Living Shadow* as set down by Mr. Maxwell Grant, my raconteur, and do find it a true account of my activities upon that occasion. I have therefore arranged that Mr. Grant shall have exclusive privilege to such further of my exploits as may be considered of interest to the American public.

— THE SHADOW

With such a send-off, the story just couldn't miss. As Maxwell Grant, a pen name that was concocted for use with The Shadow stories only, I was ostensibly under The Shadow's orders as much as the agents who obeyed his bidding or as the hapless victims of conniving criminals whom only The Shadow could rescue from the brink of doom. Even the title of the first story, *The Living Shadow*, established The Shadow as an actual personage and the central theme in the minds of avidly susceptible readers. The titles of the next two novels, *The Eyes of The Shadow* and *The Shadow Laughs*, continued the same motif.

In those early stories, The Shadow moved in and out of the affairs of friend and foe, not only as a cloaked figure, but as a master of disguise who could adopt various personalities, even doubling as a crook in order to confuse other criminals. Actually, there was nothing that The Shadow couldn't do, which made it all the easier to describe the things he did do. From those, he developed not only his own personality, but his own background. Whatever he had to have, he saw to it that he had it and Maxwell Grant said so.

Early in the game, it became evident that The Shadow, whoever he was, needed a million dollars or more to knock down criminals who were thriving during the Depression. So he identified himself as a wealthy resident of suburban

New Jersey answering to the name of Lamont Cranston. Then, when even Maxwell Grant was convinced that The Shadow had disclosed his actual identity, it turned out that he was simply doubling for Lamont Cranston when the millionaire was taking extended trips abroad. By switching from Cranston to other identities, including his cloaked self, he continually kept enemies off his trail.

This, however, could cause complications whenever Cranston returned home, but The Shadow offset those by switching to the personality of George Clarendon, a man-about-town whose favorite habitat was Manhattan's exclusive Cobalt Club. He played that role long enough to lure crooks along a false trail from which he vanished, never to reappear as Clarendon. Until then, The Shadow had often visited police headquarters, doubling for a dull-mannered janitor named Fritz, in order to listen in on the reports of Joe Cardona, an ace detective. But with Clarendon permanently gone from the Cobalt Club, Cranston was free to appear there and cultivate the acquaintance of Police Commissioner Weston, a regular member, who frequently summoned Joe Cardona to confer on crime developments after the ace detective had been promoted to inspector.

Meanwhile, The Shadow conducted his own investigations in the seclusion of a black-walled room that served as his sanctum. Under the glow of a bluish light, his hands opened reports from agents and inscribed orders that they were to follow. His identifying token, a scintillating girasol, or fire opal, gleamed from the third finger of his left hand, flashing rays that exerted a hypnotic effect upon many persons whom he encountered while on the rove.

One analyst who read The Shadow novels closely came up with the opinion that the somber, eerie, isolated atmosphere of the sanctum undoubtedly aided The Shadow in reasoning out his brilliant deductions and battle plans with no fear of secret watchers who might attack him. This analysis was dated back to The Shadow's role as a spy in World War I, when, as an American air ace called the Dark Eagle, he pretended to be shot down over Germany and, using disguises by day and black garb at night, worked his way back to the Allied lines, releasing many prisoners and guiding them along the route to safety.

From this, the analyst assumed that The Shadow "had to work out his plans in out of the way places or at night; and the constant fear of being seen or found out no doubt left a major impact on his way of thinking or manner of working." Hence The Shadow's need for a secure sanctum when he returned to the United States and decided to combat the postwar crime wave that was rampant there.

Actually, this shows the remarkable impact that The Shadow, through Maxwell Grant, had upon the constant readers of his chronicles. Among the millions of words devoted to his current adventures, there were probably only several hundred referring directly to his earlier career. Those formed a separate section of The Shadow's archives, to which Maxwell Grant had only occasional access, hence analytical readers were forced to form their own theories. But in this instance, it went wide on two counts:

First, The Shadow had recourse to his sanctum only when operating within range of his fixed base in Manhattan, never when adventures carried him far afield. Again, in none of his numerous adventures was the word "fear" ever applied personally to The Shadow; indeed, he could be well described as totally unemotional throughout. It was The Shadow's utter impassivity that won him loyal agents who supported him in his campaigns against crime. As his forays expanded, The Shadow came into conflict with formidable antagonists, whose own cryptic identities became titles for the stories in which most of them met their deserved doom, notably, *The Silent Seven*, *The Black Master*, *The Crime Cult*, *The Blackmail Ring*, *The Ghost Makers*, *Kings of Crime*, and *Six Men of Evil*.

These involved spy rings, murder cults, mad scientists, and haunted houses, which in turn brought new agents and specialists into The Shadow's fold. At times, The Shadow's exploits became topical: when New York police were baffled by a real-life terrorist who signed himself "Three X," The Shadow met and conquered his fictional counterpart in the form of "Double Z." These themes could prove prophetic, too: *The Black Hush* foreshadowed New York City's "blackout" by thirty years, while another novel, *The Star of Delhi*, called the turn on a jewel robbery that occurred two decades later.

Most important, however, were the supervillains who developed during The Shadow's saga. The mere turning of "shadow into substance" produced new prospects, most notably a parade of intermittent rivals, such as the Cobra, the Python, the Condor, the Green Hoods, the Hydra and the Voodoo Master. During most of this expansive period, which included a total of 125 novels written during a six-year period, The Shadow so identified himself as Lamont Cranston that their personalities virtually merged and became a classic in their own right. This gradually lessened the value of other identities that The Shadow assumed whenever occasion demanded, but when matters neared a crux, he was ready with the answer.

In a novel titled *The Shadow Unmasks*, the real Lamont Cranston was injured in a British air crash, forcing The Shadow to revert to his real self, that of an aviator named Kent Allard, who had disappeared in a flight over the Guatemalan jungle years before. The Shadow took off secretly for Yucatan and emerged from the wilds with two body-guards from a tribe of Xinca Indians who had presumably worshipped him as a "bird god" during those lost years, though actually he had been combatting crime as The Shadow, all that while.

In due course, The Shadow reverted to the Cranston guise but occasionally switched to Allard, one advantage being that he could team with the real Cranston, who by now was familiar with The Shadow's ways and always will-ing to go along with them. In due course, The Shadow reverted more and more to the Cranston role, so that Allard became almost forgotten, except on rare occasions when his identity could prove helpful in diverting crooks from Cranston's trail. In the opinion of some readers, The Shadow apparently "felt more comfortable when he was Cranston," but perhaps it was the readers who felt that way. Whichever the case, it worked out as intended.

This tied in with the initial concept of The Shadow, a feature which was preserved throughout the series. Always, his traits and purposes were defined through the observations or reactions of persons with whom he came in contact, which meant that the reader formed his opinion from theirs. Since The Shadow's motto was "Crime does not pay," that convinced the readers — like The Shadow's own agents — that he could do no wrong. That, in simpler terms, meant that although he might be misinformed or unaware of cer-tain circumstances, he never made mistakes. By the old rule "What is sauce for the goose is sauce for the gander," what-ever applied to the reader applied to the writer. It was up to Maxwell Grant to maintain The Shadow's image con-stantly in mind and portray it faithfully and consistently.

Thanks to the frequency with which the novels appeared — twice a month for ten consecutive years! — the reactions of readers were both rapid and frequent, thereby serving as guidelines for future novels. Many stories involved a "proxy hero," whose fate was a bone of contention between The Shadow and the villains with whom he was currently concerned. Therefore, no fixed style of writing was required, since the "proxy" rather than The Shadow was temporarily the central character. Keen analysts have classified The Shadow novels in three patterns — the "classic," the "thriller," and the "hard-boiled" — and these frequently could be used in combination, producing a diversity of types which kept up the tempo and sustained reader interest through a constant expectancy that usually resulted in the unexpected.

This gave The Shadow a marked advantage over mystery characters who were forced to maintain fixed patterns; and that, in turn, made it easy to write about him. There was never need for lengthy debate regarding what The Shadow should do next, or what course he should follow to keep in character. He could meet any exigency on the spur of the moment, and if he suddenly acted in a manner totally opposed to his usual custom, it could always be explained later by The Shadow himself, through the facile pen of Maxwell Grant.

A noteworthy example was the question of The Shadow's girasol. It was constantly described as "a magnificent fire opal, unmatched in all the world," and in an early novel, The Shadow stated that it had come from a collection of rare gems long owned by the Russian czars. In a later novel, this was countered by a claim that the girasol was the eye of a Xinca idol given to The Shadow when he landed in the jungle as Kent Allard. Serious-minded readers were prompt to point out the discrepancy in these conflicting tales, but the answer was readily found by a search of The Shadow's archives.

Fire opals are found only in Mexico and since an idol normally has two eyes, it was obvious that one could have been stolen, thus finding its way into the czarist collection, from which The Shadow obtained it. Arriving in Yucatan, as Allard, The Shadow, by showing the mate to the remaining eye, naturally won the loyalty of the Xinca tribe and was given the idol's leftover eye. So he actually had *two* girasols, each "unmatched" as it is practically impossible to find two opals that are exactly the same. Hence each story was correct, according to which girasol The Shadow happened to be wearing at the time.

The Shadow's very versatility opened a vast vista of story prospects from the start of the series onward. In the earlier stories, he was described as a "phantom," an "avenger," and a "superman," so he could play any such parts and still be quite in character. In fact, all three of those terms were borrowed by other writers to serve as titles for other characters who flourished in what might aptly be styled "The Shadow Era." Almost any situation involving crime could be adapted to The Shadow's purposes; hence the novels ran the gamut from forthright "whodunit" plots to forays into the field of science fiction. The most inimitable of The Shadow's features was his laugh, which could be weird, eerie, chilling, ghostly, taunting, mocking, gibing, sinister, sardonic, trailing, fading, or triumphant.

Often, when a story ended on such a note, the very echoes of The Shadow's mirth would set up the pattern for the next novel. It might involve unfinished business, or some theme suggested during the development of the story, or a way by which surviving crooks might think they could turn the tables on the victorious master. Always, in the finishing chapter of a story, The Shadow was really on the go, so that new situations naturally sprang to mind and unfinished plots would readily crystallize. Also, from my recollections as an author, I can definitely say that at the climax of a story, the mood that I adopted when writing as Maxwell Grant was invariably at a peak.

The final rule was this: put The Shadow anywhere, in any locale, among friends or associates, even in a place of absolute security and almost immediately crime, menace, or mystery would begin to swirl about him, either threatening him personally or gathering him in its vortex to carry him off to fields where antagonists awaited. Always, when The Shadow defeated some monstrous scheme, he would be spurred on to tackle something bigger; while, conversely, master criminals, learning that one of their ilk had been eliminated, would logically profit by that loss and devise something more powerful to thwart The Shadow.

In the story of *The Crime Master*, one supercriminal actually made all thoughts of evil profit or ill-gotten gains subordinate to his real purpose, which was to obliterate The Shadow and thus win the everlasting acclaim of crimedom. In all his well-calculated schemes of robbery and murder, he left loopholes that would enable The Shadow to counteract the impending crime, but only at risk of putting himself in traps from which escape would prove impossible.

To set up the snares, the Crime Master used a large board with hundreds of squares representing the scene of crime-to-be, with dozens of men of various colors, representing police, detectives, criminals, lookouts, and victims. When the board was all set, he added a single black piece to represent The

Shadow; then, from there, he worked out moves and countermoves, like a chess game in reverse, since the king was already in check at the start; and the purpose was to keep him from getting out of it, rather than merely adding stronger checks toward an ultimate mate.

Needless to say, The Shadow did get out. That was his forte throughout all his adventures. Always, his escapes were worked out beforehand, so that they would never exceed the bounds of plausibility when detailed in narrative form. And that was the great secret of The Shadow.

Maxwell Grant

(Walter B. Gibson)

Michael
Shayne

Brett Halliday

Private-detective stories traditionally involve tough guys who are not afraid to use their guns or their fists, who spend most of their time drinking and womanizing, and who are more often than not deeply cynical. Mike Shayne, the big redhead with the fists of a Paul Bunyan, breaks that stereotypical mold. Although he uses his fists in virtually every one of his more than sixty cases, he seldom uses his gun, relying more often on his brain. True, he has a strong partiality to cognac, but that somehow seems to fit the good-humored Shayne — the most famous private investigator in Miami.

Michael Shayne, Private Detective, a short-lived radio series, featured Jeff Chandler in the title role. And Richard Denning portrayed Shayne in thirty-two one-hour episodes of a 1960 television series. A dramatic version of Murder Is My Business *had a short stage run in 1948. But the* Michael Shayne Mystery Magazine *(which quickly became* Mike Shayne Mystery Magazine*) has been on the newsstands since September 1956. There have also been twelve Shayne films.*

Brett Halliday was one of the many pseudonyms of Davis Dresser, a prolific pulp fiction writer and author of countless Western, love, sex, adventure, and mystery stories for a variety of publications. He formerly owned Torquil & Company, a publishing firm which produced the Shayne novels for many years. One of the founding members of the Mystery Writers of America, Dresser lived in Santa Barbara, California, until his death at the age of 72 early in 1977.

Michael Shayne

by Brett Halliday

I FIRST SAW the man I have named Michael Shayne in Tampico, Mexico, many, many years ago. I was a mere lad working on a coast-wise oil tanker as a deckhand when we tied up at Tampico to take on a load of crude oil. After supper a small group of sailors went ashore to see the sights of a foreign port. I was among that group.

We didn't get very far from the ship, turning in at the first cantina we came to. We were all lined up at the bar sampling their tequila when I noticed a redheaded American seated alone at a small table overlooking the crowded room, with a bottle of cognac, a small shot glass, and a larger glass of ice water on the table in front of him. He was tall and rangy and had craggy features with bleak gray eyes which surveyed the scene with a sort of quizzical amusement. He appeared to be in his early twenties, and while I watched him he lifted the shot glass to his mouth and took a small sip of cognac, washing it down with a swallow of ice water.

I don't know what caused me to observe him so closely. Perhaps there was a quality of aloneness about him in that crowded cantina. He was a part of the scene, but apart from it. There was a Mexican playing an accordion in the middle of the room and several couples were dancing. There were other gaily dressed senoritas seated about on the sidelines and some of the sailors went to them to request a dance.

I don't know what started the fracas. Possibly one of the sailors asked the wrong girl for a dance. Suddenly there was a melee which quickly spread to encompass the small room. There were curses and shouts and the glitter of exposed knives. We were badly outnumbered and getting much the worst of the fight when suddenly out of the corner of my eye I saw the redheaded American shove the table away from him and get into the fight with big fists swinging.

Each time he struck, a Mexican went down — and generally stayed down. I was struck over the head by a beer bottle and was trampled on by the fighting men. I must have lost consciousness for a moment because I was abruptly aware that the fight had subsided and I was lying in the middle of a tangle of bodies with blood streaming down my face from a broken head. Then I was dragged out of the tangle and set on my feet by the American redhead. He gave me a shove through the swinging doors and I stumbled and went down, to be picked up by my comrades who were streaming out the door behind me.

We got away from there fast, back to the ship where we patched up broken heads and minor knife cuts.

We went to sea the next morning and none of us knew what happened to the redhead after we left the cantina.

I didn't see him again until many years later in New Orleans. I had quit the sea as a means of livelihood and was barely eking out a precarious living by writing circulating library novels.

I stopped by at a smoke-filled bar in the French Quarter for a drink and I glanced back over the rest of the room as I ordered a drink at the bar.

There I saw him! Sitting alone at a booth halfway down the room with a shot glass and a larger drink of ice water before him.

There could be no question that it was he. Several years older and with broader shoulders than I remembered, but with the same look of aloneness in his bleak gray eyes.

I paid for my drink and carried it back to his booth with me. He looked puzzled when I slid into the booth opposite him, and I quickly reminded him of the fight on the Tampico waterfront and told him I was the sailor whom he had dragged out of the fight and shoved outdoors.

A wide grin came over his face and he started to say something when a sudden chill came over his features. He was looking past me at the front door and I turned my head to see what he was seeing.

Two men had entered the bar and were making their way toward us. He tossed off his cognac and slid out of the booth as they stopped beside us. He said harshly to me, "Stay here," and started down the aisle with one burly man leading the way and the other following close behind. Thus they disappeared in the French Quarter, and I've never seen him again.

But I have never forgotten him.

Years later when I decided to try my hand at a mystery novel, there was never any question as to who my hero would be. I gave him the name of Michael Shayne because it seemed to fit somehow, and wrote *Dividend on Death* and began sending it out to publishers and getting it back with a rejection slip.

All and all, it was rejected by twenty-two publishers before I gave up on it and laid it aside on a shelf.

In the meantime I had written another mystery novel under the pseudonym of Asa Baker. It was titled *Mum's the Word for Murder* and was written in the first person, laid in El Paso. It was rejected by only seventeen publishers before Frederick Stokes brought it out.

Then came one of those coincidences that do occur in real life. Soon after *Mum's the Word for Murder* was published, I was visited by a salesman from Stokes who had my book in stock. He was accompanied to Denver where I was then living by a salesman from Henry Holt and Company (one of the few publishers who had not had the opportunity to reject *Dividend on Death*). I invited the two of them out to my home for dinner that night, and during the course of a mildly alcoholic evening I was congratulated by both of them on *Mum's the Word for Murder*.

I thanked them but told them I had a much better mystery written and laid away after twenty-two rejections. The Holt salesman told me that Henry Holt was just starting a new mystery line, and suggested that I send *Dividend on Death* to them. I did so, and Bill Sloane (then editor at Henry Holt) liked it and sent me a contract.

Thus, Michael Shayne was finally launched.

I had not thought of it as the first of a series when I wrote it, but Bill Sloane wrote and asked me for a second book using the same set of characters, and I did *The Private Practice of Michael Shayne*.

The first book had been the story of Phyllis Brighton, a very young and very lovely girl who was accused of murdering her mother. She fell in love with Shayne during the course of the book and tried to make love to him as it ended. Shayne was many years older than she, and he patted her paternally on the shoulder and advised her to come back after she had grown up.

I used her as a subsidiary character in the second book, and they were engaged to be married as the book ended.

Twentieth Century–Fox bought *The Private Practice of Michael Shayne* as a movie to star Lloyd Nolan, and gave me a contract for a series of movies starring Nolan as

Shayne. For this, they paid me a certain fee for each picture starring Shayne, promising me an additional sum for each book of mine used in the series.

But they didn't use any of my stories in the movies. Instead, they went out and bought books from my competitors, changing the name of the lead character to Michael Shayne. I was surprised and chagrined by this because I thought my books were as good or better than the ones they bought from others, and I was losing a substantial sum of money each time they made a picture.

I finally inquired as to the reason from Hollywood and was told it was because Shayne and Phyllis were married and it was against their policy to use a married detective.

Faced with this fact of life, I decided to kill off Phyllis to leave Shayne a free man for succeeding movies. This I did between *Murder Wears a Mummer's Mask* and *Blood on the Black Market* (later reprinted in softcover as *Heads You Lose*).

I had her die in childbirth between the two books, but alas! Fox decided to drop the series of movies before *Blood on the Black Market* was published, and the death of Phyllis had been in vain. I have had hundreds of fan letters asking what became of Phyllis, and now the unsavory truth is told.

With the movies no longer a factor, in my next book, *Michael Shayne's Long Chance*, I took Shayne on a case to New Orleans where he met Lucile Hamilton and she took the place of Phyllis as a female companion. I brought her back to Miami with Shayne as his secretary, and in that position she has remained since.

I don't know exactly what the situation is between Shayne and Lucy Hamilton. They are good comrades and she works with him in most of his cases, but I don't think Shayne will ever marry again. He often takes Lucy out to dinner, and stops by her apartment for a drink and to talk, and she always keeps a bottle of his special cognac on tap.

He has only one real friend in Miami: Timothy Rourke, crime reporter on one of the Miami papers. Rourke is tall, lean, and slightly disheveled appearing, a boon drinking companion for Shayne. He accompanies Shayne on most of his cases, hoping to get an exclusive story after the case is ended.

Shayne is also on good terms with Will Gentry, Miami's chief of police. Gentry likes and admires Shayne, and is inclined to look the other way when Shayne oversteps the strict letter of the law in solving a case.

On the other hand, Shayne's sworn enemy is Peter Painter, chief of detectives of Miami Beach, across Biscayne Bay from Miami. They have had numerous clashes when a case takes Shayne into Painter's territory, from which Painter always emerges as second best.

I know nothing whatever about Shayne's background. As far as I am concerned he came into being in Tampico, Mexico, some forty years ago. I don't know where or when he was born, what sort of childhood and upbringing he had. It is my impression that he is not a college man, although he is well educated, has a good vocabulary, and is articulate on a variety of subjects.

He has no special or esoteric knowledges to help him solve his cases. A reader can identify with him because he is an ordinary guy like the reader himself. He solves his cases by using plain common sense and a lot of perseverance, and absolute fearlessness.

When confronted with a problem, he assesses it from a practical viewpoint, following out each lead doggedly until coming up against a stone wall, then dropping that lead and following up the next one until it peters out.

He carries a gun seldom, trusting to his fists to get him out of any trouble he gets into. As a result he has taken some bad beatings as he goes along thrusting himself into danger.

In several of my books I have mentioned that Shayne was an operative for a large detective agency before setting up in Miami on his own, and as a result he has friends in different cities throughout the country on whom he can call for information or help if a case requires it.

He is well known and trusted by the criminal elements in Miami, who respect his closemouthed integrity and are willing to pass on information not available to the police.

He depends on no special gadgets or devices such as James Bond uses, depending on his fists and an occasional handgun to carry him through.

On all of his cases, I try to give the reader exactly the same facts and information as Shayne possesses at any one time.

That just about sums up Michael Shayne as he has been depicted in sixty-odd books.

Brett Halliday

Virgil
Tibbs

John Ball

In the Heat of the Night *won the Edgar Allan Poe Award of the Mystery Writers of America as the best first novel of 1965. It introduced Virgil Tibbs, a homicide detective with the Pasadena, California, Police Department, who has subsequently appeared in four additional novels and three motion pictures. He is the most important black detective in mystery fiction but, ironically, in the decade of Black Power, Black Militants, Black Panthers and other shibboleths of racial consciousness and pride, Tibbs prefers the word "Negro," feeling that it has its own dignity. If the truth be known, he prefers not to think in terms of race at all, generally regarding himself and others simply as people, ignoring the question of color and race as often as possible. It works well for him, gaining him the respect and affection of virtually all who come in contact with him — except the bad guys. He is determined and relentless, employing a thorough knowledge of police procedure in his pursuit of criminals. He is also not above using physical force when there is no alternative. As a student of both karate and the advanced martial art of aikido, Tibbs does not often finish second-best.*

John Ball, formerly a pilot, music critic, newspaper columnist, broadcaster, science lecturer, and public relations director for an aerospace institute, now devotes his full time to writing, collecting jade, studying Oriental culture, and practicing the martial arts. He is the Board Chairman of The Mystery Library project of the University of California, San Diego Extension, and editor of its introductory publication, The Mystery Story. *The 66-year-old author lives in Encino, California.*

Virgil Tibbs

by John Ball

MRS. DIANE STONE, secretary to Chief Robert McGowan of the Pasadena Police Department, was on the phone. "The chief has approved the release to you of the details concerning the Morales murder," she told me. "He has authorized you to go ahead with it at any time, if you want to."

Of course I wanted to: the unraveling of the case via the patient, intelligent investigation work of the department in general, and Virgil Tibbs in particular, would need no embellishment in the telling. As I always do in such instances, I called Virgil and suggested a meeting. Two nights later we sat down to dine together in one of Pasadena's very fine restaurants.

The atmosphere was conducive for the conversation to follow despite the fact that the lights were so dim the menus should have been offered in Braille. By the time that the main course had been put in front of us we had gone over the Morales case in detail and Virgil had filled me in on several points which had not previously been made public. As always, I agreed to publish nothing until the department had read the manuscript and had given it an official approval. This procedure helped to eliminate possible errors and also made sure that I had not unintentionally included information which was still confidential.

"When did you first know that it was murder?" I asked.

"When I found that the TV set was tuned to the wrong channel," Tibbs answered. "The UCLA basketball game had been on at the time of Morales's death. That appeared all right on the surface, but when I checked on the point, I learned that he had no interest at all in basketball and didn't understand the game. A show that he was known to watch regularly was on another channel at the same time, so something was obviously wrong."

The waitress brought ice tea and I stirred my glass. "I have a letter from Otto Penzler," I said.

Virgil nodded recognition. "The co-author with Steinbrunner of the *Encyclopedia of Mystery and Detection*? I have a copy."

"Otto has asked me for a piece about your background. How much may I tell him?"

I should insert a footnote here. Virgil Tibbs is a basically quiet, sometimes almost self-effacing man. He is genuinely modest. He has mentioned to me more than once that my accounts of some of his cases have proved somewhat embarrassing to him. However, Chief McGowan feels that these books help to explain the police function to the citizenry at large and to show how modern, enlightened police departments function. The outcome of that difference of opinion is predictable.

"I know that you have McGowan behind you on this," Tibbs said. "Otherwise I'd ask you to drop it, our personal friendship aside. All right: I was born in the Deep South as you know. I was about five, as I recall, when my father sat down with me and on a fine spring afternoon explained that we were Negroes and therefore I could expect to face prejudice, dislike, distrust, and even hatred during all of my life. It was the greatest shock I have ever known; I lay awake all that night wondering why God had made me different when

I hadn't asked Him to. When I finally got control of myself, I began to understand some things I had already noticed.

"Then Dad had another talk with me. He explained that things were getting better, slowly but definitely. His great hope for me was that I would have some opportunities, particularly in education, that had been denied to him. He spoke of Dr. Carver, Walter White, John Hammond, and other influential people who were helping. This is before Ralph Bunche and Martin Luther King became prominent, of course."

The attractive waitress came and refilled Virgil's coffee cup. Her pleasant manner attested that times had indeed changed, and for her as well: she was Korean-American.

"When I was about seventeen," Virgil continued, "one of my friends was murdered — because of his color. When that happened I didn't rant and rave, but I did feel a terrible determination. I made up my mind that if I ever could, I would try to do what I could to stop such senseless violence and to deal with those who were responsible for it."

"You certainly accomplished that," I noted. "You've already taken a number of murderers out of circulation. Not to mention drug dealers and the like. But please go on."

Tibbs ate a little before he continued. I knew that I was putting him over the hurdles, exhuming some painful memories in his mind, but he has the intelligence to overcome such distractions.

"I came to California and managed to get into the university. I worked my way through, washing dishes, doing some janitor work, shampooing cars, and whatever else I could find. I took up social sciences principally, and other subjects that might prepare me for my goal. I wanted to be a policeman."

As he ate a little more, I paid attention to my own plate

and said nothing. I knew that he would continue when he was ready.

"When I was still a freshman I was worried that I wouldn't be able to make the weight requirements; I was quite thin. One day some members of the All-America Karate Federation gave a demonstration on campus. I was tremendously impressed and went down to see about lessons. I had very little extra money and wanted to find out if I could work out my tuition in some way. John, I think that was the first time in my life that I met a group of people, talked with them, and was never conscious of the fact that we had different ethnic origins. Most of them were Japanese, of course, and they understood. They gave me a scholarship. Two years later I was chosen for a special class; it was taught at first by George Takahashi, then, later, by Master Nishiyama himself. You know his standing."

"The best in the world," I commented.

"Believe it," Tibbs said. "What he did to us I don't think I could live through again, but I reached the brown belt level and went into competition under his direction. The art suited me; physically and mentally I responded to its disciplines and the things that we were taught. Nine years after the first day that I walked in, Nishiyama gave me my black belt.

"That's about it, John. I graduated, took my degree, and then looked for a police department where a Negro applicant would be acceptable. Pasadena was having an examination and I took it."

The girl came again, charmed us both with a smile, and took away the dinner plates. Virgil had some more coffee.

"Is that enough?" he asked me.

"Yes," I answered. "The rest is pretty well known."

"One thing," Virgil added. "You can put this in for me, if you want to. If people want to call me black I don't mind, but I prefer something else. My first choice is to have my origins ignored, and within the department, that's the way that it is. I don't like the idea of sorting people out by colors; if I called Jim Lonetree 'red,' he'd probably slug me. And if anybody called my partner, Bob Nakamura, 'yellow,' I'd resent it very much. If I have to be classified, then call me a Negro. It's a dignified, proud word — my father taught me that."

I signaled for the check. "Thank you," I said. "I'll pass this on to Otto, and let him take it from there."

We stopped together in the parking lot outside before we said good-night. Tibbs looked around him, taking in the pin-pointed sky overhead and then the clusters of vehicles that were parked in orderly rows. As he did so I looked at my friend again. Still in his thirties, five feet nine, weight not a great deal over a hundred and sixty. Although I was dressed informally, he had on a subdued Italian silk suit and a tie that had come from one of the best shops. Despite his dark complexion, his features were aquiline in their molding; his nose was straight and well defined, his lips were slightly on the thin side. At one time I had suspected that his heritage might be mixed, but he had denied that. He had known all four of his grandparents and there had been no question of their origins.

"There's something I wish you would put into your story," he said, breaking the silence. "So many people overlook it. Police work is a team effort, from relatively simple matters up to major investigations. We don't have any room for prima donnas, and none of us work in a vacuum.

"It's a ceaseless war that we're engaged in, and some of the people we fight for, and take our chances for in some pretty dangerous situations, hate our guts in return for what we do."

"I know it," I said.

We shook hands and parted, leaving in our respective cars. I hit the westbound freeway and headed back for Encino.

Fifteen minutes out of Pasadena I tuned the radio to the all-news station to find out what, if anything, was going on. Or, more properly, what was going on that had been made public. The two are seldom if ever the same. After a few minutes the announcer broke into the steady flow of his edited copy to air something that had just come in. A body had been found in an alley in the western section of Pasadena, where most of the thrift shops were congregated.

I was going home for what remained of an essentially quiet evening. The body could be an OD, an alcohol pass-out, or even natural causes. But there was, of course, the possibility of foul play, a very old and time-worn expression that could be compressed into the single fatal word *murder*.

Before long I would be comfortable and deep in the pages of a good book. Virgil Tibbs might not have that privilege, much as I knew he would value it. If indeed it was murder, then in all probability he was already back at work.

John Ball

Dick
Tracy

Chester Gould

There are but two claimants to the title of most famous detective in the world — Sherlock Holmes and Dick Tracy. Both have added their names to the language as virtual synonyms for intelligent, relentless, effective crimefighters. It is logical, then, to learn that Chester Gould, the cartoonist who created Dick Tracy, is an ardent fan of the illustrious English detective and drew his cartoon character to resemble him.

The success of the Dick Tracy strip exceeded the wildest hopes and speculations of everyone involved with its creation. Beginning modestly with the Chicago Tribune *syndicate in 1931, the strip today is syndicated throughout the world to some 800 newspapers with a readership exceeding 100 million.*

Although he is 77 years old, Chester Gould continues to develop the plots of the Dick Tracy series, and he draws the characters himself. Another artist, Rick Fletcher, fills in the backgrounds; Gould's late brother Ray did the lettering. Chester Gould has never missed a deadline and has never run out of ideas. (He does confess that he runs out of ideas every week, but he manages to pull himself out of a seemingly hopeless hole just in time to meet his deadlines.)

Among Mr. Gould's most notable contributions to the idiom of the American language, aside from the name of his detective — and characters as famous as "The Mole," "The Brow," and "Flattop" — are two of Dick Tracy's philosophical saws: "Little crimes lead to big crimes," and "Crime does not pay." Chester Gould still lives and works in Woodstock, Illinois.

Dick Tracy

by Chester Gould

IN THE 1920s, the United States was bleeding, literally and figuratively, through the dark, dry days of the Prohibition era. Illegal bootlegging activities, which had begun quickly but modestly after the Volstead Act was passed, became more and more overt with each passing month. The rate of related crimes and every type of terrible violence which accompanies them spread like the relentless cancer it was. Innocent people, who at first believed they were simply taking the path of least resistance by offering no objection to the criminal activities taking place all around them, were soon caught in a hopeless tangle of fear. They were frightened by the threats of rival underworld gangs to each other. As the wealth and power of the mobs mushroomed, the battle for law and order seemed beyond prayer. Criminals had corrupted not only those victims who closed their eyes to the bootlegging, robbery, extortion, and murder occurring on every side, but also the very people being paid to protect the decent, law-abiding citizens who were powerless on their own. Policemen, lawyers, judges, and politicians all were added to the payrolls of the mobs, and the last small chance for justice appeared doomed forever.

The police, and the rest of the law-enforcement community, simply were not doing the job. Something had to be done; someone had to do it. That is when Dick Tracy arrived on the scene — the modern equivalent of a knight in shining armor on his white stallion. The country didn't need a detective to sit in an armchair and theorize about crime and criminals. It didn't need a policeman to calmly and rationally discuss the situation with thugs. It needed someone who was as tough as the gangsters were, who would use some of their own methods, if necessary, to counteract their menace. It needed someone who would physically pursue crooks and shoot them dead, right on the spot, if that was the only effective method of ridding society of their foul presence. Dick Tracy was that man.

It was during these years that I attended Northwestern University in Chicago — the very heartland of gangsterdom — and supported myself by doing free-lance cartooning and commercial artwork. Wanting to make my career in that area, I submitted cartoon strips to Captain Joseph Medill Patterson of the Chicago Tribune Syndicate. Although I submitted countless ideas from 1921 through 1931, nothing seemed to work.

Then I began to think about the times, about the state of the world, and figured I might as well try something that no cartoonist had ever attempted before — a strip about a real crimefighter who dealt with criminal activity in a realistic way. Most cartoon strips were comics — that is, they were funny, or tried to be, anyway. Those which had dealt with crime at all generally had hinted at the violence, letting it occur offstage, so to speak. But I thought killing and robbing and shooting and kidnapping and all the other acts of violence needed a realistic counteraction by the forces of law. I wanted to portray that in my strip. I thought people could understand that approach, and that type of detective in those situations, and truly make the strip a part of their experience, a part of their lives.

Although the country was in the midst of the Depression, with families starving and jobs as rare as honest politicians, crime was on the minds of the vast majority of the population. In 1931, a poll was taken to determine the "paramount problems" facing the United States and "Prohibition" was ranked first, "Administration of Justice" was second, and "Lawlessness" third. Clearly, the American public was concerned about the breakdown of respect for the law. It seemed to me that if the real-life police couldn't do the job of restoring confidence in the law, and if they couldn't go out and catch the gangsters, I would create someone who could.

So, after submitting more than forty ideas to Captain Patterson, I sent him six strips with this kind of straightforward, hard-hitting, tough detective. He was called "Plainclothes Tracy." Patterson liked the idea and he liked the detective, but he didn't like the name very much — too long, he said. Since detectives were called "dicks" in those days, especially in the "hard-boiled" language of the underworld and even more especially in the detective stories of the time, he suggested "Dick Tracy" as a name. It stuck.

Although a lot of people think of Tracy as a purely two-fisted cop, he is actually very cerebral and solves more cases with his brains than he does with his fists. Because of this intellectual capacity, and because Sherlock Holmes is the greatest detective of them all, I decided to make Tracy look like Holmes: straight acquiline nose, square chin, generally sharp features.

When Captain Patterson accepted the idea of Dick Tracy, he decided to waste no time in getting it off the ground. He gave me only two weeks in which to prepare the first couple of weeks' worth of strips. The initial story line (suggested by Captain Patterson, by the way) saw Dick as just a citizen, "an ordinary young fellow." It is in the middle of his proposal to Tess Trueheart that thugs break into her home and try to rob the life savings of her father. When he resists, Mr. Trueheart, a kindly and hardworking grocer, is shot to death. His wife suffers a breakdown and must be taken to a hospital and his daughter Tess is kidnapped. Tracy, although not a member of the police department, volunteers his services to the force. He pursues the hoodlums for approximately a month, finally nabbing them and their boss — "Mr. Big." Appointed to the plainclothes squad of the city police force, he has remained there ever since. In the four serial films about him, curiously enough, he is portrayed as a member of the Federal Bureau of Investigation.

Tracy doesn't age much in the strip, although many of the other characters do. On Christmas Day, 1949 (eighteen years after his proposal), Dick marries the still young and beautiful Tess Trueheart, and two years later they have a little blond daughter, Bonnie Braids.

In addition to being a cerebral and physical detective, depending upon what each situation calls for, Dick Tracy also has the good sense to use the most modern techniques and equipment that science has managed to develop. Sometimes, in fact, he uses technological devices that real-life police can't use because they haven't been invented yet. These devices are not far-out gadgetry; they are merely logical extensions of currently available equipment or concepts.

When Tracy began using the atom-powered two-way wrist radio back in 1946, it was science fiction. Today, of course, in its considerably altered form, it is science fact. He also used a crude type of "voice print" called a "Voice-O-Graf" long before it became one of crime detection's most valuable tools, and he was the first policeman to use closed-circuit television as a burglar alarm and as a silent, unseen monitor of potential crime areas. Called "teleguard" then, today it is one of the most frequently used and effective methods of crime prevention.

Tracy spends a great deal of time in the police lab, where he has a reputation for knowing how to use much of the complex paraphernalia of the modern laboratory: microscopes, lie detectors, X-ray and telescopic cameras, and other electronic equipment. He also boasts a good working knowledge of chemistry, ballistics, fingerprinting, psychology, and handwriting analysis.

In the 1950s, Dick Tracy and his associates became involved in more areas that were considered science fiction, most notably the trip to the moon and the meeting with the Moon-Maid. Some people thought this was pretty far-fetched, but look at what has happened since then. Sure, there was no Moon-Maid when we landed on the moon, but the scientific achievement of making the lunar landing is now an old story. And many of the other things portrayed in those strips will come to pass — the same kind of moon stations that Diet Smith had, for instance. And there is no doubt that those stations will have to be protected — by armed forces, in all likelihood — and so will everything else that we want to keep.

On more traditional cases, especially in the 1930s and 1940s, Tracy has combatted an extraordinary rogue's gallery. The villains in his adventures are often considered ugly, and they are, but they are far more ugly on the inside. All murderers are ugly, regardless of their visage. But when someone reads a Dick Tracy comic strip, there is never a question or doubt about who the bad guy is. The villains

are vicious, cruel, and ugly people, and neither Tracy nor I
(nor readers) feels the slightest remorse when they get
what's coming to them.

Mumbles (he is called that even by his friends) has a
member of his gang always with him to translate his im-
peded speech to others. When he says, "Whrz acob?" he
has actually said, "Where's the cop?" Perhaps not surprisingly, he is a singer. His girl friend's name (she fingers him
when she learns he is a crook) is Kiss Andtel.

Flattop, a professional killer, is imported by a gang of
black marketeers to "hit" Tracy. Because of his short, wide
head, he is named for the descriptive jargon used for the air-
craft carriers that were so much in the news at that time.

The "Blank" is a faceless criminal who rescues Dick
Tracy's adopted son, Junior, but murders former members
of his own gang in various bizarre ways. His real name is
Frank Redrum (murder spelled backwards), a former convict believed killed in a prison escape but who actually managed to elude the law. At the end of his adventure, the face,
which has no eyes, nose or mouth, is revealed to be a piece
of flesh-colored cheesecloth glued over his real face.

The Mole, with the face of a huge rodent, lives in an
underground sewer and provides a hideout for other crooks.
Food is secretly delivered each day, he has dug a tunnel in
which he and his occasional guests can walk and exercise,
and he has little need (or, evidently, desire) to surface. Having once promised former members of his gang a free hideout for life, he prefers to eliminate them, one by one, taking
their money. When captured, he says, "It was fun."

Other villains include the Brow, a spy whose tall forehead
has half a dozen highly prominent ridges. Littleface Finny,
whose oversized head has a huge forehead and large cheeks,

has eyes, nose and mouth squeezed into a tiny area in the middle of his face. When he is forced to spend a night in a deep freeze, he gets frostbitten and must have his ears amputated — just before Tracy nabs him. Pear Shape gets his sobriquet not from the shape of his head or face, but of his entire body. He is a swindler in the weight-reducing business. Shaky is nervous. Pruneface looks as if he had a face made of wax which has been too long in the sun; his wife is equally unattractive. B.B. Eyes, a tire bootlegger, appears to be in a perpetual squint with two tiny dots to reveal the location of his eyes.

Some of Tracy's friends and associates have been in the strip since its inception and new ones appear from time to time while others fall by the wayside. Some change more quickly than others, following a natural aging process, while others change hardly at all.

When Tracy joined the force, his superior was Chief Brandon, a good, competent, and honorable man. When Brilliant, the young scientist who had invented the two-way wrist radio, is murdered, Chief Brandon blames himself, feeling that he had not provided enough protection to the threatened scientist. Although it was impossible for him to have prevented the killing, he resigns. Some years later, he reappears in the strip as the operator of a garden shop called "Lawn Order."

Tracy's partner, and the man with the best sense of humor on the force, Pat Patton, takes over as the new chief. Dick was offered the job, of course, as befits the ace of the department, but he prefers to allow his friend to take the position because he likes to be on the street, fighting crime with his fists and gun as well as with his brain. Patton, by the way, loses most of that sense of humor when he takes the higher office because he thinks it inappropriate for a man at his level to make jokes.

Tracy's new partner is Sam Catchem, not so new after fifteen years.

Early in their careers, Gravel Gertie and B.O. Plenty (the B.O. stands for Bob Oscar) are outlaws, but they reform and are living as itinerants until Tracy brings them together. They marry and have a daughter, Sparkle Plenty, who grows up to be a beautiful married woman herself (to cartoonist Vera Alldid).

Junior, needless to say, has matured a good deal through the years. He, too, is married, with his own child, and is a responsible and valuable member of the police department, working as an artist.

Liz has played a prominent role in the police procedure since she joined the force some years ago. She is one of the most necessary people in the department, constantly demonstrating the huge need for policewomen.

You can have only one hero in a strip, or you lose your readers, but I think it's important to keep some of the old familiar faces nearby. It is like having a family. You may not always want to be around them, but it's nice to know they are there. It is this sense of comfortable familiarity that keeps readers coming back for more, and keeps them wanting to know who will do what to whom next. Dick Tracy is someone people have come to know down the years, and they care about him and his associates, just as they know and care about Sherlock Holmes and Dr. Watson and the sitting room at 221B Baker Street and Professor Moriarty.

Much has been made of the fact that Tracy was one of the first "hard-boiled" detective heroes, and that he was perhaps the first of the American exponents of the "police procedural" style of combating crime. He simply realized he had to be realistic, and those methods and attitudes were the only way to effectively fight crime in the gangster era, just as they were the most effective method of fighting the war on espionage, and just as they are the most effective way of dealing with the rampant crime of today. It was a combination of the times — the Prohibition era — and my boyhood idolatry of Sherlock Holmes that made Dick Tracy the man he was in 1931 — and the man he is today. And the man he will always be.

Inspector
Van der Valk

Nicolas Freeling

Inspector Van der Valk of the Amsterdam police department is unmistakably a creature of the twentieth century, with all its complexities and apparent paradoxes. Among the things he passionately hates are bureaucracy and bureaucrats; yet he is himself a member of that government officialdom. His politics are leftish. He loves his wife but has no aversion to enjoying other pretty women. Though considerable time has passed since he himself was young, he is especially attuned to the problems of young people. After ten years as an inspector on the police force of Amsterdam, he was made chief inspector of the Juvenile Brigade. A good cop, he nevertheless occasionally circumvents the rules and often employs bizarre methods to achieve success.

After ten successful books (The King of the Rainy Country *won the Edgar Allan Poe Award from the Mystery Writers of America as the best novel of 1966*), *Nicolas Freeling committed a shocking, if not unprecedented, act for an author: he killed his hero. (Sir Arthur Conan Doyle, or Professor Moriarty, once threw Sherlock Holmes over a cliff at the Reichenbach Falls but resurrected him.) Dead for five years now, and much lamented, Van der Valk seems unlikely to have further adventures.*

Freeling's first mystery, Love in Amsterdam, *may have compensated in part for his once having been arrested for a theft he had not committed. Born in London, the 50-year-old author lived for a time in France, Ireland, and the Netherlands, and now resides again in Bas Rhin, France. His deep knowledge of that country is reflected in his several recent novels involving Inspector Henri Castang of the Police Judicaire.*

Inspector Van der Valk

by Nicolas Freeling

THE LEGEND runs that Alexandre Dumas came from his working room, the face distorted by tears, saying, "I have killed Porthos." A version I find nearer reality runs, "I killed Porthos; it was a necessity." But the tears are believable, for a character one has lived with for ten years is the writer's closest kin, and this fictional deathbed is fratricide.

Nobody found it easy to forgive me the death of Van der Valk. Editors with big reproachful eyes began planning (they are a cynical tribe) posthumous adventures; angry old ladies sputtered fiercely about my callousness. As though it were my fault . . . We speak of a character in fiction "being alive" and we mean just that. He obeys the rule of life, which is death. The professional police officer, and we tend to forget this, accepts that his life is more fragile than most, a fact that profoundly influences his manner of living. In fiction, to be sure, there are plenty of figures who could not possibly die, and go on interminably, even surviving their creators, but then they never were alive . . .

Van der Valk is buried close to my home and I am reminded of him daily: I see him as vividly present and intensely alive. Which he is, for as long as one of his books is owned and re-read. Stendhal, who had small success during his lifetime, hoped only for one reader in a hundred years' time. The man of course fills my room; he always did. Physically, to be sure, he was a solid presence. Large-boned, he took a size forty-five in shoes and left them sticking out for people to trip over. Big hands, too, with flat well-shaped nails, not always very clean, just as his shoes were not always polished: a job that bored him. Wide mouth in a heavy jaw, filled with large white teeth, and a harsh metallic voice which though quiet made itself heard anywhere. He could and did keep still when it was needed, with enviable concentration and a cop's patience, but a low boredom-threshold led him to roam restlessly about the room; paperwork made him grunt and pick his nose.

The nose too was large, reddened where he rubbed it and showing broken veins from drinking too much. Ears large and flat, with a good shape. Only the eyes were small, of a sharp electric blue, flat and hard, and could become frightening. He was of course a peasant, with the slyness and cunning one finds in backward rustic corners, but he became furious if one said so, being vain of his birth and upbringing in an earthy, crowded quarter of central Amsterdam. His father was a jobbing carpenter with a taste for fine joinery, and he could never withhold his respect from any man with skill in his hands.

He was intensely Dutch, characteristically fond of crude personal remarks followed by a guffaw: obstinate, brutal, pragmatic, and given to lavatory humor. He did not have the unimaginative insensitivity: he acted it, but this was police protective coloring. He could be — like most people — cruel, vindictive, and petty, but never for long. A generous and open person, the quickest way to reach him was to show simplicity and spontaneity. Any show of self-importance, and he would take pains to arrange a banana skin beneath your feet.

He loved form in things: he could always be captivated by a person, a building, a picture with a sense of form, and even a wash basin or a park bench that was well designed caught his eye and gave him pleasure. He was bored by sport, though it kept the beer at bay and speeded up metabolism. It was the shape and balance of a good slalom skier or an attacking out-half that excited him. He loved above all his French wife because she was so well designed.

Arlette was his entire secret: he knew it and was fond of saying so. Of both his personal equilibrium and his professional career. It would be true also to say that he used her, with a Dutch sense of pragmatism: she was the sharpest and handiest of his tools. She disliked hearing details of police work — life was sordid enough as it was — but her judgments of persons, situations, hypotheses would be asked for, carefully heard, stored away, and thought about. She stretched the man, enlarged him, gave him suppleness where he was stiff and rigid. He was always a feminist, and a libber before the term was invented, and was forever saying how immeasurably police work would be improved, more competent as well as more human, by using women more. He was, too, one of those men who find women easier and more understanding to talk to than other men. It was amusing that Arlette had no wish whatever to be libbed: she took pride in her status as housewife, was as obstinate as he himself, and determinedly a *"femme d'interieur."* She had few friends, and with them generally talked children and clothes. When she went out without him it was to concerts, for music was her passion, and on subscription evenings he was left ruthlessly in front of the television set. Her home was a fortress, and the fortress was for him; a large but shabby and old-fashioned flat, since they had only his pay to live on. He was known for not taking bribes. Not so much because of honesty, for he was dishonest in plenty of ways, saying bluntly that without dishonesty a cop could not function: independence was more precious. A bent cop can never get off the hook: take favors, and you will be asked for them.

The fortress thus badly needed new curtains and new carpets. It was full of flowers, but most Dutch houses are (this is one of the nicest things about Holland). Arlette, being French, spent much more on food than on clothes. Dutch food is penurious in the extreme, and she came from the Var, where it isn't much better . . . One can make good food only by taking much time and trouble, and she did both because he was a big man with a healthy appetite. Some people would find this stupid, even ignoble. Marriage seen as dinner-on-the-table, and doubtless plenty of rice-pudding sex to follow! (Certainly; Arlette was an intensely beddable woman.) Van der Valk would not have bothered arguing the point. Not that he ever cared much what opinion people formed of him, and least of all critics: one imbecile once called him a sexual fascist, at which he guffawed. The grub is good, he would say, paraphrasing Brecht; the ethics will be better as a consequence.

Briefly, Arlette and a very closely knit family life made him what he was. He had his job; hers was him . . .

They also had two children, both boys, and in later life, when these reached student age, they adopted a little girl. The books make small mention of the children, for the technical reason that children are very difficult to handle in telling a story. It should be realized that children, both his own and other people's, were extremely important to Van der Valk.

His beginning, eighteen years ago, sprang from my boredom with existing crime writers' platitudes. I could not see

any point or interest in a character (be it the English amateur, mannerisms-and-manservants, or the beat-up Cal-Flor
eye; the species never flourished in Salt Lake City) who
was no more than tired mechanical catalyzer of a denouement that stayed obvious no matter how many surprise
twists it could be given. The whole business of crime writing rested upon a false premise: that it was a somehow in-
ferior genre, not to be taken seriously. Was not the answer
to present a crime tale that introduced people one could
care about, with problems that were ours? In my youthful
enthusiasm I overlooked the difficulties of overcoming nine-
teenth-century prejudice, in this as in other moral questions
deeply rooted.

The first and essential factor was a "detective" who would
be a recognizable human being, a member of society, who
worried about the childrens' inability to pay attention in
class and the cost of shoe repairs, and whose car would not
start on foggy mornings. He would be a professional cop,
because when we have a crime to contend with in the world
we do not call Mr. Chose the philosophy don, or Viscount
Machin: we scream for the despised fuzz. My man would
be an officer, because he had some education and intelligence.
Such a man would be a middle-grade career officer in a well-
disciplined, unpolitical metropolitan police force. The city
of Amsterdam fitted the case perfectly. The first detail was
to find a name, for once a character has a name and address
he is in business, defined, as it were, in length and breadth.
I recalled an Officer of Justice, to give the public prosecutor
his Dutch title, with whom I had once had a none too sympathetic meeting, and whose name was Van der Valk . . .

The man had ideals, while knowing perfectly that they
are a sore expense which a cop can ill afford. Being just,

flexible, understanding, et cetera et cetera, toward a public incurably cowardly and egoistic, as well as generally brutish; easier said than done. The policeman's trade is squalid and underpaid, as well as governed by a pack of regulations. In his earliest, crudest shape, Van der Valk took on consistency through these oppositions. You know that dishonesty pays, that your promotion is compromised, that inhumanity is inherent in the rules. You wish to do right? — the law forbids it. You wish to do good? — the regulation excludes it. This was his raw material. Why do you persevere? You aren't, we hope, going to come up with a lot of clichés about the alleviation of suffering.

The next set of equations concerned power. Criminal-brigade cops possess a good deal, and abuse it. In all civilized countries there are elaborate mechanisms to protect the public from tyranny, and to bridle excess zeal. These laws and instructions are largely self-defeating, since they are largely ineffectual, while managing to stay a considerable hindrance to the cop. The courts have a tendency to be more hostile toward the cop than the criminal: the public has a shamefaced sympathy for the fellow who's been caught . . . The cop represents might, and be it in civil or criminal law we know that might has always abundant means of wearying out the right. Yet any intelligent man can see the dangers of dispensing subjective brands of justice.

Van der Valk, facing these hard questions and not always taking the easiest or most entertaining way out, was never my creature. From the beginning he refused to be manipulated; bolting off in unexpected directions, ignoring the dictates of the plot, disregarding the convenience of the other characters and invariably of me. Hard on the scribbler, in perpetual need of some exciting event to keep his story moving. But the cop didn't have it easy either, brought up sharp by trifling matters like perjury or sadism.

He had plenty of weaknesses, worst perhaps his absurd indulgence toward pretty girls, which got him into a variety of bad fixes. Still, this self-indulgence showed too a refusal of stereotyping. All literature is full of virtuous bores, but one never likes d'Artagnan better than when he stops being heroic to play that really abominable trick on Milady. Arlette's hard-boiled eye kept Van der Valk from jumping out of the window dressed in the maid's clothes, but only just. Getting himself shot by that tiresome and spoiled young woman Anne-Marie Marchal served him right: he should have had more sense. And he was lazy to be sure, and habitually drank too much. Still, there are more unattractive vices. He had small vanity and was rarely self-satisfied; hated petty meanness and avarice. And he punctured the self-important: no wonder so many critics detested him.

The refusal to fit into a pat little mold, to be a plastic thing that makes the motor go (like a car's distributor cap) was of course his downfall. For a writer to pursue a character through a prolonged series without renewal is a sure sign of one thing: that his only continuing object is to make money. The result, be it Kojak or the Scarlet Pimpernel, is a butler-figure, something with about six fixed positions and attitudes, totally predictable and as alive as frozen mutton. Van der Valk refused this fate. After ten books in as many years I noticed that he was beginning to parody himself; I did not want the downhill slide to go further.

There were other considerations too, of course. I no longer lived in Holland and had no longer the everyday contact with the tissue of existence there. The backgrounds would have ceased being exact, slipping into the nonsense

chambers of commerce print for handouts. As well as degenerating increasingly toward cardboard, Van der Valk,
in the pattern of streets and houses that was his, would have
slipped out of focus. The sort of thing that happened, in
fact, to Maigret, whose Third Republic anachronisms in
modern Paris became embarrassing.

By killing him off, in fact, I made sure he would stay
alive . . . This is tricky ground, where the writer falls
easily into sentimentalisms and the nauseatingly sweet attitudes of anthropomorphism. I talk to the flowers, and they
confide in me: do they now. But against this, one must place
the undisputed fact that for a great many people an imaginary character has vastly more life than the zombies we
meet in our trivial round. It isn't in the least surprising that
people write "Frodo Lives" on the subway wall; it is more
surprising, and sad, that they should find it necessary to
point it out . . . One can test the fact anywhere: if you go
down, say, to Key Biscayne you will find that ex-President
Nixon is a very shadowy personage compared to Travis
McGee.

To find him a successor was, again, a task I underesti-
mated. I had not realized the strength of this character who
had lived for so long in my workroom until I found myself
copying his speech patterns. He lay with a paralyzing
weight upon the first books in the genre that I tried next,
and the streets of Amsterdam had a folklore quality I found
stultifying. Only now, in fact, do I feel the indispensable
sense of distancing that keeps us friends.

I have many more reasons for gratitude toward him. Over
those ten years I served my apprenticeship as a writer, and
it was Van der Valk that kept my family and myself fed
and clothed. He was a constant and unselfish companion.
He had the agreeable habit of seeing the funny side to

domestic catastrophe, and was a powerful defense against invasion by vanities or pretensions. Toward the soapy sales talk of Mr. Buy-and-Sell he brought sharp points that punctured, and better still a sense of true values that must be defended at all cost. For the skipping antics of politicians he had always a mocking eye and a scathing tongue, and for parish-pump thinking (a disease that does not flourish only in Holland) he had a good-humored contempt that brought oxygen into our lives in moments of great disillusion and discouragement.

My gratitude to him will last as long as my life.

Bibliography
and
Filmography

Roderick Alleyn

Books:

1938 *Artists in Crime* (Furman)

1938 *Death in a White Tie* (Furman)

1939 *Overture to Death* (Furman)

1940 *Vintage Murder* (Sheridan)

1940 *Death at the Bar* (Little, Brown)

1940 *Death of a Peer* (Little, Brown; British title: *Surfeit of Lampreys*)

1941 *Death in Ecstasy* (Sheridan)

1941 *Death and the Dancing Footman* (Little, Brown)

1941 *Enter a Murderer* (Pocket Books)

1941 *The Nursing Home Murder* (Sheridan; in collaboration with Dr. Henry Jellett)

1942 *A Man Lay Dead* (Sheridan)

1943 *Colour Scheme* (Little, Brown)

1945 *Died in the Wool* (Little, Brown)

1947 *Final Curtain* (Little, Brown)

1949 *A Wreath for Rivera* (Little, Brown; British title: *Swing, Brother, Swing*)

1951 *Night at the Vulcan* (Little, Brown; British title: *Opening Night*)

1953 *Spinsters in Jeopardy* (Little, Brown)

1955 *Scales of Justice* (Little, Brown)

1956 *Death of a Fool* (Little, Brown; British title: *Off with His Head*)

1958 *Singing in the Shrouds* (Little, Brown)

1959 *False Scent* (Little, Brown)

1962 *Hand in Glove* (Little, Brown)

1963 *Dead Water* (Little, Brown)

1966 *Killer Dolphin* (Little, Brown; British title: *Death at the Dolphin*)

1969 *Clutch of Constables* (Little, Brown)

1971 *When in Rome* (Little, Brown)

1972 *Tied Up in Tinsel* (Little, Brown)

1974 *Black as He's Painted* (Little, Brown)
1977 *Last Ditch* (Little, Brown)

John Appleby

Books:

1937 *Seven Suspects* (Dodd, Mead; British title: *Death at the President's Lodging*)
1937 *Hamlet, Revenge!* (Dodd, Mead)
1938 *Lament for a Maker* (Dodd, Mead)
1939 *The Spider Strikes* (Dodd, Mead; British title: *Stop Press*)
1940 *A Comedy of Terrors* (Dodd, Mead; British title: *There Came Both Mist and Snow*)
1941 *The Secret Vanguard* (Dodd, Mead)
1941 *Appleby on Ararat* (Dodd, Mead)
1942 *The Daffodil Affair* (Dodd, Mead)
1943 *The Weight of Evidence* (Dodd, Mead)
1945 *Appleby's End* (Dodd, Mead)
1947 *A Night of Errors* (Dodd, Mead)
1951 *The Paper Thunderbolt* (Dodd, Mead; British title: *Operation Pax*)
1952 *One Man Show* (Dodd, Mead; British title: *A Private View*)
1954 *Dead Man's Shoes* (Dodd, Mead; British title: *Appleby Talking;* 23 short stories)
1957 *Appleby Talks Again* (Dodd, Mead; 18 short stories)
1957 *Death on a Quiet Day* (Dodd, Mead; British title: *Appleby Plays Chicken*)
1958 *The Long Farewell* (Dodd, Mead)
1959 *Hare Sitting Up* (Dodd, Mead)
1961 *Silence Observed* (Dodd, Mead)
1962 *The Crabtree Affair* (Dodd, Mead; British title: *A Connoisseur's Case*)
1966 *The Bloody Wood* (Dodd, Mead)

1968 *Death by Water* (Dodd, Mead; British title: *Appleby at Allington*)

1969 *Picture of Guilt* (Dodd, Mead; British title: *A Family Affair*)

1970 *Death at the Chase* (Dodd, Mead)

1971 *An Awkward Lie* (Dodd, Mead)

1972 *The Open House* (Dodd, Mead)

1973 *Appleby's Answer* (Dodd, Mead)

1974 *Appleby's Other Story* (Dodd, Mead)

1976 *The Appleby File* (Dodd, Mead; 18 short stories)

1977 *The Gay Phoenix* (Dodd, Mead)

Lew Archer

Books:

1949 *The Moving Target* (Knopf)

1950 *The Drowning Pool* (Knopf)

1951 *The Way Some People Die* (Knopf)

1952 *The Ivory Grin* (Knopf)

1954 *Find a Victim* (Knopf)

1955 *The Name Is Archer* (Bantam; 7 stories)

1956 *The Barbarous Coast* (Knopf)

1958 *The Doomsters* (Knopf)

1959 *The Galton Case* (Knopf)

1961 *The Wycherly Woman* (Knopf)

1962 *The Zebra-Striped Hearse* (Knopf)

1964 *The Chill* (Knopf)

1965 *The Far Side of the Dollar* (Knopf)

1966 *Black Money* (Knopf)

1968 *The Instant Enemy* (Knopf)

1969 *The Goodbye Look* (Knopf)

1971 *The Underground Man* (Knopf)

1973 *Sleeping Beauty* (Knopf)

1976 *The Blue Hammer* (Knopf)

1977 *Lew Archer, Private Investigator* (The Mysterious Press; 9 stories)

Films:
1966 *Harper* (Warner Brothers), with Paul Newman
1974 *The Underground Man* (Paramount TV), with Peter Graves
1975 *The Drowning Pool* (Warner Brothers), with Paul Newman

Father Bredder

Books:
1959 *The Saint Maker* (Dodd, Mead)
1960 *A Pact with Satan* (Dodd, Mead)
1961 *The Secret of the Doubting Saint* (Dodd, Mead)
1963 *Deliver Us from Wolves* (Dodd, Mead)
1964 *Flowers by Request* (Dodd, Mead)
1966 *Out of the Depths* (Dodd, Mead)
1968 *A Touch of Jonah* (Dodd, Mead)
1970 *A Problem in Angels* (Dodd, Mead)
1972 *The Mirror of Hell* (Dodd, Mead)
1973 *The Devil to Play* (Dodd, Mead)
1977 *A Corner of Paradise* (St. Martin's Press)

Flash Casey

Books:
1942 *Silent Are the Dead* (Knopf)
1943 *Murder for Two* (Knopf)
1946 *Flash Casey, Detective* (Avon; 4 novelettes)
1961 *Error of Judgment* (Knopf)
1962 *The Man Who Died Too Soon* (Knopf)
1964 *Deadly Image* (Knopf)

Films:
1936 *Women Are Trouble* (M-G-M), with Stuart Erwin
1937 *Here's Flash Casey* (Grand National), with Eric Linden

Pierre Chambrun

Books:
1962 *The Cannibal Who Overate* (Dodd, Mead)
1964 *The Shape of Fear* (Dodd, Mead)
1966 *The Evil That Men Do* (Dodd, Mead)
1967 *The Golden Trap* (Dodd, Mead)
1968 *The Gilded Nightmare* (Dodd, Mead)
1969 *The Girl Watcher's Funeral* (Dodd, Mead)
1971 *The Deadly Joke* (Dodd, Mead)
1972 *Birthday, Deathday* (Dodd, Mead)
1973 *Walking Dead Man* (Dodd, Mead)
1974 *Bargain with Death* (Dodd, Mead)
1975 *Time of Terror* (Dodd, Mead)
1976 *The Fourteen Dilemma* (Dodd, Mead)

Inspector Cockrill

Books:
1941 *Heads You Lose* (Dodd, Mead)
1944 *Green for Danger* (Dodd, Mead)
1946 *The Crooked Wreath* (Dodd, Mead; British title: *Suddenly at His Residence*)
1948 *Death of Jezebel* (Dodd, Mead)
1953 *Fog of Doubt* (Scribner; British title: *London Particular*, 1952)
1955 *Tour de Force* (Scribner)
1968 *What Dread Hand* (London: Michael Joseph; no American edition; 15 stories of which 3 are about Cockrill)

Film:

1946 *Green for Danger* (Independent Producers), with Alastair Sim

Captain José Da Silva

Books:

1962 *The Fugitive* (Simon & Schuster)
1963 *Isle of the Snakes* (Simon & Schuster)
1963 *The Shrunken Head* (Simon & Schuster)
1965 *The Diamond Bubble* (Simon & Schuster)
1965 *Brazilian Sleigh Ride* (Simon & Schuster)
1967 *Always Kill a Stranger* (Putnam)
1968 *The Bridge That Went Nowhere* (Putnam)
1969 *The Xavier Affair* (Putnam)
1971 *The Green Hell Treasure* (Putnam)
1975 *Trouble in Paradise* (Doubleday)

Nancy Drew

Books:

1930 *The Secret of the Old Clock* (Grosset & Dunlap)
1930 *The Hidden Staircase* (Grosset & Dunlap)
1930 *The Bungalow Mystery* (Grosset & Dunlap)
1930 *Mystery at Lilac Inn* (Grosset & Dunlap)
1931 *The Secret of Shadow Ranch* (Grosset & Dunlap)
1931 *The Secret of Red Gate Farm* (Grosset & Dunlap)
1932 *The Clue in the Diary* (Grosset & Dunlap)
1932 *Nancy's Mysterious Letter* (Grosset & Dunlap)
1933 *The Sign of the Twisted Candles* (Grosset & Dunlap)
1933 *Password to Larkspur Lane* (Grosset & Dunlap)
1934 *The Clue of the Broken Locket* (Grosset & Dunlap)
1935 *The Message in the Hollow Oak* (Grosset & Dunlap)
1936 *Mystery of the Ivory Charm* (Grosset & Dunlap)
1937 *The Whispering Statue* (Grosset & Dunlap)

1937 *The Haunted Bridge* (Grosset & Dunlap)
1939 *The Clue of the Tapping Heels* (Grosset & Dunlap)
1940 *The Mystery of the Brass Bound Trunk* (Grosset & Dunlap)
1941 *Mystery at the Moss-Covered Mansion* (Grosset & Dunlap)
1942 *The Quest of the Missing Map* (Grosset & Dunlap)
1943 *The Clue in the Jewel Box* (Grosset & Dunlap)
1944 *The Secret in the Old Attic* (Grosset & Dunlap)
1945 *The Clue in the Crumbling Wall* (Grosset & Dunlap)
1946 *Mystery of the Tolling Bell* (Grosset & Dunlap)
1947 *The Clue in the Old Album* (Grosset & Dunlap)
1948 *The Ghost of Blackwood Hall* (Grosset & Dunlap)
1949 *The Clue of the Leaning Chimney* (Grosset & Dunlap)
1950 *The Secret of the Wooden Lady* (Grosset & Dunlap)
1951 *The Clue of the Black Keys* (Grosset & Dunlap)
1952 *Mystery at the Ski Jump* (Grosset & Dunlap)
1953 *The Clue of the Velvet Mask* (Grosset & Dunlap)
1953 *The Ringmaster's Secret* (Grosset & Dunlap)
1954 *The Scarlet Slipper Mystery* (Grosset & Dunlap)
1955 *The Witch Tree Symbol* (Grosset & Dunlap)
1956 *The Hidden Window Mystery* (Grosset & Dunlap)
1957 *The Haunted Showboat* (Grosset & Dunlap)
1959 *The Secret of the Golden Pavilion* (Grosset & Dunlap)
1960 *The Clue in the Old Stagecoach* (Grosset & Dunlap)
1961 *The Mystery of the Fire Dragon* (Grosset & Dunlap)
1962 *The Clue of the Dancing Puppet* (Grosset & Dunlap)
1963 *The Moonstone Castle Mystery* (Grosset & Dunlap)
1964 *The Clue of the Whistling Bagpipes* (Grosset & Dunlap)
1965 *The Phantom of Pine Hill* (Grosset & Dunlap)
1966 *The Mystery of the 99 Steps* (Grosset & Dunlap)
1967 *The Clue in the Crossword Cipher* (Grosset & Dunlap)
1968 *The Spider Sapphire Mystery* (Grosset & Dunlap)
1969 *The Invisible Intruder* (Grosset & Dunlap)
1970 *The Mysterious Mannequin* (Grosset & Dunlap)
1971 *The Crooked Banister* (Grosset & Dunlap)

1972 *The Secret of Mirror Bay* (Grosset & Dunlap)
1973 *The Double Jinx Mystery* (Grosset & Dunlap)
1974 *Mystery of the Glowing Eye* (Grosset & Dunlap)
1975 *The Secret of the Forgotten City* (Grosset & Dunlap)
1976 *The Sky Phantom* (Grosset & Dunlap)
1977 *The Strange Message in the Parchment* (Grosset & Dunlap)
1978 *Mystery of Crocodile Island* (Grossett & Dunlap)

Films:
1938 *Nancy Drew, Detective* (Warner Brothers), with Bonita Granville
1939 *Nancy Drew, Reporter* (Warner Brothers), with Bonita Granville
1939 *Nancy Drew, Trouble Shooter* (Warner Brothers), with Bonita Granville
1939 *Nancy Drew and the Hidden Staircase* (Warner Brothers), with Bonita Granville

The 87th Precinct

Books:
1956 *Cop Hater* (Permabooks)
1956 *The Mugger* (Permabooks)
1956 *The Pusher* (Permabooks)
1957 *The Con Man* (Permabooks)
1957 *Killer's Choice* (Permabooks)
1958 *Killer's Payoff* (Permabooks)
1958 *Lady Killer* (Permabooks)
1959 *Killer's Wedge* (Simon & Schuster)
1959 *'Til Death* (Simon & Schuster)
1959 *King's Ransom* (Simon & Schuster)
1960 *Give the Boys a Great Big Hand* (Simon & Schuster)
1960 *The Heckler* (Simon & Schuster)

1962 *The Empty Hours* (Simon & Schuster; 3 novelettes)
1961 *Lady, Lady, I Did It!* (Simon & Schuster)
1962 *Like Love* (Simon & Schuster)
1962 *The Empty Hours* (Simon & Schuster; contains 3 novelettes)
1963 *Ten Plus One* (Simon & Schuster)
1964 *Ax* (Simon & Schuster)
1965 *He Who Hesitates* (Delacorte)
1965 *Doll* (Delacorte)
1966 *Eighty Million Eyes* (Delacorte)
1968 *Fuzz* (Doubleday)
1969 *Shotgun* (Doubleday)
1970 *Jigsaw* (Doubleday)
1971 *Hail, Hail, the Gang's All Here!* (Doubleday)
1972 *Sadie When She Died* (Doubleday)
1973 *Let's Hear It for the Deaf Man* (Doubleday)
1973 *Hail to the Chief* (Random House)
1974 *Bread* (Random House)
1975 *Blood Relatives* (Random House)
1976 *So Long as You Both Shall Live* (Random House)
1977 *Long Time No See* (Random House)

Films:
1958 *Cop Hater* (United Artists)
1958 *The Mugger* (United Artists)
1963 *High and Low* (Continental Distributing: Japanese), set in Yokohama
1972 *Without Apparent Motive* (Twentieth Century–Fox), set in Nice
1972 *Fuzz* (Twentieth Century–Fox), set in Boston
1978 *Blood Relatives* (Filmel: French), set in Montreal

Fred Fellows

Books:
1959 *Sleep Long, My Love* (Doubleday)
1960 *Road Block* (Doubleday)
1961 *That Night It Rained* (Doubleday)
1962 *The Late Mrs. D.* (Doubleday)
1962 *Born Victim* (Doubleday)
1963 *Death and Circumstance* (Doubleday)
1963 *Prisoner's Plea* (Doubleday)
1964 *The Missing Man* (Doubleday)
1965 *End of a Party* (Doubleday)
1966 *Pure Poison* (Doubleday)
1968 *The Con Game* (Doubleday)

Inspector Ghote

Books:
1965 *The Perfect Murder* (Dutton)
1966 *Inspector Ghote's Good Crusade* (Dutton)
1968 *Inspector Ghote Caught in Meshes* (Dutton)
1968 *Inspector Ghote Hunts the Peacock* (Dutton)
1969 *Inspector Ghote Plays a Joker* (Dutton)
1971 *Inspector Ghote Breaks an Egg* (Doubleday)
1972 *Inspector Ghote Goes by Train* (Doubleday)
1973 *Inspector Ghote Trusts the Heart* (Doubleday)
1974 *Bats Fly Up for Inspector Ghote* (Doubleday)
1976 *Filmi, Filmi, Inspector Ghote* (Doubleday)

Matt Helm

Books:
1960 *Death of a Citizen* (Gold Medal)
1960 *The Wrecking Crew* (Gold Medal)
1961 *The Removers* (Gold Medal)
1962 *The Silencers* (Gold Medal)

1962 *Murderers' Row* (Gold Medal)
1963 *The Ambushers* (Gold Medal)
1964 *The Shadowers* (Gold Medal)
1964 *The Ravagers* (Gold Medal)
1965 *The Devastators* (Gold Medal)
1966 *The Betrayers* (Gold Medal)
1968 *The Menacers* (Gold Medal)
1969 *The Interlopers* (Gold Medal)
1971 *The Poisoners* (Gold Medal)
1973 *The Intriguers* (Gold Medal)
1974 *The Intimidators* (Gold Medal)
1975 *The Terminators* (Gold Medal)
1976 *The Retaliators* (Gold Medal)
1977 *The Terrorizers* (Gold Medal)

Films:
1966 *The Silencers* (Columbia), with Dean Martin
1966 *Murderers' Row* (Columbia), with Dean Martin
1967 *The Ambushers* (Columbia), with Dean Martin
1968 *The Wrecking Crew* (Columbia), with Dean Martin

Duncan Maclain

Books:
1937 *The Last Express* (Doubleday)
1937 *The Whistling Hangman* (Doubleday)
1941 *The Odor of Violets* (Little, Brown)
1943 *Blind Man's Bluff* (Little, Brown)
1945 *Death Knell* (Morrow)
1945 *Out of Control* (Morrow)
1947 *Make Mine Maclain* (Morrow; 3 novelettes)
1952 *You Diet Today* (Morrow)
1954 *Blind Allies* (Morrow)
1957 *Reservations for Death* (Morrow)
1958 *Clear and Present Danger* (Doubleday)

1960 *The Aluminum Turtle* (Dodd, Mead; British title: *The Spear Gun Murders*)
1961 *Frankincense and Murder* (Dodd, Mead)

Films:
1938 *The Last Express* (Universal), with Kent Taylor
1942 *Eyes in the Night* (M-G-M), with Edward Arnold
1945 *The Hidden Eye* (M-G-M), with Edward Arnold

Mark McPherson

Books:
1943 *Laura* (Houghton Mifflin)

Film:
1944 *Laura* (Twentieth Century–Fox), with Dana Andrews

Lieutenant Luis Mendoza

Books:
1960 *Case Pending* (Harper & Row)
1961 *The Ace of Spades* (Morrow)
1962 *Extra Kill* (Morrow)
1962 *Knave of Hearts* (Morrow)
1963 *Death of a Busybody* (Morrow)
1963 *Double Bluff* (Morrow)
1964 *Root of All Evil* (Morrow)
1964 *Mark of Murder* (Morrow)
1965 *The Death-Bringers* (Morrow)
1965 *Death by Inches* (Morrow)
1966 *Coffin Corner* (Morrow)
1966 *With a Vengeance* (Morrow)
1967 *Chance to Kill* (Morrow)
1967 *Rain with Violence* (Morrow)
1968 *Kill with Kindness* (Morrow)

1969 *Schooled to Kill* (Morrow)
1969 *Crime on Their Hands* (Morrow)
1970 *Unexpected Death* (Morrow)
1971 *Whim to Kill* (Morrow)
1971 *The Ringer* (Morrow)
1972 *Murder with Love* (Morrow)
1972 *With Intent to Kill* (Morrow)
1973 *No Holiday for Crime* (Morrow)
1973 *Spring for Violence* (Morrow)
1974 *Crime File* (Morrow)
1975 *Deuces Wild* (Morrow)
1977 *Streets of Death* (Morrow)
1977 *Appearances of Death* (Morrow)
1978 *Cold Trail* (Morrow)

Mr. and Mrs. North

Books:

1936 *Mr. and Mrs. North* (Stokes; a collection of non-mystery vignettes)
1940 *The Norths Meet Murder* (Stokes)
1941 *Murder out of Turn* (Stokes)
1941 *A Pinch of Poison* (Stokes)
1942 *Death on the Aisle* (Lippincott)
1942 *Hanged for a Sheep* (Lippincott)
1943 *Death Takes a Bow* (Lippincott)
1944 *Killing the Goose* (Lippincott)
1945 *Payoff for the Banker* (Lippincott)
1946 *Murder Within Murder* (Lippincott)
1946 *Death of a Tall Man* (Lippincott)
1947 *Untidy Murder* (Lippincott)
1948 *Murder Is Served* (Lippincott)
1949 *The Dishonest Murderer* (Lippincott)
1950 *Murder in a Hurry* (Lippincott)
1951 *Murder Comes First* (Lippincott)

1952 *Dead as a Dinosaur* (Lippincott)
1953 *Death Has a Small Voice* (Lippincott)
1953 *Curtain for a Jester* (Lippincott)
1954 *A Key to Death* (Lippincott)
1955 *Death of an Angel* (Lippincott)
1956 *Voyage into Violence* (Lippincott)
1958 *The Long Skeleton* (Lippincott)
1959 *Murder Is Suggested* (Lippincott)
1960 *The Judge Is Reversed* (Lippincott)
1961 *Murder Has Its Points* (Lippincott)
1963 *Murder by the Book* (Lippincott)

Film:
1941 *Mr. and Mrs. North* (M-G-M), with Gracie Allen and William Post, Jr.

Patrick Petrella

Books:
1959 *Blood and Judgment* (Harper & Row)
1973 *Amateur in Violence* (Davis; 4 of the 11 stories are about Petrella)
1977 *Petrella at Q* (Harper & Row; 1 novelette and 11 short stories)

Superintendent Pibble

Books:
1968 *The Glass-Sided Ants' Nest* (Harper & Row; British title: *Skin Deep*)
1969 *The Old English Peep Show* (Harper & Row; British title: *A Pride of Heroes*)
1970 *The Sinful Stones* (Harper & Row; British title: *The Seals*)
1971 *Sleep and His Brother* (Harper & Row)
1972 *The Lizard in the Cup* (Harper & Row)

Quiller

Books:

1965 *The Quiller Memorandum* (Simon & Schuster; British
     title: *The Berlin Memorandum*)
1966 *The Ninth Directive* (Simon & Schuster)
1969 *The Striker Portfolio* (Simon & Schuster)
1971 *The Warsaw Document* (Doubleday)
1973 *The Tango Briefing* (Doubleday)
1975 *The Mandarin Cypher* (Doubleday)
1976 *The Kobra Manifesto* (Doubleday)
1978 *The Sinkaing Executive* (Doubleday)

Film:

1967 *The Quiller Memorandum* (Twentieth Century–Fox),
     with George Segal

Inspector Schmidt

Books:

1935 *Murder at the Piano* (Covici-Friede)
1936 *Ring Around a Murder* (Covici-Friede)
1937 *Murder Half Baked* (Covici-Friede)
1938 *Murder on the Nose* (Doubleday)
1939 *Bird Walking Weather* (Doubleday)
1939 *The Corpse with the Purple Thighs* (Doubleday)
1940 *The Corpse Wore a Wig* (Doubleday)
1941 *Here Comes the Corpse* (Doubleday)
1941 *Red Is for Killing* (Doubleday)
1942 *Murder Calling "50"* (Doubleday)
1946 *Dead on Arrival* (Doubleday)
1946 *The Original Carcase* (Doubleday)
1947 *The Twin Killing* (Doubleday)
1948 *The Starting Gun* (Doubleday)
1948 *In Cold Blood* (Doubleday)
1949 *Drop Dead* (Doubleday)

1949 *Coffin Corner* (Doubleday)
1950 *Blood Will Tell* (Doubleday)
1951 *Death Ain't Commercial* (Doubleday)
1952 *Scared to Death* (Doubleday)
1952 *The Corpse with Sticky Fingers* (Doubleday)
1953 *Give the Little Corpse a Great Big Hand* (Doubleday)
1953 *Dead Drunk* (Doubleday)
1954 *The Body in the Basket* (Doubleday)
1955 *A Dirty Way to Die* (Doubleday)
1956 *Dead Storage* (Doubleday)
1956 *Cop Killer* (Doubleday)
1957 *Dead Wrong* (Doubleday)
1958 *The Three-Time Losers* (Doubleday)
1959 *The Real Gone Goose* (Doubleday; British title: *A Real Gone Goose*)
1961 *Evil Genius* (Doubleday)
1963 *Murder's Little Helper* (Doubleday)
1965 *Mysteriouser and Mysteriouser* (Doubleday; British title: *Murder in Wonderland*)
1966 *Dirty Pool* (Doubleday; British title: *Bait for a Killer*)
1967 *Corpse Candle* (Doubleday)
1968 *Another Day — Another Death* (Doubleday)
1969 *Honest Reliable Corpse* (Doubleday)
1970 *Killer Boy Was Here* (Doubleday)
1976 *Two in the Bush* (Doubleday)
1976 *My Dead Body* (Doubleday)
1977 *Innocent Bystander* (Doubleday)
1977 *The Tough Get Going* (Doubleday)

The Shadow

Films:

1937 *The Shadow Strikes* (Grand National), with Rod La Rocque

1938 *International Crime* (Grand National), with Rod La Rocque

1940 *The Shadow* (Columbia serial), with Victor Jory

1946 *The Shadow Returns* (Monogram), with Kane Richmond

1946 *Behind the Mask* (Monogram), with Kane Richmond

1946 *The Missing Lady* (Monogram), with Kane Richmond

1958 *Bourbon Street Shadows* (Republic), with Richard Derr

Michael Shayne

Books:

1939 *Dividend on Death* (Holt)

1940 *The Private Practice of Michael Shayne* (Holt)

1940 *The Uncomplaining Corpses* (Holt)

1941 *Tickets for Death* (Holt)

1941 *Bodies Are Where You Find Them* (Holt)

1942 *The Corpse Came Calling* (Dodd, Mead)

1943 *Murder Wears a Mummer's Mask* (Dodd, Mead)

1943 *Blood on the Black Market* (Dodd, Mead)

1944 *Michael Shayne's Long Chance* (Dodd, Mead)

1944 *Murder and the Married Virgin* (Dodd, Mead)

1945 *Murder Is My Business* (Dodd, Mead)

1945 *Marked for Murder* (Dodd, Mead)

1946 *Blood on Biscayne Bay* (Dodd, Mead)

1947 *Counterfeit Wife* (Ziff-Davis)

1948 *Blood on the Stars* (Dodd, Mead)

1948 *Michael Shayne's Triple Mystery* (Ziff-Davis; 3 novelettes)

1949 *A Taste for Violence* (Dodd, Mead)

1949 *Call for Michael Shayne* (Dodd, Mead)
1950 *This Is It, Michael Shayne* (Dodd, Mead)
1951 *Framed in Blood* (Dodd, Mead)
1951 *When Dorinda Dances* (Dodd, Mead)
1952 *What Really Happened* (Dodd, Mead)
1953 *One Night with Nora* (Torquil/Dodd, Mead)
1954 *She Woke to Darkness* (Torquil/Dodd, Mead)
1955 *Death Has Three Lives* (Torquil/Dodd, Mead)
1955 *Stranger in Town* (Torquil/Dodd, Mead)
1956 *The Blonde Cried Murder* (Torquil/Dodd, Mead)
1957 *Weep for a Blonde* (Torquil/Dodd, Mead)
1957 *Shoot the Works* (Torquil/Dodd, Mead)
1958 *Murder and the Wanton Bride* (Torquil/Dodd, Mead)
1958 *Fit to Kill* (Torquil/Dodd, Mead)
1959 *Date with a Dead Man* (Torquil/Dodd, Mead)
1959 *Target: Mike Shayne* (Torquil/Dodd, Mead)
1959 *Die Like a Dog* (Torquil/Dodd, Mead)
1960 *Murder Takes No Holiday* (Torquil/Dodd, Mead)
1960 *Dolls Are Deadly* (Torquil/Dodd, Mead)
1960 *The Homicidal Virgin* (Torquil/Dodd, Mead)
1961 *Killer from the Keys* (Torquil/Dodd, Mead)
1961 *Murder in Haste* (Torquil/Dodd, Mead)
1961 *The Careless Corpse* (Torquil/Dodd, Mead)
1962 *Pay-Off in Blood* (Torquil/Dodd, Mead)
1962 *Murder by Proxy* (Torquil/Dodd, Mead)
1962 *Never Kill a Client* (Torquil/Dodd, Mead)
1963 *Too Friendly, Too Dead* (Torquil/Dodd, Mead)
1963 *The Corpse That Never Was* (Torquil/Dodd, Mead)
1963 *The Body Came Back* (Torquil/Dodd, Mead)
1964 *A Redhead for Mike Shayne* (Torquil/Dodd, Mead)
1964 *Shoot to Kill* (Torquil/Dodd, Mead)
1964 *Michael Shayne's Fiftieth Case* (Torquil/Dodd, Mead)
1965 *The Violent World of Michael Shayne* (Dell)
1966 *Nice Fillies Finish Last* (Dell)
1966 *Murder Spins the Wheel* (Dell)

1966 *Armed . . . Dangerous . . .* (Dell)
1967 *Mermaid on the Rocks* (Dell)
1967 *Guilty as Hell* (Dell)
1968 *So Lush, So Deadly* (Dell)
1968 *Violence Is Golden* (Dell)
1969 *Lady Be Bad* (Dell)
1970 *Six Seconds to Kill* (Dell)
1970 *Fourth Down to Death* (Dell)
1971 *Count Backwards to Zero* (Dell)
1971 *I Come to Kill You* (Dell)
1972 *Caught Dead* (Dell)
1973 *Kill All the Young Girls* (Dell)
1973 *Blue Murder* (Dell)
1974 *Last Seen Hitchhiking* (Dell)
1974 *At the Point of a .38* (Dell)
1976 *Million Dollar Handle* (Dell)
1976 *Win Some, Lose Some* (Dell)

Films:

1941 *Michael Shayne, Private Detective* (Twentieth Century–Fox), with Lloyd Nolan
1941 *Sleepers West* (Twentieth Century–Fox), with Lloyd Nolan
1941 *Dressed to Kill* (Twentieth Century–Fox), with Lloyd Nolan
1941 *Blue, White and Perfect* (Twentieth Century–Fox), with Lloyd Nolan
1942 *The Man Who Wouldn't Die* (Twentieth Century–Fox), with Lloyd Nolan
1942 *Just Off Broadway* (Twentieth Century–Fox), with Lloyd Nolan
1942 *Time to Kill* (Twentieth Century–Fox), with Lloyd Nolan
1946 *Murder is My Business* (PRC), with Hugh Beaumont

1946 *Larceny in Her Heart* (PRC), with Hugh Beaumont
1946 *Blonde for a Day* (PRC), with Hugh Beaumont
1947 *Three on a Ticket* (PRC), with Hugh Beaumont
1947 *Too Many Winners* (PRC), with Hugh Beaumont

Virgil Tibbs

Books:

1965 *In the Heat of the Night* (Harper & Row)
1966 *The Cool Cottontail* (Harper & Row)
1969 *Johnny Get Your Gun* (Little, Brown; revised and re-titled *Death of a Playmate* by Bantam)
1972 *Five Pieces of Jade* (Little, Brown)
1976 *The Eyes of Buddha* (Little, Brown)

Films:

1967 *In the Heat of the Night* (United Artists), with Sidney Poitier
1970 *They Call Me Mister Tibbs!* (United Artists), with Sidney Poitier
1971 *The Organization* (United Artists), with Sidney Poitier

Dick Tracy

Films:

1937 *Dick Tracy* (Republic serial), with Ralph Byrd
1938 *Dick Tracy Returns* (Republic serial), with Ralph Byrd
1939 *Dick Tracy's G-Men* (Republic serial), with Ralph Byrd
1941 *Dick Tracy vs. Crime, Inc.* (Republic serial), with Ralph Byrd
1945 *Dick Tracy* (RKO), with Morgan Conway
1946 *Dick Tracy vs. Cueball* (RKO), with Morgan Conway
1947 *Dick Tracy's Dilemma* (RKO), with Ralph Byrd
1947 *Dick Tracy Meets Gruesome* (RKO), with Ralph Byrd

Inspector Van der Valk

Books:

1963 *Love in Amsterdam* (Harper & Row)
1964 *Because of the Cats* (Harper & Row)
1964 *Question of Loyalty* (Harper & Row; British title: *Guns Before Butter*)
1965 *Double Barrel* (Harper & Row)
1966 *Criminal Conversation* (Harper & Row)
1966 *The King of the Rainy Country* (Harper & Row)
1968 *Strike Out Where Not Applicable* (Harper & Row)
1969 *Tsing-Boom* (Harper & Row; British title: *Tsing-Boum*)
1971 *The Lovely Ladies* (Harper & Row; British title: *Over the High Side*)
1972 *Auprès de ma Blonde* (Harper & Row; British title: *A Long Silence*)